Not Today

A Dora's Rage Mystery

Book 1

Not Today
A Dora's Rage Mystery
Book 1

First Edition

By David E. Feldman

For my sons

CONTENTS

PROLOGUE

THEN

The young couple lay back on the boy's parents' bed, which was soft and plush, covered with thick comforters, fluffed pillows, and an appliquéd blanket that smelled sweetly of fabric softener and the girl's lavender perfume. At either side of the bed were twin, stained wood night tables, and a matching headboard rose from behind the blankets and pillows.

The boy's parents had gone to a restaurant, then a show in the city, so he knew they wouldn't be home anytime soon. He had also known she would agree to come by. He could tell by the excited buzz he felt whenever they looked at each other. He knew she felt that buzz, too.

She had gone along with everything—the empty house, the beer, the bed. And when he gently lifted her chin to kiss her, she had closed her eyes and become still, waiting.

Kissing was wonderful. He had never kissed anyone like this before. His only kissing experience had been a year earlier with one of his cousins, and that had been with their mouths closed. Anne's lips were warm and soft and seemed to be made for his. When she opened her mouth and swirled her tongue around his, the boy was startled, then delighted.

They kissed for quite a while and writhed in one another's arms, mussing the covers and each other. They were eager and ardent, and they couldn't get enough of one another.

For the boy, there was nothing but this moment—this kissing and the urge for more. He cupped the back of her head, holding her against him, thrilled that she pressed back. He quickly realized he did not have to hold her, that his hands were free for other things.

They kissed faster and harder, more urgently, taking tiny breaks to breathe, pressing their faces to one another's necks, inhaling one another's scents, as their hands began to fly.

He ran his fingers down her arms, over her jeans, and up her back. He did this again and again, as she pressed forward, angling her body toward him, encouraging him.

He felt for her blouse buttons and struggled to undo them, his fingers shaking. He hoped she didn't notice, but she seemed as eager as he was, pushing away his hands and undoing the buttons herself before flinging her blouse open and guiding his fingers inside her bra.

Her breast was soft and light, gentle and fragile. He sighed with joy that this moment was happening, right here and now. He would have stopped time if he could, but he was too preoccupied to give it, or anything else, much thought.

She had taken her blouse off entirely and slid over to one side so she could run her palm over the front of his pants, pressing hard, as he pressed back. She tried to pull him on top of her, but he held himself to one side and tried to unbutton her jeans. However, he couldn't manage to slip the button through its hole with one hand.

"Let me," Anne whispered. In seconds, she had kicked off her pants, giggling as one of her feet got stuck in a pant leg. She kicked repeatedly, frantically, comically until he helped slide her foot free. Then he sat back, unsure of what to do next.

She showed him, and he looked at her in surprise. "You've done this?"

She shook her head and whispered, "Thought about it … read about it."

And then they were doing it. The boy had lost the ability to think; there was only feeling and doing, and a joy that made him want to cry.

He was pushing hard against her, and she pushed back … at first.

He heard her call his name and had the vague notion that something was not right. She called again. Perhaps she had called a few times, but he was pushing *hard*, and Anne was bouncing off the bed, sliding toward the headboard with each bounce.

He opened his eyes and saw the fear in hers. While some part of him wanted to know why, at the same time, his body, this thing they were doing, had a mind of its own.

She said his name again and pushed against his hips with the heels of her palms, trying to push him off her.

"You can't … you can't … Stop! You've got to … *stop!*" She yelled the last word at the same moment as he thought he heard the crunch of tires on gravel outside.

He clapped a palm over her mouth and focused his attention on listening for the sound of car doors. Anne was bucking and making muffled noises, but the boy, panicked, pressed his hand harder over her mouth and focused on the sounds.

She clawed at his arm, and he looked down, realizing he was suffocating her. He took his hand away, all while trying to hear what was going on outside.

"Let! Me! Up!" Angrily, she tried to push herself onto an elbow. "*Let me...*"

She was yelling now, and the boy could only think of being caught by his parents, so he pushed down hard against her collarbone, just as she was trying to sit up. When he pushed, her head slammed back against the oak headboard. Then a small sound, like a sigh, passed between her lips ... her last sound.

Chapter 1

NOW

Officer Francesca Hart had just gotten home from work and was changing out of her uniform and into a pair of old, black jean shorts and a T-shirt. As it was chilly, she decided to add a sweater.

Felix, an enormous grey and white striped Maine Coon cat, rubbed against her calf, jumping and pressing against her.

"Who's a wonderful cat?" Franny cooed, scratching the back of the thick mane of fur that encircled his neck, which of course had been Felix's goal all along.

Franny looked at her phone, deciding what music to listen to. She was partial to Chopin, particularly piano sonatas. Her stereo system, a surround sound wonder with elite Bose speakers that ran throughout the apartment, was connected to an app in her phone.

As she was about to select "Piano Sonata Number 2," her phone rang. The number came up as "Unknown," and she was about to press *End Call* but decided that she might do better telling this person, assuming the caller was a person and not a computer, not to call directly.

"Hello?"

"Officer Hart?" The caller's voice had a metallic tinge, as though disguised.

"Who is calling?"

"I'm calling about a crime."

"How did you get this number? To report a crime, call 911, or the station's direct line—516-555 …"

The person continued, "This crime happened a long time ago and was never solved. It was reported as something else—a tragic accident. But trust me; it was a murder, and the coverup led to a corrupt cancer that's spread all over Beach City."

"Hey," Franny said in her firm, no-nonsense cop voice, "you can't call here. We have a crime hotline … Hello? Hello?" She held the phone away from her face. The caller had hung up.

Forgetting about the music, she sat down on the edge of her bed, deep in thought.

9

● ● ●

Route 24 was a two-way street lined with storefronts and dogwood trees, featuring banks, garden apartments, a tattoo parlor, several nail salons, realtors, gyms, delis, a diner, and two physical therapy practices. It was Beach City's main drag and was bisected by a wide, grass median that was planted with flowers in the spring and summer. As busy as it was, the street also featured a growing percentage of empty storefronts, growth that matched that of local internet-related businesses, which were cheaper and easier to run and could serve populations regardless of locale without the investment of brick and mortar. The empty storefronts made garbage collection slightly easier than it had been in the past.

Deborah "Dora" Ellison and Maurice "Mo" Levinson took turns running ahead, past the empty stores, and pulling the garbage cans and bundled refuse into the street until the truck caught up. They then lifted and tipped their containers into the truck's bin and jumped up on one of the twin rear platforms, with a wave to Estéban, the driver, signaling it was okay to drive on.

Despite having enough seniority to drive, Dora preferred to be a "tipper," one who rides on the back of the truck and tips the trash into the rear bin. Mo's career trajectory had been the opposite. Though he was a few years older than Dora—thirty-seven to her twenty-eight—he had once been a driver, but had lost that favored position as the result of some infraction or disfavor with the city and was now, like Dora, a "tipper."

As they pulled up in front of a series of low, brick garden apartments, both Dora and Mo jumped down and began hoisting bags, bundled refuse, and trash can contents into the back bin. The complex had twenty units, so there was quite a bit of garbage strung along the curb. They would be there a while.

When they were about halfway through, a young man in a black T-shirt, khaki shorts, and beige moccasins ran out of an apartment and began yelling at Mo.

"Hey! You ran over my garbage can last week! Now I gotta buy a new one!"

"Nah, we didn't," Mo argued.

"I was there. I saw you! I watched you do it through my window!"

"I don't even drive," Mo said wearily.

They finished the load, and he and Dora pulled themselves up onto their platforms. Mo signaled Estéban to drive on, but the young man was standing in front of the truck, blocking its path.

Mo began waving his arm in a circle, indicating that Esteban should go around the man.

"You drove last week," the man said. "I saw you. Do I gotta call downtown?"

Mo leaped down from his perch, strode over to the young man, and began bumping him with his chest, pushing the man backward. Mo stood six-feet-two-and-a-half and weighed nearly two hundred and thirty pounds; he was at least a head taller and quite a bit wider than the young man.

"Yeah?" Mo taunted. "Gonna call downtown?" He bumped the guy back a step. "Ya gonna? Ya gonna? Really? Go ahead and call! Why aren't ya calling? Huh?"

Dora rolled her eyes and sighed. Then she jumped down from her perch and started toward the fracas. Though she was a large woman—five-eleven and two hundred forty-five pounds—she was deceptively light on her feet and moved with unusual physical confidence. "All right, Mo. That's enough. Mo! Enough!"

But Mo wasn't backing off.

"The asshole started this." He again bumped the young man, who was looking less sure of himself. "Let's see him finish it. How 'bout it, tough guy? Wanna take it to another level? Huh, pal?"

Panicked, the young man looked to Dora for help.

She stepped between them and pressed her palm to Mo's chest. "I said enough. The man's a resident, a taxpayer."

Finally getting the message, Mo seemed to shrink in stature.

"That's right." The young man pointed a finger, his anger rising again.

Dora held up her hand, her simple gesture forceful, authoritative.

The young man grew silent.

"We're done here." Dora leaped back up to her perch and waved to Estéban.

Mo reluctantly climbed aboard the other side, and then Estéban revved the engine, threw the transmission into gear, and the big yellow-green truck bucked with the gear change and lurched forward.

As they arrived on the next block, Dora called to Mo, "By the way, last week? You filled in for Estéban on Tuesday when his kid was sick. You drove."

Mo didn't answer.

Chapter 2

On her way home, Dora stopped at the market to pick up a *challah*. She was thinking ahead to a quiet evening at home with the love of her life, doing one of her beloved puzzles. She loved the way the pieces came together—disparate, separate bits that became larger, more recognizable segments, which came together with momentum and logic, as the big picture slowly took shape.

Puzzles were one of her favorite activities. She had such an active, wandering mind, often not in a good way. Puzzles occupied her inner hamster-on-a-wheel, monkey mind as little else did. She was aware of her challenges. She knew that her subconscious was preoccupied with abandonment and hurt, tending to react with anger, even rage. She was okay with that. The rage was better, she felt, than hurt. Her therapists tended to disagree.

Fuck them, she thought. They didn't have to live with her memories.

As she waited in the ten-items-or-less line, she watched a thin teenaged boy in a dirty T-shirt and denim jacket one spot in front of her argue with a blocky, white-haired, sixty-something, florid-faced man with too many items for the line.

"That's not right, and you know it," the boy whined. "This is ten items or less."

The white-haired man, who was much larger than the boy, stared back for a moment, pretending to look surprised. "Very impressive. The boy can count." Done with the boy, he turned away and faced forward, as the woman in front of him paid. He took the divider from behind her items and slid it to the space behind his.

"You should be over there," the boy persisted, pointing to the next line, where three people waited with full carts.

The white-haired man turned toward the boy again. "You know what? You're right. It says ten items or less, and I have eleven, so"—he took a step toward the boy, looming over him—"whatcha gonna do about it?"

Dora closed her eyes and counted to ten. She hated this kind of shit, and it seemed to find her so often. When she opened her eyes, the man was still staring at the boy and had taken another step closer to him.

"Sir," Dora said wearily, "the boy happens to be right, not that it's the biggest deal in the world."

The man raised his eyebrows and looked at Dora then at the boy. "You his mother? You don't look alike."

Dora shook her head. "Concerned citizen." She shrugged a bit sheepishly. "And I ... well, I have this thing about bullies."

The white-haired man thrust his face close to Dora's. "Well, citizen with a thing about bullies, I'm checking out right here, in this line."

Dora looked the man steadily in the eyes as she surreptitiously slid an open palm between his legs, closed her hand around the man's privates, and squeezed ... hard. Then she shook her head. "I don't think so."

The man let out a yip, like a dog whose tail has been stepped on.

Dora brought her arm up, as though to brush back her hair, and purposely jostled the man's arm so that the carton of eggs he was holding fell to the floor. She stepped on the carton, making sure to crush every egg, as the man gasped and fought for air.

She smiled at the man. "And if you want to make a complaint about how some girl bullied you, be my guest."

Wounded and terrified, the man moaned softly, staring back at her.

She turned to the boy, who was grinning.

"Thank you!" the boy breathed.

"Unfortunately," Dora told him, "the man's right. He does have ten items ... now, without the eggs. So, if you don't mind, why don't we just let him go?"

The boy thought about it then nodded. "I see what you mean." He stepped back, making sure to avoid the broken eggs.

• • •

From the moment Dora walked through the door of their apartment, she knew what Franny had planned. It wasn't the music, but the warm, homey aromas that gave away Franny's plans.

Dora paused just inside the door to listen to the Chopin sonata that Franny was practicing on her keyboard. It was lovely. The piano lent a grave beauty to their apartment.

Dora stood momentarily in the doorway, soaking in the sensory experience of being in her favorite place with the woman she loved. The apartment was decorated in modern black and white, with vertical blinds as room dividers, soft track lighting, a white couch with zebra striped pillows, and white, shell chairs.

She pulled off her heavy, orange sanitation gloves and black, steel-toed boots then removed her bird's egg blue hard hat and her reflective orange coveralls. She would soon add thermal long johns, sweats, and possibly even a woolen *balaclava* on the coldest winter days.

She tore off her socks then padded to the refrigerator in search of a beer. Her feet, sweaty after a long, hard day of tipping garbage and supporting her considerable bulk, kissed the cold kitchen tile with every step.

"Babe!" she called without slowing down. She opened the fridge, took out a bottle of Sam Adams, and twisted off its top.

Something warm and furry brushed her leg.

"Not you, Felix; my other babe." She reached down to stroke the cat, brushing back the thick fur around Felix's neck. He was the king of their apartment and was treated like one. She scooped him into her arms and spoke to him in her doggy voice. "But I wuv you, too. Yes, I do." She put him down again and watched him walk away as though he had not a care in the world.

"Where is she?" Dora whispered. "Where's our girl?"

Felix circled back and rubbed against her thigh. Saying just about anything in this tone brought Felix running, knowing he could expect a massage or a snack.

The music stopped.

"Hello, babe!" came Franny's reply. A moment later, Franny floated into the kitchen, a dark and slender vision in jean shorts and an orange and brown wool sweater.

Dora marveled that Franny didn't seem to walk. Her years of dance lessons had given her the lovely ability to glide.

Dora put down the beer and held her arms wide. "Officer Hart!"

Franny giggled and allowed herself to be hugged and held. They kissed their ritual four times. "*Mwah, mwah, mwah, mwah.*"

Franny nodded toward the twin, silver Kiddish cups, the lighter and matching candlesticks, and the *challah* Dora had bought, all waiting on the counter.

"Ready for Shabbat?" Franny asked.

Dora nodded, took hold of the lighter, and lit a candle.

"Baruch, atah, Adonai ..."

Dora loved that Franny not only accepted her religion, but joined in. Franny accepted just about everything about her. She didn't go along with the supposedly politically correct term "sanitation engineer," but was fine with "garbage man," which Dora preferred, despite its incorrect gender reference. Franny also didn't mind Dora's weight. "You're perfect as you are," she would say. "Just enough of you to love." Franny was fond of saying, and her actions bore that out. Franny's blanket acceptance of her was evidence to Dora of Franny's honest love.

"Movie tonight?" Franny asked later, as Dora was clearing, washing, and drying plates.

Dora shook her head. "Fight's tonight ... and my puzzle." Dora often worked on a puzzle while she watched her beloved MMA.

"Uh-oh," Franny said, smiling. "Nice knowing you."

"Watch with me. I could use the company. Uh-oh." She lifted a used, glass mayonnaise jar from the garbage. "What's this?"

Franny feigned ignorance. "Never saw it before in my life."

"It goes in recycled."

"It certainly does."

Dora looked at her with loving amusement. "You're so cute when you pout."

"So, I'm not cute when I'm not pouting?"

Dora shook her head, still smiling.

Fifteen minutes later, they were entwined on the couch, watching preliminary bouts or, more accurately, Dora was riveted to the fights, while Franny worked on a crossword on her iPad, her head nestled back against Dora's pillowed chest.

Dora kept up a running commentary on the fights, while Franny nodded and continued her crossword.

"This guy was a Brazilian BJJ national runner up two years ago. It'll be interesting to see what he does against a striker like this Czech."

"BJJ?"

"Brazilian Jiu-Jitsu."

"National runner up? Mmm ... Where?"

Dora looked at Franny, eyebrows raised. "Brazilian runner up in ... um, Brazil? Look at him! He's a beast. How can they be in the same weight class? There's no way! And there's *no* way he's clean."

A musical phrase issued from Franny's iPad, signifying the successful completion of her crossword. She wriggled with the tune then looked up. "Probably bulked up after the weigh in."

Dora looked at her, impressed. "You, my darling, are probably right."

The match began.

"There you go, there you go! That's what you do with an aggressive striker—front leg roundhouse to the lead leg. Oooh ... that's gonna hurt later. He's gonna shoot ... Gonna shoot ... Nice sprawl! Don't circle into his power, don't—Whoa, way to swing for the fences! See, Fran? He swung, missed, went too far, and the BJJ guy is all over him, got him down, mounted—ground and pound. And ... takes his back!"

When Dora leaned forward to focus on the TV, Franny sat up, watching Dora with a combination of fascination and curiosity. An idea occurred to her.

"And ... there it is—the tap!" Dora sat back, winded.

A commercial for tacos had come on.

Franny paused. "You ever think of doing that?"

"Making tacos with hot sauce? Tomorrow?"

Franny shook her head. "No, babe. MMA."

"MMA? I don't understand."

"Fighting."

"Yeah, I know what it is, but you want me to—huh?"

"I think you should do it." Franny sat up and leaned into Dora, her elbows on Dora's knees. "You're physically the strongest person I know—mentally, too. Male or female. And that includes everyone on the BCP. You know and really love this sport. You'd be great at it."

Dora stared back at her, baffled. "That's fucking nuts."

Franny paused then gently added, "Not to mention, you have a level of rage that could use some channeling."

Dora pushed her away. "Only toward the deserving few."

Franny shook her head. "Look, on the BCP, they taught us to fight. I had to fight ... guys. Big guys, with joint locks and wrist controls. You could whip most of them now. With a little training, all of them."

Franny could see that Dora was entertaining the idea, if only for momentary amusement.

"You think?" She looked at Franny, eyes wide. "Really?"

Franny nodded and typed something into her iPad. "I saved something for you." She found what she was looking for then held up the device. "Local league for women is up and running. Mostly made up of martial arts schools, but ... open tryouts."

Dora didn't have to lean close or squint to read what was on the screen —her eyesight was 20/10. "Oh. My. God. I'm gonna do it!"

"Matches are with gyms in some surrounding towns, as well as intramural."

"You sure they take women?"

Franny pointed at the screen. "They *want* women. Check it out!"

Dora had the wide-eyed innocence of a child at Christmas or, in her case, Hanukkah.

Franny looked at Dora for a long moment. "Babe, I have this thing going on at work. Well, not at work, but related to work ... sort of."

Dora waited, but Franny didn't go on. "And ...?"

"And ... I can't talk about it."

"You lost me. A thing at work you can't talk about? So, why are you bringing it up?"

"Because I *want* to talk about it."

"Oh, for fuck's sake! This could go on all night. Darlin', you want to talk about it, talk about it. You don't want to talk about it, don't!"

"I do want to, because it explains ... some things."

"Okay, let's try this." Dora patted Franny's hand. "What does it explain?"

"Everything."

"Oh, so you're involved with string theory at work? No, Stephen Hawking, it doesn't explain *everything*." She shook her head. "Maybe we ought to get back to this when you're really ready."

Franny took a deep breath. "Someone reached out to me that I think has connections in town, like high up in town."

Now Dora was listening. "You are a trustworthy person. One of the main reasons you're my girl."

"He—at least, I think it's a he—says he has information about a local crime. A murder. And how that murder is connected to some kind of city-wide corruption."

"So? You're a cop—investigate!"

"Do you know how many BS tips we get?"

"So, don't investigate. Your call."

"Babe, I'm telling you because I trust you enough to be my sounding board."

• • •

Cliff Jamison had been the Beach City Beach Patrol Director for seven years. The job was a far more active one during the busy beach season that began on Memorial Day and ran through Labor Day, during which a significant portion of Beach City's revenues came from beach passes, both seasonal and daily, than it was during the off season. Cliff was tasked with overseeing issues related to beach safety, erosion, litter, and marine life, along with the wellbeing of beachgoers and conditions on the beach.

Today, however, Cliff was concerned about a text he had received. The text was similar to texts he received every few months, sometimes more frequently; texts where tasks that were expected of him were laid out, texts that were expected to be obeyed, destroyed, and disavowed.

That Mrs. Cavaletti, who's been complaining about dogs leaving little presents all over her beach, is now banned from the beach. Her husband, Ralph, is also banned. Her sons, Philip and Greg, are banned, and that includes surfing. Let me be clear; they may not surf. I'm aware that she's called your office, but now she's gone to the

Facebook groups and to The Chronicle and made accusations about the council and the mayor. She's determined to make the city look bad, and we can't have that. While dogs are not allowed on the beach, and we do want you to continue to enforce that, you might look the other way if a dog or two happens to want to do its business over on Monroe, where she lives.

The text was signed *J.H.*

It was an all but impossible text to enforce. How was Cliff to keep members of the Cavaletti family from using a public beach that they had every right to use? How was he to even know if they were on the beach? Beach passes had tiny squares corresponding to the days of summer, into which holes were punched by high school kids working summer jobs. There were no names on summer beach passes. It was a crazy request, but it had been made by J.H.—it had to not only be obeyed, but eagerly obeyed.

Cliff sighed. He would have to assign lifeguards to keep an eye out for the Cavalettis. Removing them from the beach would not be a problem, not if J.H. wanted them gone. Any complaints the Cavalettis made would be ignored.

Cliff shook his head. *Beach City ...*

Chapter 3

"What do you think?" Charlie Bernelli Jr. pointed his coffee cup toward the cement and glass construction across the street. Several sections of its cement façade were festooned with colorful art deco panels, whose lines and shapes continued on other panels, separated by the negative shapes of the underlying material.

"Nice," Charlie Sr. said. "Put it to good use." He then turned toward his son. "So, how does it feel being back in Beach City?"

Charlie Jr. shook his head. "I don't know. I love the beach and the boardwalk, and some of the old hangouts, but some of the memories … not so good."

"Yeah, I know."

Charlie Jr. didn't answer. He was thinking about how the day he had dreamed of had finally arrived.

The Bernelli Group was back in business; same town, new location, new ownership—a younger Bernelli at the helm. He was proud and excited, and he was grateful that his father had paved the way for some of his long-time clients to return to the firm, while he did his best to add his own.

"Wonder what kind of reception you'll get. You kind of tore up this town," his father mused.

"Not worried about it."

Charlie Sr. nodded then chuckled. "And the girls you went around with"—he shook his head—"some were as bad as you."

"Not girls. *Girl.* Singular. And Christine was a good Catholic school girl."

His father chuckled. "Well, when some of those Catholic school girls get to high school … watch out!"

Father and son stood together, looking at the façade of their ad agency.

"What about the boy?" Charlie Sr. asked quietly.

Charlie Jr. continued to look at the building across the street while folding his arms across his chest. "What about him?"

"How 'bout you keep in mind he's a person."

Now his son turned to face him. "How about—"

"I know you don't want to hear it, but our children are human beings and deserve to be treated as such. C's grandmother and I believed that from day one."

Charlie Jr. didn't answer right away. He let the silence between them grow and solidify before he said, "And the result of your approach has been three generations of alcoholics, gambling addicts, and serial philanderers."

"You watch your mouth, son."

"Or what? You'll deck me? You don't believe in corporal punishment."

To his son's surprise, the senior Bernelli laughed. "I'm not saying give the boy enough rope to hang himself. I'm saying being a dad means supporting him, as well as being strict."

The son shrugged. "Sometimes support means letting him sit in his own shit. Anyway, financial support and a roof over his head won't be an issue. He won't be in my care, at a least for a bit. He'll be in the state's care, as he has been for two years—first, prison; now a halfway house."

They stood another few moments together.

"Guess we'll see." Charlie Sr. sipped his coffee. "Look." He nodded toward a garbage truck that was making its way noisily toward them. "How many female garbage men—or is it garbage women?—have you seen?"

They watched for a bit. Charlie Jr. said nothing.

"Look at how she sweeps the can up in the air with one hand then flips it over," Charlie Sr. marveled. "That's one strong girl!"

Charlie Jr. still said nothing.

"I piss you off?" Charlie Sr. looked at his son. "Can I count on you to stay out of trouble?"

"Pop, I'm forty-two. I can have a drink without driving or taking a swing at anyone. Besides, at this point, it's not your business."

Charlie Sr. nodded. "Fair point." He clapped his son on the back. "I trust you, son."

"Good." Charlie Jr. smiled. "'Cause I was about to ask if I could taste your coffee; make sure that's all it is."

Charlie Sr. turned and stared at his son in mock anger. They both burst out laughing.

If someone would have told Charlie Jr. that he would be reopening The Bernelli Group in his old hometown, he never would have believed them. Yet, here he was, back in Beach City. The memories had been pushing into his consciousness, but he had pushed them away. That was then. He had little desire to relive such extremely wild oats.

He crossed the street, wandering his eyes over the exterior of the building, their building. He patted the base of one of the decorative panels. "The construction looks good. Best-looking building in Beach City."

"Not saying much," the elder Bernelli muttered. Then he sniffed the air. "You really can smell the sea around here, can't you?" He sipped his coffee and caught up with his son, who nodded.

"Depends on the tides and the winds, I suppose," came the son's answer. "Kind of combines vacation and work."

Charlie Jr. held the door for his father, who pointed with his coffee toward the garbage truck, which had passed their building and was receding in fits and starts. "Or, could be garbage day."

His son shook his head as he followed his father through the door and up the short steel staircase. "Give the place a chance, Pop. Don't be so cynical."

Charlie Sr. didn't bother turning around, his footsteps echoing in the stairwell as he said, "Wait till you're my age."

• • •

Charlie Jr. spent his morning sowing what he hoped would prove to be fertile ground at City Hall, a six-story brick edifice almost completely fronted by dark blue tinted, floor-to-ceiling windows. A row of black and white police vehicles was parked along one side of the building—squad cars, the newer SUVs and, toward the back, now that beach season was over, the off-road four wheelers used for beach patrol and rescues.

The only work on Charlie's desk was social media and SEO for their four long-term clients, all attorneys, and, of course, the cold calls, lunches, and meetings with new prospects. He had plenty of time to go downtown, meet the local authorities, make sure his business was looked upon favorably, and schmooze a bit.

The city clerk's office was a large, open room, bisected by a dark wood veneer half-wall, topped by a blue faux marble countertop that separated civil servants from the public. To one side was a row of five cubby office spaces, separated by chest-high portable dividers. The other side was filled, floor to ceiling, with filing cabinets, which were in the long process of being transferred to digital servers.

He had been hoping that the clerk, Christine Pearsall, with whom he had some history, would meet with him, but she was out.

Charlie's current task was simple: offer a few polite words of introduction to the assistant clerk, along with assurances that all ordinances, rules, and suggestions would be happily adhered to, and The Bernelli Group would be off to a City-Hall-approved start.

That accomplished, as he left the building and was walking across the town square, between the two rows of water fountains, he thought he heard his name called.

"Mr. Bernelli?" the call came again. An authoritative yet friendly baritone that carried well over the sound of the cascading water and passing traffic.

He turned, seeing a tall, slightly stooped, bald man in grey sweatpants, striped with yellow, and a matching striped, yellow Polo shirt striding toward him, a palm outstretched.

"Mark Morganstern!" The man's grip was loose, despite his size and obvious fitness.

Charlie smiled, making sure to keep his expression a bit shy and deferential. "Mr. Mayor, what a wonderful surprise!"

The mayor shrugged. "I keep it pretty informal. Most call me Mark, or Mayor Mark. Whatever works for you is fine. Say, how old would you say I am?"

"Putting me on the spot first time I meet you? Ha! Thanks. I don't know … sixty?" He put out a hand. "Charlie Bernelli Jr. My dad founded our agency here then moved us to New York City, and now I'm taking over."

The mayor seemed suddenly interested. "So I heard. Advertising, right?"

"That's right. Ran Fortune 100 newspaper and radio campaigns in the city … Manhattan." He paused, considering his next words carefully. "Do you know of any opportunities locally?"

"I'm glad you asked. You know, I've been thinking, we've been looking at starting a local, tourist campaign. Print and TV. You do those?"

Charlie grinned. This was turning into a pretty good day. "Sure do!"

"I figured. Give Christine, in my office, a call."

"But, don't you already have a contract—"

"Oh, I do," the mayor interrupted with a sheepish look, "but I can do more or less what I want. Probably not entirely kosher, but I've had some success over the years and have built up enough trust that no one gives me a hard time … other than my wife, of course." He grinned. "Eighty-four."

"Excuse me?"

"I'm eighty-four years old."

"You're putting me on!"

"Nope. Swim two miles then walk three, every day. And sometimes I bike after that!"

Charlie shook his head in wonder as he took a gold-plated business card case from his pocket, flipped it open, and held it out. "My new cards. Please, Mr. Mayor."

The mayor took one and looked at it. "Very nice. Wishing"—he scrutinized the card—"The Bernelli Group much success. I'll be in touch." Without waiting for an answer, he turned and strode back toward the building, waving to the left at two uniformed police officers then to the right at a fifty-ish man and a young woman. The mayor stopped, said a few words to each, patted them on the arm, and then continued on into City Hall.

• • •

Tom Volkov ran his hand back through his thinning salt and pepper hair. "I see what you're saying, Sarah, but—"

"But nothing." Sarah got up from the chair and took a step toward Tom's desk. She was thirty-five, with short brown hair, and wore a simple business suit that was unremarkable, except that it, and the rest of her attire, were entirely black. She had long been Tom's best writer, reporter, and video editor. Since canceling their print edition and streamlining the company so as to deliver their news online and via app only, job titles had merged, their descriptions blurred. Now she was his *only* writer, reporter, and video editor, excepting himself, of course.

He tried not to wonder if he would one day be doing all *Chronicle*-related work alone. He hoped not. Sarah was more than competent. She was cheerfully earnest, with more than a dash of take-no-shit thrown in, a good quality to have in a reporter. He suspected she would not be easily replaced.

Their office "suite," if it could be called that, was tiny. Neither of their two offices had doors and the wall between them was thin, crumbling sheet rock. They could hear one another's phone calls, along with everything that went on in the conference room, which was essentially the hallway outside their offices painted with thick, off-white acrylic, lined with wall-mounted shelving, also painted white, which contained loose-leaf binders housing printed records of each of their daily editions going back twenty-two years, to the time when Tom had founded the newspaper.

"Look, one person has a problem with their building permit, okay," she continued. "That could be anything—a genuine, building-related issue, even a grudge, or a misunderstanding. But twelve people, all of whom were thorns in the city's side? Coincidence? I don't think so. Certainly worth looking into, don't you think? And it's not like I have so much other crucial work to do."

Tom didn't answer right away. Whatever he might say would be the tip of the truth's iceberg. The pressure he was under was emphatically no one's business, other than his and the city's. He could always explain that choosing which stories to prioritize for upcoming issues of *The Beach City Chronicle* was a challenging responsibility, and because it was his responsibility, she would have no say in the matter, regardless of her opinion.

In this "era of Trump," the notion of "news" hardly applied. At least, not as it had in the past. People's attentions were drawn to Facebook's politics-of-blame-and-rage pages, or puppy dogs and kittens, or juicy neighborhood gossip. Especially rage. People homed in on stories that pissed them off. Rage sold. Whether or not the catalyst of the rage was a true story was not so important to the powers that be. What *was* important? Ad revenue.

End of story.

He shook his head, thinking of his grandmother. The old rag papers had it right all along. Grandma Jen had read them religiously, no matter how ridiculous their stories. In fact, the stories she dwelled on most had headlines like: "Movie Star Has Martian Baby" or "Dog with Two Heads Runs for Congress." She had waved away his strident claims that such articles were nonsense. There were no news stories *about* their being nonsense—further proof of their veracity, as far as she was concerned. What made the stories true to Grandma Jen was the fact that they were in the paper. She was not alone.

He missed her every day.

The factual stories that made *The Chronicle* nowadays were fires, arrests, and local City Hall events. Everything else was something someone said, or insinuated, or an accusation or counter-accusation. What happened was but a small portion of "the news." What it *meant* was a much larger and more important portion.

Many of their stories nowadays were obvious smears, but they drew eyeballs … and advertisers. These were based, not on fact, but on editorial —i.e., his—opinion, so they required little time beyond what was spent making them up and doing just enough research for them to appear truthful. They could not be disproved since they were, at root, conjecture or opinion. "So and so is a bum." That was the editorial board's—i.e., his— opinion. This had become an industry trend.

What he chose not to dwell on was how sixth-grade-style, schoolyard bullying had also become an industry standard. He also chose not to dwell on the source of some of his smears. He knew enough not to bite the hand that fed him. The city was one of *The Chronicle's* primary sources of advertising and influence.

Tom was accommodating and gracious when he picked up his phone to find representatives of city departments on the line, whether Animal Control, Beach Patrol, Parks and Recreation, City Clerk, Building Department, Community Development, Comptroller, Civil Service, Fire

Department, Water and Sewer, Transportation, Police Department, Tax Bureau, or the Bureau of Alcohol and Firearms Licensure. Volkov knew well enough on which side his bread was buttered.

He was pretty sure that committing to investigating Sarah's notion that those who ran afoul of the city and had axes to grind might run afoul of city departments when issues, such as the need for a building permit or liquor license, came up was not in his or *The Chronicle*'s best interest.

He shrugged in Sarah's direction. "Twelve people could be something, or not. If we decide to pursue it, I'll let you know."

Sarah knew a dismissal when she heard it. With a dramatic sigh and a stream of inaudible epithets, she stormed from the room. He overheard her slamming desk drawers a few feet, and one thin wall, away.

He sat stock-still for a moment, the weight of Sarah's disapproval sinking in. Sarah had a way of activating his atrophied sense of guilt. They both knew he buried many real news stories—not all of them, nowhere near all of them; not even the really important stories, or so he told himself. Still, he thought of himself as a journalist, and the fact was that he buried stories because he was pressured to do so. That didn't sit well with Sarah and, truth be told, it didn't sit well with him. It didn't sit well at all.

His cell phone rang. *The Chronicle* had "cut the cord," which meant they no longer had telephone landlines, another budget-saving measure masked as a "modernization." He waited another ring, knowing Sarah could easily answer. Taking calls was part of her job description, but he knew she was too passive-aggressive to pick up when she was angry.

He took his phone from his pocket and looked at it, but there was no name, and he didn't recognize the number. "*Chronicle,*" he answered.

• • •

"*Yid gadal, v'yid kadash, shmei raba ...*"

Irene Volkov sat in Anne's room, saying *Kaddish*. On her daughter's bureau were photos of Anne, along with articles of Anne's clothing, her favorite Backstreet Boys CD, and several lavender-scented candles. Anne had loved the smell of lavender.

Irene kept the candles lit in perpetuity. Twice a day, she recited *Kaddish* then spoke to Anne, relating the high or low points of her day, her thoughts about whatever was in the news, and the goings on in her life. She would tell her daughter how much she was missed and, as time went on, Irene began sharing more private thoughts and memories. Nowadays, much of her life was spent in front of the shrine to Anne. She had come to accept that her daughter was no longer physically present, but she firmly believed that Anne remained with her, could see and hear her, and knew what her mother said and, perhaps, thought.

Irene felt a little badly that Tom was less and less a part of her life, but that was the way things went. Little of daily life interested Irene nowadays and, unfortunately, that applied to Tom and his work, as well as just about everything that passed for news. Her time with Anne had become the most important part of her life. Irene Volkov believed she was following her daughter, as best a living person could, to a spiritual realm, where they coexisted.

"... *aleinu v'al kall Yisrael, v'imru, amein.*" She sighed then brightened, inhaling the scent of lavender and gazing at the flickering candles. "We've had our first real cold spell of the fall. You never much liked the cold, since we could no longer pretend the summer was hanging around. Hopefully, you don't get too cold there."

• • •

Charlie had an idea. The Bernelli Group was the new kid on the block and breaking through the resistance of existing business relationships in Beach City was a challenge he was prepared to meet. And now he had an in.

He performed a Google search for local newspapers and found *The Beach City Chronicle*, as local as you could get. Beyond *The Chronicle* was the county, which had no newspaper, followed by a Long Island regional paper. *Starting as local as possible would be best*, he thought. He could branch out from there.

"Hi, my name is Charlie Bernelli. To whom am I speaking ...?"

"Tom Volkov. How can I help you, Mr. Bernelli?"

"Ah, Mr. Volkov—"

"Please. Tom."

"Okay, Tom, then. I own a little ad agency here in Beach City ... The Bernelli Group..."

"The Bernelli Group..."

"Well, we're new .... Actually, we were here maybe fifteen years ago. Run by my dad, also named Charlie."

"I knew I'd heard the name somewhere. I remember your father. I hope he's still with us."

"He is. Thank you. Tell me, what do you do at *The Chronicle?*"

"I'm the founder and owner," he chuckled, "and I do just about everything."

"Really? An owner! And you answer the phones?"

"How can I help you, Mr. Bernelli?"

"Of course, certainly. The reason for my call is that I would like to discuss a possible ad campaign we're considering for a new client...."

"Well, that's wonderful. Do you mind if I ask who the client is?"

"Well, I can't say who yet, but trust me; they're a name you'd know ..."

Eight minutes later, Charlie hung up and felt the familiar rush of adrenaline that came with new business. The campaign would be a winner, cementing the company's business relationship with the city and the community.

His discomfort at being the newcomer, an outsider, had evaporated. He casually wondered if enthusiasm and excitement burned more calories than calm. He was ravenous.

He checked Google Maps for the nearest diner and found a place called Cobb's, a third of a mile away.

• • •

Jesse Healy was disgusted. He had taken his case to the court, and city court judge, Cheryl Rose, had ruled against him. He had lived in Beach City all his life, voted, faithfully paid his taxes, seen his children attend and graduate Beach City schools, and yet here he was, homeless. Well, technically homeless. The home he and his wife, Marla, had bought and made their own was apparently now owned by the city. Eminent domain, it was called. Part of the city's plan to stave off another Superstorm Sandy. Well, fuck that, and fuck them!

Telling off Clyde Franklin, the Building Department supervisor, had felt good. Next stop? The newspapers. He would go first thing tomorrow. He had already called and left a message with a Sarah somebody for a Mr. Volkov.

The blue Mustang inched along the curb two houses from Jesse's. A lanky young man with floppy bangs emerged from the car, wearing a UPS uniform, carrying a package and a computer tablet.

• • •

Franky Patella had been in prison for six years. He was thirty-five now and had been arrested many times and served time twice. He didn't mind going to jail. Why should he? There, he was fed, clothed, and given a place to sleep. And he could take care of himself.

Franky's father had been killed in a motorcycle accident when Franky was seven. Prior to that, his father had been a mid-level enforcer for a local "organization." His father's absence and his mother's morphine and crank addiction led him to believe that you had to be not only tough but willing to be brutal to succeed in life. And if you can terrorize and terrify the other guy, so much the better. Your status, your superiority, your place at the top of the hierarchy was that much higher and that much more secure.

He had hung around the teenage and twenty-something gangs and criminals, and was challenged and often beaten by them in his pre-teen and teen years, but he refused to leave them because they were the only tribe that accepted him. He had nowhere else to go. He did not consider trying to fit in elsewhere because he had never been provided with any viable alternative; even if he had considered working his way into some other group, he would not have believed anyone but the least socially acceptable groups would want him. He had lived with that belief even as a child, when he had argued with a neighbor's son and had whipped the other boy's face with a thin, green lawn stake, which had made a soft whistling sound.

Little Franky had liked that, and had found a baton that built on the idea in the back of a paramilitary magazine, and now was rarely without it.

He found his own brand of acceptance by dominated every group he chose to join—which were few and far between—with, not only violence, but brutality. His willingness to butcher terrorized most opponents, potential rivals and companions alike, leaving him alone at the top by something like default most of the time. Once he found his way into City Hall, first as a messenger and then as The Messenger, he had found a semi-official tribe who would reward his unique abilities and proclivities and could offer him the shelter of the law in return.

Typically, within a day or two in prison, all sorts of opportunities presented themselves. He had been given the job of caring for the cell block's plants and flowers. In a real way, that job had sustained him, had given him something to love, something that would never, ever hurt him.

With the other inmates, he had to quickly demonstrate dominance, which he did well. Really well. It was always the same—he would pick out the strongest or, better, the leader, then beat him bloody, which never failed to give him satisfaction. In a real sense, the satisfaction was physical, even sexual. Be fast. Be first. Be brutal. Be so vicious that no one could stand against him, because such viciousness was unimaginable and disheartening, even in prison. What scared even the toughest among the inmates was the fact that he didn't stop, even when the other person was out cold. That scared just about everyone, so it became one of Franky's favorite tactics.

Now, on the outside, he was usually unarmed. He played a mental game with the messages he sent, challenging himself to find a weapon at hand. Other times, he brought his baton-blade. Either way, once faced with that barely contained rage and the expertise behind it, the expertise with a knife that could remove an eye or a tongue without causing unconsciousness, the results, the surrender, inevitably followed. Every. Single. Time.

He knew nothing about Jesse Healy. He didn't have to. Once this guy saw what was coming, it would be over; the guy's insides would turn to water.

He rang the bell.

• • •

Cobb's Diner looked about like every other diner Charlie had ever seen, with a few small exceptions. There were the usual cashier and counter areas, two rotating chrome and glass showcases of cakes and pies, multiple glass coffee pots—with red tops for regular, green for decaf. There were wood booths padded with thick vinyl—red to sit on, turquoise backrests, and red head rests. The red and turquoise reflected faintly off the curved metallic ceiling area above the windows. The floors were metallic gold tile squares, divided by dark silver borders. In the corner of each gold tile were smaller white tiles. Clearly, the owner had his, or her, own sense of decor and ambience.

What set the aesthetic of Cobb's Diner apart from other diners were two differences. The diner was lit by circular sconces above the aisles, while hanging over each table was a single lighting pendant of polished metal, its bulb facing downward so that patrons could read their menus. The rest of the diner remained dimly lit, perhaps for the comfort of late-night patrons who might not appreciate bright lights.

The other difference was that the seating, apart from the counter area, was comprised entirely of booths. Cobb's lacked free-standing tables. Charlie had noticed this as soon as he had walked in and appreciated the diner's nod to the patrons' comfort. Most people, when given the choice, would opt for a plush booth over a hard, wooden chair.

The owner—Cobb, presumably—was a big-boned man in his late fifties, about six-foot-three, with a tousled, full head of grey hair, deep set eyes, and a ready grin. He held out an arm, palm up, a "sit anywhere" gesture.

Charlie nodded, returned the smile, and found a booth.

After a moment, the owner sidled over.

"You must be Charlie Bernelli." He extended his hand, and Charlie shook it.

"How'd you know?"

"Small town. Everyone knows everyone. 'Cept you. And being as how you're a player of sorts, word gets around."

"A player?"

"Of sorts. Agency owner, right?"

Charlie nodded, as though he understood and agreed, then looked at the big man. "You must be ..." He flipped the menu to its cover. "Mr. ... Cobb?"

The man barked a laugh and started to put out his hand before realizing he had already done that and pulled it away again. "Horace, not George."

"Or Ty." Charlie smiled.

Horace Cobb pointed at Charlie as though the joke was one that he had never heard and chuckled. "But tell me; why open an ad agency in a little beach town like this? You think there's enough work here to support it?"

Charlie nodded. "I do. Besides, my clients are all over." He gestured to the other side of the table. "Why don't you join me?"

Horace Cobb smiled. "Don't mind if I do. Coffee? On me."

"Thank you."

"Carolyn," Cobb called in the direction of the counter area. "Two coffees."

The waitress, who was in her forties and had a worn-out yet focused look, must have had the coffees poured and ready to bring over, as she appeared almost instantly, setting the cups and saucers in front of them before sliding milk and sweeteners to the center of the table.

Cobb smiled vaguely in her direction as she disappeared.

Charlie continued, "We're near enough to the city that we can do some business there. And I figure, even in a small town, businesses have to advertise — maybe on buses, railroad platforms, or on the radio and even TV. And, of course, there's digital. You got a daily paper, right?"

Cobb nodded. "It's online now, but yes. And you might have some work with the city. That *is* a bit of luck."

Charlie shrugged. "Far from a sure thing, but I met the mayor, and he sounded optimistic. Seems like a nice guy."

Horace Cobb gave a long belly laugh, and Charlie was struck by the difference between the man's offhand chuckle and this laugh, which was deeper and shook the man's broad shoulders.

"Yes," he said when he caught his breath, "he does."

Chapter 4

Again with the water!

Shmuel Schwartz was frustrated. He was trying to boil water, and there was no water! He called the city and was told there were no hydrant flushings or other Water Department work in his vicinity today. He had even splurged to pay a plumber for a house call and was told that the problem was not in the house, nor with the pipes running from the street. The problem was that he had no inbound water from the city's system. He did not understand, so he called a neighbor, Mrs. Ida Steinglatz, who said she had plenty of water and to come by and fill up a container any time. Then, he called the city again to explain what the plumber had told him, and they had said they would get back to him.

That had been yesterday.

How was this possible?

Then he had a thought. Last month, he had called to complain about his water bill being ridiculously high, and when he hadn't liked the official's tone, he had gone downtown to let them know it, then wrote a letter to the newspaper.

Could there be a connection? Could a city official be that petty?

• • •

The doorbell chimed, and then chimed again.

Dora was leaning back in one of the white swivel chairs, paying close attention to something on her iPad. "Can you get it?" She glanced at Franny, who was on the couch across the room reading, then at the door.

The bell chimed again.

Dora looked up. "So, I'm closer?"

Franny raised her right eyebrow then went back to her book, a *Jack Reacher* mystery. She liked Jack Reacher for many of the reasons she liked Dora. If he were a woman and a real person, she might have loved him, too.

The bell chimed again, followed by a muffled, "Hello?"

Dora bounded out of her chair with a loud sigh. She opened the door to find a man who looked to be in his early forties. His longish, blond hair was streaked with grey and combed straight back, giving him a lion-esque appearance. He wore a tan suit and a warm smile as he held out a hand.

"Charlie Bernelli."

Dora looked him over, trying to imagine what he was selling. She didn't take his hand. "Can I help you?"

"I think you can." The smile remained. "Might we talk inside?" He tried to peer around her, but Dora automatically shifted along with his gaze, blocking Franny from his view. The move came naturally, a protective instinct.

She didn't answer right away. That, too, was an extension of her personality and other aspects of her life—read them before they read you.

Finally, she said, "Depends."

Charlie pressed his lips together. "Of course. Well, I'm the owner of a small ad agency—The Bernelli Group. We're new in town. Actually, we're *back* in town, after many years, and we may be producing an ad for the city, and we'd like you to be the focus of it."

Confused, Dora didn't answer right away. "An ad? You want *me* in an ad? Me?"

"Yes."

"What's this ad for?" She looked down at herself. "Some kind of food?"

"Well, I thought to have you sign an NDA before getting too far into the details, but I guess it's okay to tell you, since you aren't in our business. It's essentially a tourism ad for the city."

"I'm sorry, I don't understand. You want to show a picture of me and expect people to come here, as in to the beach?" She was starting to think the man might be a few bananas shy of a bunch.

The smile was back. He nodded quickly. "Very much so, assuming we produce the ad correctly. Have you ever heard of Rosie the Riveter?"

She frowned and shook her head. "No."

From behind her came Frannie's voice. "She was a symbol of women supporting the war ... as in World War II."

Dora turned, still not understanding, then noticed Charlie move to see behind her and shifted again to block his view.

"Exactly!" Charlie agreed. "I watched you work recently, and I think you'd be a great spokesperson for the city, assuming they'd allow it."

Still suspicious, Dora stepped back and to one side, allowing Charlie to enter the apartment.

At that moment, Franny's cell phone rang. She picked it up, listened, and then hurried into the bedroom.

"Even if I believe what you're telling me," Franny was saying as she went, "I'm not in a position to do anything about this. I'm just a local cop."

"You're missing the point," came from the metallic-tinged voice.

"And what is the point?"

"Many years ago, there was a murder that was covered up. It was called an accident and, in a way, it was, but it was also a crime. The coverup grew into a lot of coverups and spread through Beach City like a corrupt virus. And now ... it's everywhere! This city is utterly corrupt, but it all started with the murder coverup."

"A virus? That's everywhere? Corruption? Is Beach City any more corrupt than—"

There was a *click*, and then a dial tone.

• • •

His alarm had been going off for quite some time. He reached out and patted its spot, but the thing just continued to beep. Then Jesse Healy opened his eyes.

He was in a hospital room. The alarm was some kind of monitor. He had tubes protruding from every entrance and exit of his body, and several places that were neither. He was covered in bandages.

He had not shut off his alarm clock; he had not, in fact, moved at all.

Why was he here? How long would he be here? What exactly was wrong with him? And what would his future be?

He remembered being in his apartment, having beer, watching a romantic comedy on his iPad, then ... nothing. He had so many questions.

None, however, addressed where he would live, given the city's repossession of his home.

• • •

Fred Yanatta sat in his red Ford 150, listening to the Grateful Dead on XM Radio. He didn't want to go into his house, knowing that Estelle, his wife, would have questions about his day. He loved his wife. They had been married for thirty-two years. Fred was used to telling Estelle about his day, and Estelle was accustomed to listening. But these last few years had been an ever-increasing shitstorm.

He was the fire chief. His job was putting out fires and seeing to the safety of the public. The fact that someone at City Hall wanted to slow down his department's response to certain homes was criminal! It was insanity! And the worst of it was the combination of rewards offered, penalties levied, and embarrassments revealed made the requests, which were more orders than requests, nearly impossible to resist. Did he want his pension? Did he want to quietly tender his resignation?

The last thing he wanted to do was talk to Estelle about any of this. She would have opinions and would be pretty vocal about sharing them.

So, he sat in his truck, singing along with the lyrics.

"You know better, but I know him ..."

Chapter 5

The courtroom on the top floor of City Hall doubled as a venue for large Beach City events, to which the public was invited. Tonight, the room was nearly filled with residents, many of whom Tom Volkov knew.

The mayor was making his way up the center aisle, smiling and warmly greeting everyone by name, taking them by the hand, asking about their homes and families, listening to their responses in the practiced manner of a career politician, and filing the information away to bring up the next time he saw them, as evidence of his deep compassion.

Mayor Mark shook hands with the two existing council members whose terms were not currently up, Chase Craig and Valerie Nussbaum. Then he made his way to the two lecterns behind which stood the two current candidates, Jeremy Anderson and Agatha Raines.

It was an open secret that everyone knew that the mayor, the department chairs, and everyone at City Hall favored Mr. Anderson, whose company, Anderson Consulting, had been doing business with the city for just over a decade. There had never been any overt signs of favoritism, other than the awarding of the city's advertising contracts to Mr. Anderson's company and the silence faced by anyone who uttered the phrase "conflict of interest."

Once the candidates were seated, Tom, who was at a table facing the podium and was the event's moderator, waited for the mayor to finish his greeting *shtick* and sit down at the center of the podium.

Tom cleared his throat and spoke into his microphone, "Welcome everyone. The *Beach City Chronicle* is pleased to present the candidates for the vacant city council position. On my left is Jeremy Anderson, the Republican's candidate and incumbent, and on my left is Agatha Raines, the Democrat's candidate and challenger. Each will have two minutes to present his or her opening remarks, which will be followed by questions on a variety of local issues that were submitted to *The Chronicle* by Beach City readers. Following your answers to those questions, you will be given a few minutes to present closing arguments, which may or may not reflect the topics covered here this evening. Is everyone clear on the process? Any questions? Now would be the time." He paused, looked at both candidates and at the assembled residents, then nodded and swiped a finger several times across the surface of a tablet that rested on the table in front of him.

"The order in which you will answer was decided a few moments ago via the flip of a coin. Jeremy Anderson won the toss and will go first.

"Mr. Anderson ..." Tom looked down at the tablet, reading aloud, "the decor, beauty, and image of the city will be the subject of some of the items on the upcoming council docket and budget. What is your philosophy regarding the image of Beach City?"

Jeremy Anderson was a tall, thin man in his mid-fifties, with a crown of wispy gray hair and a pencil-thin, brown mustache, flecked with gray. He retained what was either the remains of a deep summer tan or a tanning booth facsimile and wore a blue, pinstriped suit and red tie, held in place by an American flag tie pin.

He nodded gravely and cleared his throat. "Thank you for the question, Tom. As the owner of Anderson Consulting, Beach City's"—he cleared his throat again—"premier ad agency, I'm uniquely qualified to offer an opinion on our city's branding. After all, my work helps to create that branding. But I'm a citizen first, a taxpayer and a resident who believes in the ongoing growth and prosperity of our community. I care about the safety of our citizens, and so, when I read about the random violence that affected one"—he looked at a piece of paper—"Jesse Healy, I thought it my civic duty to speak out for the need for increased law and order, specifically a beefed-up police force that will help keep residents, who may be out at night, or any other time, safe and secure."

There was mild applause.

He went on, "I also look forward to the completion of the Clean Community, including Clean Seniors, Clean Living, and Clean Acres, which will afford residents of all ages beautiful, state-of-the-art communities in which to live."

Agatha Raines leaned forward in her seat. "But are you in favor of the tax breaks the developers were given?"

"Ms. Raines," Tom Volkov chided, "please wait your turn."

Agatha shook her head, muttering, "Millionaire builders not having to pay their fair share ..."

Jeremy Anderson cleared his throat. "I'll answer that. My answer is yes. Tourism represents millions of revenue dollars each year, in beach passes and dollars spent at our many wonderful restaurants, coffee shops, pubs, surf shops, and many other establishments, all of whom pay taxes. And the taxes paid by those who utilize the Clean Communities will help all of us. So, to answer Ms. Raines, I believe that, when taken in context, the tax breaks are a net positive for Beach City.

"Please, take the long view. I have worked hard as a business owner and private resident to keep our community the pristine destination it has been since the prohibition era, and I will continue to do so. Residents, voters, and taxpayers can rest assured that I have the same values when it comes to our elite brand that they do. I look forward to serving at their pleasure."

Tom paused to be sure the candidate was finished before turning to the second candidate. "Agatha Raines, same question."

Agatha Raines was in her early forties. Her normally unruly black hair was slightly streaked with grey and was pulled back in a bun. She wore a forest green blouse and a simple, navy blue skirt. Her chocolate-colored complexion was highlighted by gold-rimmed glasses that sat on the tip of her nose and over which she now peered, eyebrows raised, first at Tom, then at her opponent. "My idea of branding runs a bit deeper than my opponent and his ad agency might be accustomed to," she began.

There was a rustling around the room, residents shifting uncomfortably in their pews.

"You see, branding, per se, ought not to be the priority of the council. Sure, it's an issue, but it isn't *the* issue. The beauty of our city has long been undermined by the way justice, or what some might refer to as the day-to-day business affairs of our city, has been dispensed. Beach City has many fine attributes, but we don't all have access—equal access—to these benefits. It is my hope to be a voice of equality and justice on the council, which is balanced in favor of the wealthiest two percent of our homeowners and local businesses, at the expense of the other ninety-eight percent."

Tom stared at his tablet screen, as though searching for the script that Ms. Raines might have departed from. He looked up and saw that Mayor

Mark, too, was watching her with what looked to Tom to be detached interest. The mayor shifted his gaze to Tom.

Agatha Raines looked around the room and smiled, and her smile—it was a joyous smile—transformed her, lighting her from within. "I see I am confusing some of you. So, let me explain. The beauty of Beach City cannot be denied. The ocean, the beaches, the sun—all of God's great gifts —are ours to enjoy. But these are not ours. We do not own them. They are everyone's, to enjoy equally."

Jeremy Anderson chuckled. "Ms. Raines, no one would deny that what you say is true ..."

Agatha Raines looked at her watch. "I believe it is still my turn, Jeremy. I would like to continue my opening statement." She looked at Tom, who nodded ascent.

Jeremy Anderson raised an eyebrow and sat back.

"What I am referring to is that our city employees, union members, clerical personnel, entrepreneurs, and others work hard to feed their families, while recent retirees receive obscene payouts from the city. Nearly three million dollars' worth."

Jeremy Anderson frowned. "Union retirees' contracts were guaranteed, which has nothing to do with the upcoming election."

Ms. Raines turned toward her opponent. "Still my turn, Jeremy." She let her gaze wander over the audience. "What of the doling out of so-called justice via parking tickets aimed at those who oppose the so-called will of the people? What of the beauty of our parks that is dimmed by the building permits handed out to certain favored construction companies and private interests? This favoritism is a form of corruption! And speaking of favoritism, what of the favoritism shown by the police department toward some at the expense of others?" Her voice rose a notch. "You know what I'm talking about. It's common knowledge. What of our land repurposing projects—the confiscation of land via so-called eminent domain? What of the liquor licenses, which are approved or turned down, based not so much on the establishment's fitness to serve, but on its relationships with certain members of our community?" Her voice crescendoed, and she stood, slamming her palm on the surface of the table. The sound was picked up by her microphone and broadcast throughout the cavernous room.

Several people started in their seats.

"Liquor licenses, building permits, parking tickets, summonses of all kinds, and other violations are not weapons! Nor are they gifts! They are expressions of the will of the people! They. Rep-re-sent. Laws!"

"Ms. Raines." It was the mayor. He raised a respectful hand toward Tom, asking with a gesture for permission to speak, which was granted. "Ms. Raines, you have a wonderful imagination and an admirable gift for oratory, which I'm sure stands you in good stead with children at the library when it is time to read to them. But this is not the library, and we are not children." He narrowed his eyes. "Slander and libel can have consequences."

Agatha Raines smiled, looked at the gallery, then back at the mayor. "Threats, Your Honor?"

"Facts, Ms. Raines. You've made accusations; where are your facts?"

Tom rapped his knuckles on the table. "I agree with His Honor. Let's stick to facts, Ms. Raines. Demonstrable facts. Facts which are relevant specifically to this election. If you have knowledge of some specific grievance that involves you personally, or which bears specifically on this proceeding, by all means. We all know the city is politically polarized, and that this election represents a swing vote in a split council. We've run editorials and Op-Eds supporting both points of view—"

"Both points of view? Debatable," Ms. Raines said.

"Nevertheless," Tom said, "there must be decorum. We're not here to conduct an investigation, nor to sling mud."

"I'd agree, if decorum were equally enforced. In any case, I say, let the people decide." In the space of a few moments, Agatha Raines had grown from a quiet librarian into something quite different.

"I say," Jeremy Anderson mimicked her phrase and tone, "you are making a lot of accusations that throw quite a lot of people under the bus and which reflect rumors and innuendo found in certain local Facebook groups, which are populated primarily by local losers—yes, losers—with axes to grind. People who, through their own irresponsibility, have lost jobs or … elections. Our debate was to be about current issues, the facts on the ground, and you've dragged it into the mud and gutter."

"I haven't dragged anything anywhere. What you're calling the gutter is where the facts are," Ms. Raines retorted.

The debate continued on in this way, with Jeremy Anderson, the incumbent, extolling the virtues of Beach City's status quo and parrying the incendiaries lobbed by Agatha Raines, whose oratory kept the audience spellbound.

Tom Volkov struggled to retain both order and his professional reserve, and he did his best to make sure the candidates remained within their time limits.

Tom kept his eye on Mayor Mike and was not surprised to see not a single crack in the mayor's famous, magnanimous veneer, the above-the-fray kindness and benevolence that shone from somewhere behind the white, dental-implant smile and gleaming bald pate. His response to the most vicious of Agatha Raines' charges was the sort of saddened, patronizing *tsk-tsk* and head shake a wizened parent might reserve for a prodigal child.

The public was respectfully quiet for most of the evening, occasionally gasping or politely applauding.

Eventually, Tom arrived at the final question, which he knew would be the most controversial.

"There have been reports, verified by an independent environmental company, that certain liquid, viscous effluents have been dumped into our canals and channel. To be clear, this is not rumor; it has been verified. It is fact." He paused and looked pointedly at each candidate, at the mayor, and then scanned the gallery.

Many residents were nodding, and grumbling could be heard. Three men in business suits, in the second row near the window, sat up straighter in their chairs.

"What, if anything, would your policy be about this chemical dumping? Mr. Anderson?"

Jeremy Anderson dipped his head, acknowledging the issue's gravitas. "First of all, yes, there have been reports of this substance in our waters—"

"Verified reports," Tom clarified.

"Verified reports, yes. But what is it? Where does it come from? What do we know about it?" He shrugged. "So ... there's some bad stuff in the water. I'm as against such a thing as anyone." He shook his head. "Let's determine the facts and let those determine our course of action. Making assumptions and trumpeting them in letters to the editor doesn't help anyone."

Several people in different spots of the crowd stood up and began shouting at once, pointing at the candidate, who held up his hand.

"Yes. Yes. Okay. We can all agree there is undesirable stuff in our waters," he said, enunciating slowly so everyone understood his words. "My policy will be to get to the facts. Undesirable does not mean poisonous or deadly, or even unhealthy. And we don't know where it came from."

Agatha Raines jumped to her feet. "But its chemical components match your client Julienne's waste products!"

"Excuse me, Ms. Raines. I believe it is now my turn!" Jeremy Anderson straightened his tie. "If, for instance, the chemicals were gasoline, the fact that you all own cars doesn't make you guilty. However, I do pledge to leave no stone unturned in finding out, scientifically, what this … this stuff is, how it is getting into our waters, what the laws are surrounding this situation, and seeing to it that they are enforced." He had been leaning forward, hands clasping the wooden railing that ran across the front of the courtroom's witness boxes. The mayor, too, had been leaning forward. However, when Anderson finished, he leaned back in his chair, and the mayor visibly relaxed, his smile returning to full wattage.

Tom turned to Agatha Raines. "Ms. Raines?"

She was shaking her head, her eyes locked on the three men in suits along the window. "Come on." Her tone dripped with sarcasm. "I mean, *come on*. We all know where this sludge—these *ef-flu-ents*—comes from. It's from Julienne Incorporated, verified by an independent lab, and with whom my opponent is in bed and in which my opponent has an ownership stake!"

"Outrageous!" Jeremy Anderson leaped to his feet, stabbing the air with a finger. "And the lab did not state that the effluents originated at Julienne, only that the chemical makeup was similar!"

"Identical," Agatha Raines said.

"Nonsense," Anderson countered.

Tom banged his gavel and looked from one candidate to the other. "Order. We will have order. Now, Ms. Raines, let's stick to facts."

Agatha Raines shook her head again and looked directly at Jeremy Anderson. "The analysis states that these effluents originate with manufacturing companies. How many manufacturing companies do we have along our canals? One. And it's at the intersection of our biggest canal and our channel. Any discussion that leaves the issue open-ended is a joke. And everybody knows about Mr. Anderson's relationship with—"

One of the suits jumped to his feet. "Who knows what floats downstream or upstream? You're jumping to unfair conclusions. The people—residents—need to understand that!"

Another of the suits stood up. "You're not being fair, Agatha. We take great care and expense to have our effluents stored in drums and carted away. We can document that and account for every barrel. Mr. Anderson *has* stood up for our rights in the past. His company is, in large part, responsible for our reputation, our image, our brand. We certainly pay our fair share of taxes. More than our fair share. We deserve some representation. We believe those effluents to be from gas stations and marinas dumping oil, and from small construction companies dumping paint waste, turpentine, and the like. They are *not* from our company."

The third suit stood up. "Julienne is a publicly traded company. Anyone can invest and would then have part ownership."

Beach City was home to two marinas, five gas stations, and many small construction companies, even a paint store. The owners of those companies were all in attendance, and all began yelling at once.

Tom banged his gavel until order was restored. "We will have an orderly debate, taking turns and, at the very least, being courteous. Now, I'm here as moderator, and as a member of the press, I am no special friend of the city." He looked at Anderson then at the mayor. Neither reacted. "Nor do I represent businesses." He looked at Agatha Raines. "And I will not allow slander or rumor to be a part of these proceedings."

Of one thing, Tom was sure; his readers and advertisers would be looking forward to the next issue of *The Beach City Chronicle*.

• • •

Agatha Raines moaned, braced herself with both hands on Rudy's shoulders, and bounced harder. Rudy's enormous hands held fistfuls of her ass as he lifted her up, off of him, then pulled her back down again hard. They were both sweating and panting in ecstatic exhaustion. He lifted her higher, until she was up in the air, then slammed her down again, faster and harder than before.

A long wail escaped her, like a note on a blues guitar—long and low, infused with joy and pain and longing.

Then it was his turn, puffing like a steam engine, picking up momentum until he yelled, and Agatha covered his mouth, lest the neighbors hear.

She fell down on top of her husband and licked his neck. He laughed; his eyes closed.

"Gimme some tissues," she said.

"Can't ... get up ... over there." He waved a finger toward his night table.

She slid off him then returned, tissues pressed between her thighs and a few more held out for him.

She sat next to him, and they held hands for a few moments.

"Think we did it?" Rudy asked.

Her face turned serious, shut down. "Did what?"

"Made a little boy."

Her look turned hard. "Why do you have to bring that up?" She got up and went to the window. The night outside was black and moonless.

"You gave 'em hell tonight."

She stayed at the window, nodding at the night. "I did."

"Shit, I'm sorry."

She nodded again.

"It was good to give them a taste of what the city's been doing to us all." He tried to laugh, but her look shut him down.

He tried again. "Sorry."

She held his gaze, turned, and then went into the bathroom.

• • •

Tom Volkov arrived home, exhausted. His head ached from tension and stress, and because he hadn't eaten in nine hours. He went to the refrigerator, took out a fried chicken leg, took a bite, then poured himself a tall, neat scotch and sat down in his red cloth armchair. He could hear Irene's voice coming from upstairs, from Anne's room.

He leaned to his right and turned on his Bluetooth surround sound system, took out his phone, opened Spotify, and put on a Clapton list loud enough to drown her out.

He had two more drinks then turned off the music and turned on the TV, finding his favorite show, a mystery thriller, on Netflix. He was obsessed with mysteries, murders, and detective shows, especially when the murderer is caught and the victim's family finds closure … and justice.

Chapter 6

The city clerk, Christine Pearsall, was in her mid-thirties and thought of herself as an attractive, conservative, family-minded, church-going woman, who believed that being married and having children were her responsibilities. She got along easily with just about everyone and had ample opportunities to meet men, given that she was essentially the gatekeeper at City Hall. So, she was frustrated to find herself still single.

She knew that some of her coworkers, including a few she counted as her friends, thought her values out of date and out of step, but she believed that an attitude of forgiveness toward judgmental people was admirable, so she kept her opinions to herself.

Decades ago, she had given her heart, and her virginity, to Charlie Bernelli. She had loved him and had naively assumed he was "the one," that together they would head off into the sunset, a brood of babies in tow. Charlie's drinking had gotten in the way of their relationship, but her own naiveté was at least as much to blame.

He had been a mean drunk, which had led to her drinking. Some of their troubles could be chalked up to Charlie's son, C3's, troubles. He had been attracted to the wrong crowd, had burglarized a liquor store, and had gone to jail, which had been devastating for his father. She understood, and sympathized, but was strong enough to refuse to enable Charlie's cruelty over his issues with his son.

And now, the love of her life was back in town, and she could all but hear her biological clock ticking.

She loved her job and, though she was paid well, saw her work as her civic duty. So, on days like today, when her job conflicted with her beliefs, she was anxiety-ridden. She felt no real fear about consequences—she was pretty sure God understood the difficult position she was in—but she had never mustered the courage to refuse to do as she was told. Questioning her work for Beach City was beyond her job description, and yet …

So, she looked the other way.

She scanned the "D List," which was in a spread sheet, clicked on the name and email address, then on the email designated to be sent to that address. Because so much of her job was performed in her official capacity as the face of Beach City, she had plausible deniability.

She tried to think of her work in the abstract, and usually succeeded, yet she was also aware that her deniability did not extend to God.

So, she went to the next name on the list, a Dr. Weingrad.

• • •

Dr. Jacob Weingrad pressed the intercom button.

"Mrs. Grady is here for her flu shot," Nikki, his office manager, said. "Room 2."

"Thank you." He stood up and started toward his office door when he heard the chime of an incoming email and reflexively sat down and clicked on the icon. All arriving emails held a subtle sense of excitement, as handwritten cards arriving on his birthday had when he had been a boy, though far subtler and usually with less promise. His mind flashed to a childhood memory: little Ronnie Howard singing "The Wells Fargo Wagon" in *The Music Man*.

Three emails had arrived; two were spam—a request from a politician for a donation and an email newsletter from a local chiropractor he might have once visited. The third email was meant for him but was far from the subtly pleasant surprise he associated with the sound of incoming mail. This email was from the Beach City Clerk's office. He read the email, and then he read it again. Then he took out his cell phone and, squinting at the number below the email's signature, began to dial.

"Beach City Clerk."

"Christine Pearsall, please."

"Just a moment, I'll see if she's available."

Dr. Weingrad waited, muttering under his breath, "See if she's available? She works for us, for God's sake." He had little love for City Hall, which held a portion of the keys to his practice. He believed public servants held far too much power, which was why he was a vocal proponent of term limits. He made a point, in fact, of opposing any Beach City policies he believed were self-serving, which was most of them.

Public servants were exactly that—their jobs were to serve citizens, voters —and he believed it was important to let them know it.

"I'm sorry. Ms. Pearsall is on another line. Would you care to hold?"

While he was waiting, Dr. Weingrad tried to imagine what the email was talking about. He had paid his city taxes on time, as always. So, what kind of irregularity—*emergency* irregularity, the attached letter from this … this Lenore Callahan, Receiver of Taxes, had called it—could there possibly be with his taxes? The check had cleared the bank; he had confirmation of that. And what could the email mean by "a problem with his property's survey?" Were the emergency property tax irregularity and the property survey problem somehow related? If not, why had notification of them arrived together? He felt the beginnings of his IBS, which always began with a vague pain in his side.

A sudden noise startled him, and he hung up the phone.

It was Nikki, rapping on the door. Mrs. Grady was waiting for her flu shot.

• • •

The gym, which was the concrete underside of one of Beach City's post-Superstorm Sandy raised homes, its walls covered with soundproofing and old mattresses, reeked of sweat. A faded Indian rug covered the floor and shielded anyone sitting or lying on it from the cold concrete beneath. Everyone wore mouth guards, knee and elbow pads, chest protectors, light gloves, and head guards.

The five women milling around with Dora on the thick carpet had been introduced as Whale, Wire, Axe, Touch, and Bottoms. She could see why two of them might have earned their names and briefly wondered about the others. But Shay, the dark-eyed, forty-something owner and trainer, didn't give her time.

A blow to the side of her head nearly rocked her off her feet. She whirled and saw Shay grinning in a southpaw side stance, her front leg retracting, touching the ground briefly, then quickly snapping out again, with the top side of her foot aimed at Dora's lower leg. The first kick landed and stung. Dora lifted her foot, and Shay's second kick missed, throwing the smaller woman momentarily off balance.

Shay laughed, delighted. "Oooh, nice reflexes!"

Dora was about to thank her, but Shay was no longer in front of her. She had angled off to one side, twisting suddenly, then launching a lightning left hook into Dora's kidney, causing Dora to gasp and bend forward at the waist.

What was she doing here, anyway? The question would have to wait, as Shay was quick on her feet and smaller than Dora, at about five-foot-two and about one hundred and twenty pounds, all of it fast-twitch muscle. She was literally half Dora's weight.

Before Dora could respond, Shay had dropped her level and slid in for a single leg takedown. Dora knew enough to fling her legs out and back, sprawling her weight onto Shay, her right arm around the trainer's neck in a guillotine. She smiled to herself and squeezed.

Shay turned her head into the choke, angled her chin down and in, close to her own neck, which normally would have allowed her to escape.

Normally.

But while she had never trained MMA, Dora had her own personal, street and family experience. She swung her legs around and in front of her, clasped them around Shay's torso, and then sat back, putting all of the strain on Shay's neck.

Shay struggled then quickly tapped, prompting admiring noises from the women on the sidelines.

"Oh ho!"

"Nice!"

"Wooohoo!"

"Sign the girl up!"

"Encore!"

Shay sat up, red-faced, rubbing her neck, but still grinning.

"No way you've never trained! Now you gotta join. I've never been in a guillotine I can't break."

Dora shrugged. "Till now."

• • •

Sally Freschetti, the Beach City Director of Animal Control, was a petite, single woman whose best friends were Rosie, her black lab retriever, and Skidoo, her Dalmatian, with Theodore Roosevelt, a Russian Blue cat, running a close third … only because he was less affectionate and needy than the dogs. Sally was nearly as protective of her department as she was of her pets, whom she referred to as her "besties." She believed her mission was saving the animals that she and Richie, her assistant, brought in from the neglectful and often deranged, cruel citizens that flourished in Beach City.

She got along well enough with the mayor and the other women in City Hall, none of whom had ever treated her with anything but respect. She avoided men, other than the mayor, whenever possible, not just in City Hall, but just about everywhere. And men tended to avoid her. Well, to avoid her eyes.

Despite being barely five feet tall, Sally found that men rarely looked her in the face. She couldn't help it if she was well developed. She had never asked for that.

Since the age of thirteen, she had been disgusted by the way boys and, later, men treated her. Her besties loved her for who she was and couldn't care less about boobs.

Today's text message was similar to those she had received when something specific and outside her responsibilities was expected of her. The message was worded in such a way that the action she was expected to take, while uncomfortable for her, seemed more than justified.

> *It has come to our attention that the owner of a German Shepherd named Hero, a Clarice Banacik, will be applying for a dog license within the next few days. Please note that Ms. Banacik has been reported by several neighbors as having beaten Hero on several occasions. We hope you will take her grievous behavior into account when reviewing her application. Hero would be welcome, if you recommend it, at our shelter. German Shepherds are popular here in town.*

The note was signed J.H.

Sally knew enough to take the note seriously.

What the note did not say was that, not only was its accusation not true, but that its real purpose was to address Ms. Banacik's loud, late-night parties; parties that had been the subject of several complaints and that she had been warned about several times, as well as her own ongoing complaints to the newspapers about her stuck-up neighbors and her freedoms being encroached upon by their Victorian attitudes. It was the letters to *The Chronicle* and how they might affect perceptions of the city that were the motivations behind the text.

Sally denied Hero's license without comment, and Ms. Banacik's follow-up calls about the matter were ignored. A week later, Hero was rounded up and placed in the shelter. A week after that, he had a new home on the other side of town.

• • •

Beach City had no shortage of drinking establishments, particularly in the west end, where the younger beach crowd and the tourist beach wannabes hung out. Charlie had decided to reacquaint himself with the neighborhood. So, instead of one of any number of tourist drinking establishments, he went to Rudy's, a working-class hangout, where many of the city's union employees, police, firefighters, plumbers, and assorted "regular folk" went. Rudy's was emphatically not a white collar or tourist bar, so he left his collared shirt at home and changed into a red flannel, with a T-shirt underneath, and jeans.

He sat down at the bar and tried to catch Rudy's eye, but the big man was hunched over his phone, one palm shading his eyes, his weight shifting from one leg to the other and back again, his body language tense.

The song playing over Rudy's sound system was The Beatles' "Paperback Writer," but it was played as a swinging, syncopated jazz instrumental by a trio of piano, bass, and sax. Most of the bar's patrons didn't seem to notice. Charlie listened for a while and, when Rudy hung up, nodded in his direction then put out his hand.

"Charlie Bernelli, I just opened—"

"The ad agency down the street." Rudy nodded. "Word gets around."

"I guess it does."

"Rudy Raines."

Charlie held up a finger. "I know. Say, are you related to—"

"Agatha." The man smiled. "I hope I don't lose cred for that."

"Not at all."

"What can I get you?"

"Whatever's on tap will be fine."

Rudy nodded, turned, and then froze. His expression fell.

A big-boned, white man of about fifty had entered the bar.

The man looked familiar, and Charlie realized he was the owner of Cobb's diner. Or was he? He looked somehow ... different. For one thing, he was wearing a police uniform.

Rudy beckoned to a waitress, whispered to her, then nodded toward Charlie before heading for the newcomer. Those nearest them stepped away, giving them room. The two big men bent their heads toward one another. After a moment, Rudy straightened up, his expression stunned and angry.

"Are you kidding me?" he said, loud enough for those nearest him to half-turn then turn away again, aware that the conversation did not concern them.

Cobb spoke again and, after staring at him for a moment, Rudy walked away, past Charlie and those at the bar, and into a back room. Cobb watched him go, then saw Charlie watching and strode over.

"You're the new ad guy." It was not a question.

Charlie put out his hand, and after looking at it long enough to make his point and assert some idea of dominance, Cobb put out his. They shook. Cobb's grip was tight and hard.

"George Cobb."

"I've met your brother. You look like him."

"*He* looks like *me*." Cobb laughed without humor then slapped Charlie on the shoulder a bit too hard. "What'll you have?"

"Well, I just ordered a draft, but you distracted Rudy."

"Barb! Two drafts. My tab." He pointed to the two of them, and the waitress quickly began pouring the beer.

"Good to know they run tabs here."

Cobb shook his head. "They don't."

Charlie looked at him again. "Only for cops?"

Cobb didn't answer.

"Okay ... Say, would you be the Beach City Police Chief?"

Cobb paused again, the dominance thing. "I'm a captain. Chief's a guy named Stalwell. Terry Stalwell."

Cobb smiled back at Charlie, but his eyes were appraising him. "Welcome to Beach City."

• • •

Franny had taken her phone into the bathroom and closed the door as soon as she heard the familiar, artificially-disguised voice. "First of all, I don't understand what you mean by *a murder that wasn't a murder* and how might such a thing connect to corrupt city business, which you claim is widespread?"

"You're the cop; you figure it out."

The caller hung up, so she flushed the toilet then returned to the living room and her glass of Pinot Noir.

The door opened, and Dora came in, standing breathlessly in front of Franny, arms out at her sides. "Guess what I did?"

"Tell me."

"I went to that MMA gym, you suggested and — check this out — it's part of a startup league that has real fights. They gave me a chance, and hey, I whupped the owner."

"No way!" Franny swiped the music away on her phone screen.

"It was your idea." Dora draped an arm casually around Franny, who lightly pushed her away.

"Girl, you need a shower. And I didn't say you should fight anyone! I meant you should train, to release stress."

"I'm doing that, too. Besides"—she pulled Franny closer—"you're all the stress release I need."

"But you're not going to fight, right? Not really?"

Dora was grinning at her. She shrugged. "It's not a big deal. There's a ref to make sure no one gets hurt, and the money's nothing. I'll donate it somewhere—to the hotline downtown for abused kids, all right? Listen, I can do this. I've been watching, taking notes, practicing. Shay was pretty surprised."

"Shay?"

"Our coach. I submitted *her!*"

Franny sat up and looked at Dora. "So ... when is this fight?"

"A week from Saturday. And we'll have protective gear, by the way. Please come!"

Franny lifted her head and looked at Dora again with narrowed eyes. "No! I don't want to see my girl get beat up."

"Oh, I won't get beat up. I told you. I can do this. I can *excel* at this."

"So *you* say ... before doing it. Listen." Franny tapped her thigh, and Felix promptly jumped into Dora's lap. Franny laughed. "Wise ass."

Dora laughed with her. "Make way for the king!"

Franny touched Dora's wrist with two fingers. "That phone thing, the one I heard about at work, it's to do with a murder and a coverup. He said there was a murder, but there was no murder."

"What's that supposed to mean? When is a murder not a murder? Is that a riddle? What is this, Batman?"

"Not exactly a riddle. There was a murder, but it wasn't really a murder."

Dora shook her head. "Sometimes talking to you is like pulling teeth."

"Better than getting them knocked out." Franny gave Dora a hard look then finished her wine, walked to the kitchen and poured a second glass, took a few sips, then drank down half the remainder, topped it off again, and returned to Dora.

Dora tossed Felix to the floor, stood up, and started pacing. Felix followed, rubbing against her leg. She stopped. "And, I'm guessing, you haven't told Stalwell about this?"

"What's to tell? Some guy called me. Probably nothing. When there's something, I'll tell Stalwell ... if and when."

"But you believe the part about ...? What is it? A conspiracy?"

"I do, but only partly because of the call. Remember, I work for the city. I rub shoulders with the people in City Hall."

"At the police station more than City Hall."

Franny shrugged, finished her wine, got up, went into the kitchen, and poured another. She returned and stood in the doorway, leaning against the wall, one arm folded across her middle, the other holding the glass. She gave a hint of a smile. "So, this guy suggested I take a look at how decisions are made and implemented."

Dora waited a beat then began pacing again. "At the police station?"

Franny shrugged. "I don't know. He didn't say. He said downtown, which I would take to mean City Hall, but since I'm a police officer—"

Dora scoffed. "That could mean anything."

Franny nodded. "You're right. It could mean Cobb's. That place is better than a hairdresser's—the amount of gossip flowing there. The things I hear when I stop in for coffee and eggs ... about people's private lives, about their dealings with the city, about city politics, I wouldn't be surprised if city business gets done there on a regular basis."

Dora was pacing faster. "And the owner's brother's a cop. A cop with seniority. But you really think he might mean Cobb's?"

"I don't know. If the corruption's that widespread, it might not be limited to any one place, but be more systemic."

Dora stopped pacing. "Cobb's would be a great information hub. You want to start a rumor, give it to a hairdresser, or a waitress or waiter. They know everything."

Franny nodded. "Point taken. But what's this all got to do with a murder? And what murder, for God's sake?"

Chapter 7

Charlie awoke the next morning with an ache in his heart. The feeling was so physically strong that he tried to remember what he had eaten the previous night. Then he remembered the dream. It had been about Christine Pearsall. They had been lovers, but more than that, they had been *in* love, had shared thoughts and dreams and, at times, had felt like one person. The dream had reawakened that love. Ironically, awakening had taken it away.

He would have to deal with Christine, given that she was the city clerk and he was seeking business from the city and interacting with the mayor and the powers that be. She was essentially their gatekeeper.

Well, he was a grown man and would simply deal with her professionally, as though their past had never occurred.

He turned his attention to the new Beach City tourism campaign. He was anxious to begin. He directed Michele, his office manager, to hire a local portrait photographer for the day; told Luis Martinez, his freelance designer, and Dora, the model for the shoot, to meet him at the studio at nine thirty. He would art direct, Michele would handle makeup, Luis would work up designs and comps over the next few days, while he oversaw everything, wrote copy, and came up with the slogans. They would film the TV commercial at the same time that they took the stills. Then, later, once the print comps were done, he would hire the voice over and edit the footage.

The concepts would revolve around the strength of Beach City as a destination—the powerful draw of the beach and the restaurants and bars in the West End.

The image of Dora, an everyday working woman, would connect well with other working women; some single, others married with or without children. The ad's subtext and, perhaps, some of the headlines or copy detail would either imply or state that they already had the beach crowd— the women in bikinis and the shirtless, fit men. But Beach City was more. *We're for everyone.* In fact, that would make a great headline for one of the ads: *Beach City—We're For Everyone!*

He planned to hand deliver the proofs to the mayor. He wanted to make more than an impression; he wanted to make a splash and foster a long-term relationship, begun by his proactive creativity.

As he was finalizing the project notes in his iPad, his cell phone rang.

"Charlie Junior."

"Hi, Charlie. This is Christine. Christine Pearsall."

"How wonderful to hear your voice."

"Well … I'm calling in my professional capacity as the Beach City Clerk."

"Ah …" He waited.

"The city will not be proceeding with the ad campaign."

He didn't answer right away but absorbed and began processing the information. "What?" was all he could manage.

"I said, the city will not—"

"Yes, I heard, but the mayor personally gave me the approval to go ahead. We've hired a studio and brought on a city employee as a model—"

"I understand, and I am sorry. Your conversation with the mayor was off the record. No contract was signed, so I'm afraid we can't reimburse —"

"Don't worry about it. These things happen." He took a deep breath, regaining his composure. "Not looking for reimbursement, just to maintain our good relationship. Maybe we'll work together down the road. No worries." While he did understand, he was less sanguine about the development than he let on, given The Bernelli Group's dearth of new clientele.

Eager to change the subject and a bit giddy to hear her voice with echoes of last night's dream fresh on his mind, he plunged ahead. "Perhaps … we might have a drink or lunch … to catch up."

"The city keeps me pretty busy, but um … sure. Why not?" There was a hesitation, and then she said, "Talk soon," and the line went dead.

• • •

The offices of *The Beach City Chronicle* were above a deli and up a narrow staircase that had been painted grey once upon a time. On the second landing was a door with a hand-written sign, done in a calligraphic style by someone with talent.

Charlie knocked.

A woman called, "It's open!"

He opened the door. Inside was another short hallway, painted white with thick, ancient paint, off of which were two doors. One was closed; the same voice called from within the other.

"Hello?"

He stepped into the doorway, which opened into an office.

The woman was in her mid-thirties, with short, brown hair and a freckled nose and cheeks. She was dressed entirely in black. She stood and held out a hand. "I'm Sarah, the *Chronicle's* reporter."

"Hi," Charlie said. "Charlie Bernelli Junior."

Sarah nodded. "The ad agency. I understand we'll be doing some work together—virtually, I mean."

"Pleasure. That's kind of why I'm here. Is Tom Volkov around?"

She shook her head. "Best to catch him at home." She returned to her desk and rummaged through some papers, coming up with a card. "His home address. He'll be there. Oh, and don't mind his wife."

Charlie nodded and started for the door.

"Looking forward to working with you," Sarah said.

Charlie turned. "As am I."

As he went down the stairs, he wondered what she had meant about Tom's wife.

• • •

Tom Volkov lived in what had once been a single-story cape that had been extended and dormered and, after Hurricane Sandy, lifted. The house rested on eight-foot concrete pillars, with the space below utilized as a garage. The front door was up a flight of white vinyl stairs, alongside a deck which looked out over a more or less typical middle-class neighborhood, four blocks from the beach.

Charlie pressed the bell and heard a four-note chime echo on the other side of the door. After a moment, the door was opened by a man in his forties, with salt and pepper hair and a goatee, wearing gold-rimmed glasses. His expression was guarded.

"Yes?"

Charlie put out a hand, which Tom shook. "Charlie Bernelli."

Tom's expression softened. He held the door open as Charlie entered the home, which he would have generously described as "lived in." Clothes were scattered on the backs of chairs and dishes on the counters.

"'Scuse the mess."

"No worries," Charlie answered. "I've got a boy barely out of his teens."

Charlie followed Tom into a small office.

"Is somebody there?" called an anxious woman's voice from somewhere above them.

"An ad client, honey. Everything's fine. You can stay upstairs." He smiled and indicated a worn but well-padded, black faux leather chair. "Don't mind my wife."

Charlie nodded and smiled, pretending to understand.

Tom sat down behind a small, messy desk and turned expectantly toward Charlie. "So, what can I do for you?"

"Well, we were set to start shooting the ads for the city's campaign. I hired a model, a woman who works for the city. A garbage collector, of all things. A Darla somebody."

"Oh yes, Dora Ellison. I know just who you mean." He smiled. "It's a small town. Looking forward to seeing the comps."

Charlie pressed his lips together. "That's the thing. I received a call from Christine Pearsall."

"Oh?" Tom's expression changed to one of concern.

Charlie looked Tom in the eye, searching for a clue that might help him understand. "She said the campaign's cancelled. Just like that."

"Sorry to hear it." Tom took a deep breath then let it out as a sigh. "But I suspect there'll be other opportunities."

"Tommy?" Heavy footsteps outside the office were followed by the appearance of a gaunt, disheveled woman with dyed blue-black hair, wearing a purple terry cloth bathrobe and men's beige work boots that were many sizes too big. Her eyes and mouth were pulled downward at the corners, as though by some unseen force. Her expression was panicked. "I knew we had company! I'll just go and put on some tea." Her tone turned suddenly faux cheerful. "Maybe Anne will be back in time for you to meet her! Anne's our daughter. You'll love her—everybody does!" She disappeared, and her clumping footfalls faded.

"Okay, honey." Tom had been looking Charlie in the eyes, to see if he understood. He shrugged, dropping his eyes to his desk. "My wife ... isn't well."

Charlie nodded, eager to change the subject. "Any idea why the city would suddenly cancel?"

Tom shrugged. "Don't know. City campaigns are typically handled by another agency. Could be someone spoke to you too soon or saw a conflict."

"Well, if someone spoke too soon, it was the mayor who, I would think, gets to do that," Charlie said. "I do know the city typically works with Anderson Consulting, but I had hoped there might be enough work to go around. Why would the mayor have said I'm hired if I'm not? Isn't it his call?"

"It is, but he has a way of changing his mind. Mercurial guy. Probably wanted you to like him. He's like that. Like a little kid in a way, a dangerous little kid. I have yet to meet a politician who didn't have an outsized ego—big but fragile." He gave a tiny laugh and shrugged again. "Business."

• • •

Anderson Consulting occupied the entire top floor of the tallest building in Beach City. Charlie knew he had taken a chance by visiting without calling ahead for an appointment, but he assumed there was a greater chance of being seen sooner rather than later if he stopped by spontaneously.

The floor and walls of the elevator were lined with plush, forest green carpeting and a gold script AC insignia. The hallways were similarly carpeted, floor to ceiling; soft jazz played throughout.

He told the steadily smiling receptionist his name, the name of his company, and that he was here to see Mr. Anderson. She nodded, still smiling, and turned to her computer.

"Oh, I don't have an appointment," he added.

She turned, as if seeing him for the first time, which she probably was, and blinked. The smile faltered.

"It's official Beach City business concerning the upcoming tourism campaign." He nodded, prodding her to understand.

The receptionist picked up her phone and whispered into it. She gazed into her computer and shook her head, spoke again, then listened. Her eyes widened slightly at the response, and then she turned back to Charlie.

"As it happens, Mr. Anderson is between appointments, and will be happy to see you." She pointed toward the hallway. "The office at the end."

Jeremy Anderson's office was immense and furnished as a living room, or what was sometimes called "the great room" in older mansions, with the same green carpeting, gold insignias, elegant glass and wood furniture that decorated much of the rest of the premises. One wall sported shelves that were filled with books, held in place by glass awards as bookends. A tall, brown leather chair was facing away, toward windows that overlooked Beach City and the ocean beyond. The back of the chair was too tall for Charlie to be able to see if Anderson was in it.

Charlie cleared his throat, and the chair swiveled. Anderson, on his phone, held up a finger for him to wait. He listened for a moment and said, "Yes, you should," then hung up, rose, and extended a well-manicured hand.

Charlie took it and shook. "Charlie Bernelli."

"Junior—yes, I know. I remember your father. How is he? Have a seat." Anderson sat down and leaned back, elbows on the chair's armrests.

"He's well, thank you," Charlie said. "I'll tell him you asked for him."

Jeremy Anderson nodded then waited, his fingers steepled in front of his mouth.

After a moment, Charlie said, "Ah, well, I'm here because I had a verbal agreement with Mayor ... Mayor Mark. My company was to do at least some of the creative on a Beach City tourism campaign." He waited, but Anderson said nothing. "And it seems that the city has changed its mind, or at least so the city clerk tells me. I can't seem to get a hold of the mayor at the moment."

Anderson nodded, his eyebrows went up, his hands separated in a "what can I do" gesture, and then he shrugged. "And what has this to do with me?"

"I thought you might enlighten me as to what the usual flow of business is around here. While we may be competitors on one hand, I choose to believe there's enough business for everyone, and we can work together or, if not together, in a spirit of mutual cooperation."

Anderson narrowed his eyes. He smiled, but his smile was cold, more of amusement than of warmth. "What a laudable sentiment." He leaned forward and folded his arms, one over the other, on the desk. "But, assuming you really believe it, it's incredibly naïve. My view is that I recognize that the world is a competitive, even cut-throat place, and that to be the city's premier agency, we must maintain an edge. We typically handle all the buses, bus stops, train posters, TV commercials, and so on, including tourism campaigns. I have a contract, which is both the beginning and end of the conversation. I do wish you well in a general sense, since I do not know you and bear you no grudge or animosity. This might be a little difficult to hear, but in the animal kingdom, there are predators and there are prey. The predators have an easier time of it, unless"—he chuckled—"they become prey."

Puzzled, Charlie tilted his head to one side. "This isn't the animal kingdom."

"Isn't it?" Anderson rose, a dismissal. "My suggestion would be to take your question to the source. Make an appointment with the mayor; find someone at City Hall who can help you. You're going to the hardware store for milk here." He put out a hand. "Pleasure meeting you, Charlie. I wish you the best ... to a point."

On his way to the elevator, Charlie passed a room where half a dozen young professionals were working at computers. His eye was drawn to one of the screens that was facing the door. On it was an image of a burly woman, her sleeve rolled up, making a muscle. Beneath her were words in a thick font: *"Beach City Betty works for YOU!"*

Charlie slept poorly that night, his dreams beset by work-related imagery and seemingly unrelated frustrations. In the dream, he was working up a quote, but his father, on whom he relied for advice when quoting prospective business, was nowhere to be found. The quoting software, when opened, yielded nothing but nonsense poetry. The phones rang incessantly and, when answered, no one was on the line, but music played that put the nonsense poetry to equally silly, somehow frightening music. And the phones continued to ring and ring …

He awoke in a sweat to his radio alarm playing music reminiscent of the music in his dream.

He squinted, looking around, and made a decision. Or, more accurately, a decision came to him. Several decisions, in fact.

He made what he knew others—by whom he meant his father—would say was an inadvisable decision. He would go ahead and produce the ad, fund it himself, and run it as part of a Beach City tourism campaign, in the hopes other businesses might climb on board as a cooperative effort.

The prospect was an unlikely one, even by his own head-in-the-clouds standards, yet he was set on the idea, largely because the city—and he assumed its mayor—was behaving in an unacceptable way, and it pissed him off. Cities and mayors had that right, of course, but he had a right to tilt at whatever windmills he chose, didn't he?

And the campaign would be sure to annoy Anderson Consulting. He smiled at the thought.

Unwise propositions had long been something of a forte. He didn't care. He liked the idea. He had enough money to live and, if necessary, to move his company again if he had to. And, by God, he would do whatever he thought was right, as long as he was breathing. That part, he knew his father would agree wholeheartedly with.

Once at work, he asked Michele, his office manager, to call Luis Martinez, to tell him he was rehired and to come in ASAP. Then he added, "Find me a photographer. In fact, find me a still photographer who also does video. Tell my father I'd like to see him whenever he's free to go over an ad concept. Then get a hold of that Darla, or Debra woman, the trash collector, and tell her we're going to start work on the ad within a day or whenever she's available."

His father was dubious, as Charlie knew he would be. "I thought the city's advertising was handled by another company."

"Fuck another company. We'll do it, and we'll pay for the campaign ourselves. It'll be a hit, and we'll find local companies to co-op ... and if we don't, fuck 'em."

• • •

The studio had to be at least a hundred degrees, Dora thought, with the two 500-watt lights and the large light box, not to mention the tightly closed windows meant to keep out the sound of traffic. Even so, she was barely sweating at all. She was used to working hard, often under a hot sun and heavy protective layers; hour after hour of lifting and tipping heavy garbage cans, bags, sections of trees, kitchen appliances, and the detritus of families' lives. She was a big woman, but her size, while impressive, gave little indication of her strength, which had been built up over a decade of daily, arduous work—eight hours plus, every day, rain or shine, six days per week.

"Hold still," Ramon, the photographer, said as he circled her and snapped photos, all while the 4K camcorder continued to run. "Make a muscle! Look focused! Smile!"

Michele was busy at her desk with company paperwork—accounts payable and receivable. She felt free to comment on the proceedings—that was the kind of office The Bernelli Group ran. Easy and free, though not quite democratic; a benign autocracy.

Luis Martinez, The Bernelli Group's freelance, off-again-on-again graphic designer, was working on comps in Adobe Illustrator on a MacBook, testing headlines and fonts, while Charlie looked on, commenting freely.

"Now, roll up your shirt," Ramon was saying, and Dora lifted the bottom of her shirt up over her bra. "No, no. The cuffs. Your shirt sleeves. Like an iron worker, or whatever it is you do. Right. All the way up, as close to your shoulders as you can. There you go!"

"I tip garbage," Dora said.

"Hmm?"

"I tip garbage. I'm a garbage man."

"Oh, of course. But not a man."

"It's the name of the job. I refuse to call myself a sanitation engineer."

"Hmm? Yes! That's it. Now make a muscle again. Ah!"

Charlie was standing behind Luis, who was a light brown man, just under six feet tall, with three days' worth of black on the lower half of his face. He had curly black hair and bright red, horn-rimmed glasses. He tipped his head one way then the other.

"Change the font to Futura Extra Black."

He waited while Luis did as Charlie asked.

"Now, add a tag line below the body copy, '*Yeah, YOU!*' Ah, see?"

Luis sat back, and he and Charlie admired his work.

"Tell me something," Charlie said to Luis. "How can the mayor have told me we were hired for this campaign then change his mind and refuse to take my calls?"

Luis gave a half-smile then shrugged.

Michele had been paying close attention while attending to rote paperwork in the little alcove off to one side of the office that contained her work area. Her movements were quick and sharp, her features dark and focused, her eyes avidly attentive. Charlie thought she looked like a predatory bird.

She turned away from her work toward the set, around which everyone else was congregated. "So, Charlie," she started, "how do you propose to find someone to pay for these ads?"

Charlie shrugged. "I'll figure something out. I'm sure there are businesses in town less favorably disposed toward Anderson Consulting, who'd like to benefit from being associated with a good, professional tourism campaign."

"City Hall might not like it."

"All the more reason to do it."

"I thought you wanted to play nice with City Hall."

"Well ... they started it."

"Ah ..." she mimicked him, and he was aware of it.

"Let me ask you, Michele, how much has City Hall changed these last twenty years?"

Michele pivoted toward her computer then quickly back. She lifted her chin up, then back down, then cocked her head to one side. "Not very much, other than the ways that times have changed—technology and such."

There was a knock at the door.

"Come in," Ramon called.

When no one entered, he went to the door and opened it to reveal Charlie Sr., carrying a tray holding multiple takeout cups.

"Who wants coffee?" he asked.

As everyone headed toward the kitchen, Dora stepped out from the now darkened green screen, pulled a few tissues from a box on a table, and wiped small beads of sweat from her forehead.

Charlie had been checking the computers for messages and making sure Luis had saved his files. As he was about to step out of the room, he turned back to Dora. "Join us?"

She nodded, hanging back. "I was wondering ... you're from around here—I mean, originally."

"I am."

"From what I heard, it sounds like you're finding the way the city does business to be less than fair."

"Yeah, well, politics. Someone doesn't like your face or name or color or whatever, you're out. They like the other guy, or they're his cousin, they're in."

Dora nodded. "Not just politics. Life." She stepped closer to Charlie. "Let me ask you something. Have you ever heard of a murder here in town, something maybe controversial, maybe tied up with city politics or business dealings?"

Charlie thought for a moment then shook his head. "We've had a few murders over the years—well, decades—going back to a police chief who killed the mayor. That was murder mixed up with politics, but it was way, way back. Sixty, seventy years. How recent are we talking?"

"Within a few decades, I think, though I'm not sure. Maybe something that could've been a murder but wasn't reported as such—a controversial death?"

"Why do you ask?"

Dora was noncommittal. "Some talk I overheard. Rumors floating around."

"I grew up here"—he chuckled—"to the degree I grew up at all. And my dad was here before that. Nothing rings a bell."

Dora thought for a moment. "Could be I'm not explaining it in a way that would lead you to remember."

Chapter 8

Harry Livingston, the director of the Beach City Water and Sewer Department, picked up his phone, which had just buzzed. He read the text then flipped his phone over, as though that would make the text disappear.

The Wallace Family at 72 Floyd Street claim to have complained about a broken main in front of their home, which, they claim, has led to cracked pavement. While they may be right, they have written several articles to The Chronicle, *which have unfairly singled out city officials as having some sort of vendetta against the family. Please ensure the non-functionality of their system, and the future non-responsiveness of your department to any complaints from same. - J.H.*

Harry understood that "non-functionality" meant that he was expected to create a blockage in the sewer line running from the Wallace home to the street, ensuring a backup of sewage. When the problem was called to the city's attention—specifically, to his office's attention—he was expected to ignore the complaint, which meant putting out a red-flagged memo to his department to direct any 72 Floyd Street issues to his personal attention.

All of which was illegal, of course. But all of which would be at the top of his "to do" list, given the source of the text. His reputation and job were on the line.

• • •

Elvin Johns had been watching a Knicks game on TV but had lost interest and turned the TV off when his team fell behind by twenty-five points. That was when he noticed the light flickering on his living room wall.

He went to the window opposite, took one look, and then sprinted downstairs and out into the chilly night. His beautiful Camaro, his red baby, was engulfed in flames. He was so beside himself that, if one of his neighbors hadn't called the fire department, they might not have been called at all.

When they arrived, one of the firefighters had to instruct Elvin to move farther from the flames than where he was sitting, his head in his hands, on the curb.

Of course, the fire had been set intentionally. He did not have to wait for the police report a few days later to confirm that fact to be sure. Who was crazy enough to do this? He was liked by just about everyone in the neighborhood. He was respected as a community leader, a community organizer, by just about everyone.

Elvin was known in the community as a letter writer. He had met quite a few residents of Beach City who, when they were introduced, nodded and said, "I know your name from somewhere." They knew him from his letters to the newspapers. He wrote to *The Chronicle* at least once a month, most recently about the lack of parking in the neighborhood.

The city, in its wisdom, had built a three-tiered parking facility, had bought several street sweepers, and had begun strictly enforcing alternate side of the street parking, but few in Elvin's neighborhood were satisfied. None of the apartment buildings, assuming one was too kind to call them tenements, had nearly enough parking. The problem was exacerbated by the number of illegal two-family dwellings, whose owners made ends meet by renting sections of their homes or individual rooms. Those folks needed parking, too.

With escalating anger, he had written multiple letters on the subject to the city and to *The Chronicle*, taking the council, the Beach City Community Development Department, and the mayor himself pointedly to task.

• • •

The fight card was to take place in Nineveh, Long Island, in a high school wrestling room. The venue had been secured by Willie, one of the custodians, whose wife, Janie, coached the Nineveh squad. Willie, six-three and athletic, would referee, though little intervention on his part was expected. As long as the fights were relatively clean, they would be allowed to continue.

Dora and Franny stood in the doorway between the locker and wrestling rooms. The walls and floor were padded with thick, birds-egg blue—"Nineveh Blue"—foam. The school's wrestling season was already in full swing, so the fight was held at eleven p.m. on a Friday night.

Franny wrinkled her nose. "Ugh, the smell."

Dora smiled. "Breathe through your mouth." She liked the smell of wrestling rooms. It grounded her.

She nodded toward the wall to their left. "That's our side. Make yourself comfortable. I've gotta go change."

Franny sat cross legged, with her back against the wall, as the two coaches took turns explaining the rules. Each fight would consist of three rounds of five minutes each. Fights could end via knockout, submission, or decision, which would come via Shay and Janie's consensus. Everyone was expected to observe good sportsmanship and show respect. Concussion protocols were in place via a nurse in attendance.

After a ten-minute wait, the fighters filed in. Franny recognized two; one from a drunk and disorderly arrest a few weeks earlier, the other from around Beach City in general. Each side had perhaps twenty spectators; one or two friends or family per fighter.

The Nineveh women wore blue singlets that, more or less, matched the color of the room. Dora and her teammates wore crimson, Beach City High School's traditional colors, though the team was not affiliated with the high school or the city.

Dora had a focus, an intensity that Franny could feel, as though an electric hum emanated from her eyes and ran through the room, toward the women on the other side.

The first fight was between a woman named Shirley, with the nickname "Right," who was a short, thickly muscled black woman, and "Wire," real name Sandy, who was of some Middle Eastern heritage and was a head taller and much leaner than her opponent.

The two circled one another, with Right feinting with short left jabs followed by wild, whistling right crosses. After one of these, Wire slipped low and inside, wrapped her arms around Right's calves, lifted, and turned for a takedown, instantly spinning to take her back, her legs locked around Right's middle, her forearm beneath her opponent's neck, using the opposite arm as a crank, tightening the choke. Meanwhile, Right twisted and turned, trying to dig her chin underneath Wire's forearm. After nearly a minute of futile writhing, Right tapped Wire's arm, and Dora's side of the room erupted in cheers.

The second fight was between Wanda, "The Whale," a pale, Irish-American leviathan, and a taller, broader opponent with hazelnut skin and grey-green eyes named Martina, with the nickname "No-Mas."

Each fighter was encouraged to shake the other's hand as the fight was about to begin. The instant their hands came apart, Whale hit No-Mas with a lightning left hook to the ribs, and No-Mas went down and lay still. Whale turned to her teammates, grinned, dimpled, and pretended to curtsey. Behind her, No-Mas had pushed herself up to a squatting position and launched herself at Whale's legs, driving her back to one of the neutral walls. Whale held on and managed to wrap her arms around the back of her opponent's neck for a guillotine choke. No-Mas raised her arms and slid backward, out of the choke, and began dancing around Whale, flicking jabs and the occasional front leg roundhouse just beyond Whale's reach. Now and then, she doubled up, following the left jab with a left hook to the kidneys. Whale had plenty of padding around her middle. Still, the pain of the leg kicks and kidney shots showed, and her face was being bloodied.

Whale then did what seemed impossible. She launched a lightning front left roundhouse kick at No-Mas's chin, missing by inches when No-Mas pulled in her chin and leaned slightly back. The kick's momentum spun Whale around just enough for No-Mas to leap onto her back and sink a forearm beneath the chin and, with the other arm as a fulcrum, crank the pressure on. Whale turned this way and that, trying to fling the smaller woman off, and when this didn't work, she flung herself onto her back, hoping her own immense body weight would crush and dislodge her opponent. She was wrong, and after several more seconds, her face turned bright red then white, as she passed out. The match was over.

Dora's match was next, against a broad, blonde, shredded woman nicknamed "The Crab," who appeared to have a background in bodybuilding, while somehow remaining limber. The woman was intensely focused and refused Dora's calmly offered handshake. Dora shrugged as the woman began a slow circle to Dora's left, on all fours, away from what she thought was Dora's power. The woman jabbed twice, the second of which Dora caught and held with her left fist. She turned toward Franny, grinning, and Franny shook her head and pointed to the woman who was pulling at Dora's fingers.

Dora's expression was exactly the same distracted look as when she squeezed beer cans, but The Crab's expression turned from one of serious focus to anguish. She fell to her knees, but the move was a ploy. As Dora began to change levels with her opponent, The Crab rose up and elbowed Dora in the face. Dora let go and wiped her nose, looking at the blood on her glove. She had little time to react because The Crab had tackled her at the knees and was working on an arm bar submission.

"Crab dinner!" one of her teammates yelled, as several others waved their hands while wiggling their fingers.

"No escape from The Crab," another yelled.

"In the grasp!" a third sang out.

And indeed, Dora's arm was being pulled straight, then backward, at an angle beyond straight. Dora could not reach the woman's grip to free her arm, but she was able to reach one of the woman's feet with her other arm. A moment later, the woman screamed and released her grip.

Dora swiveled around, sat atop The Crab's chest in a full mount, and began pounding her face. The screaming from the opposing side continued but only for a few seconds, as The Crab quickly lost consciousness.

One of the women on the opposing team charged at Dora, who was standing, arms over her head, winking at Franny.

"You can't do that!" the woman yelled.

"Do what?" Dora asked.

"You broke her toe!"

Blood poured from the middle toe on The Crab's left foot.

Dora looked concerned. "No idea how that happened. She must have awfully fragile toes. Must've stubbed it."

"Dora," Franny chided.

Dora snorted. "The Crab …" She gazed briefly at her still-unconscious opponent. "Not today," she said.

• • •

Dora sat in the bathroom and sobbed silently into a towel, her mouth open wide, her face covered, her shoulders shaking. She had felt the adrenaline crash coming on as soon as the fight had ended. She had been so excited, on a high during the fight. She was used to feeling on top of every situation, whether on the truck at work with Mo or at home with Franny, with strangers, and now with MMA. She was taking life on, she felt … or she had felt. Now, not so much. She was utterly drained, dragged into an emotional abyss, while her mind continued to race.

She struggled to dissect what she was feeling. Had she made a mistake, breaking The Crab's toe? Cognitively, she knew she had made the only choice open to her at the time. It had felt right. It *was* right. And she had won. Only, now she felt as though she had lost.

MMA stressed sportsmanship and mutual respect. Purposely breaking an opponent's toe was certainly against the rules. Grudgingly, she admitted to herself that she had broken the rules. She had made a mistake and felt as though she *was* a mistake. And yet, that was what she had felt she had to do.

What did Franny think? She had talked of other things on the car ride home—food shopping and work around the apartment that needed doing. Dora wished she had the courage to talk to her beloved Franny about this, but admitting weakness felt unacceptable. She would certainly tell Franny it was okay to feel this way. At the least, she would say it was crucial to know that feeling this way was not your fault!

The adrenaline intensity of the fight and the serotonin afterglow of her victory were leaching away, leaving a vacuum of empty depression. She took four slow, deep breaths. "I love myself," she repeated ten times. Then she removed her sweat-soaked clothes and took a cold shower.

Twenty minutes later, Dora was lying face down, naked, on a towel that Franny had laid over the bed. Franny was perched on Dora's butt, rubbing her shoulders, back, and upper arms with an arnica and lidocaine ointment while humming along with a classical piano piece playing over Spotify.

"What is this we're listening to?"

"You're listening?" Franny answered.

"Not by choice."

"'Prelude and Fugue Number 1' in C Major."

"Snappy title."

"Bach," Franny said.

"Oh … that feels good."

"So, about that toe …"

"I wanted to win." She pouted. "Am I bad?"

"You're hanging around me too much. Where do you think you learned about joint locks?"

"Ha! I hadn't thought of that! This was your fault!" She tried to lift and twist her head around to look at Franny. "Anyway, this league has to understand that, in a fight, everything's allowed. If I'm fighting, I'm winning. You think boxing's clean? All sorts of things happen in clinches."

"So, babe, I got another call from … that weird guy."

"And …?"

"I did a little research. I looked into this supposed murder that has something to do with the way Beach City does business."

"And …?"

"And … I found a couple of things. The death of a store owner named Sharon Wilcox, who had a pretty serious zoning board conflict with the city. She was hit by a car—hit and run."

"Witnesses?"

"A vague description of a blue sports car."

"Hmm. Oh … Yes. There!"

"Okay. Then there was a young woman named Anne Volkov. Her father is the editor and publisher of *The Beach City Chronicle*, Tom Volkov, so he has a connection to the city, in a sense, though not exactly at a level that influences the way things get done around here, and not necessarily political."

"Interesting."

"And it wasn't reported as a murder. It was intriguing enough for me to check the police report. She fell out of bed or something and hit her head. Not much more to it than that."

Dora looked thoughtful. "I'd say the first one has more promise. Sharon with the zoning problem. More likely someone with an ax to grind."

Franny nodded. "I think the same, but I'm going to dig a bit into both."

Dora agreed. "'So, who is the guy calling and what's his purpose? If you ask me—"

"Which I didn't, but go ahead."

"—I'd say he's a family member of someone who died. He's pissed about some tragedy or accident. And through his grief, he's referring to the original situation as murder."

Franny agreed. "Could be."

"Shouldn't you report these calls to the chief?"

Franny thought about this as she began karate-chopping Dora's shoulders. "Good question, but without something more specific, and more criminal, there's nothing actionable, to use a pet Stalwell phrase."

"Ooo ... Don't stop!"

"Anyway, if I were to report it, it would be to George Cobb, who has an even lower tolerance for BS than Stalwell. If I went to the chief, Cobb would be pissed. I'd be going over his head. Anyway, no, I'm not reporting the calls."

Franny slapped Dora's back with both palms. "Okay, babe, spa time's over!"

"Ten more minutes. Five more!"

"Well, since you put it that way ..." Franny smiled her little half-smile and resumed her massage.

• • •

Carl Bunsen was furious with the city. He had been living across the street from the beautiful boardwalk on East Main Street in a rent-controlled apartment since he was a little boy. Now, the city was building a double high rise and mini mall that he would be forced to look at for the rest of his life, a project that ignored numerous environmental impact studies that predicted unmanageable traffic patterns that would wreak havoc on the neighborhood's quality of life. And the worst of it was that this monstrosity would block his view of the boardwalk and ocean, a view he had woken up to every morning with a smile. A view he kissed good night every night. A view that connected him to nature.

And worse, this was to be a project whose builders would be entirely exempt from paying city taxes for decades. It was also a project he was uniquely equipped to fight, as a lawyer and as a motivated citizen. So far, he had garnered nearly twenty-seven-hundred signatures on his petition, which named the Building Department supervisor, the council, and the city itself as liable in two law suits.

He looked out the window at his boardwalk, beach, and ocean across the street. He watched a white gull circle overhead.

A blue Mustang pulled into an empty parking spot four floors below. Franky Patella got out of the car, shaded his eyes with a palm, and paused to looked up toward Carl's window. He waited until an older couple emerged from the building and, before the outer door closed, slipped into the building and headed for the stairwell.

A few minutes later, Carl's doorbell rang. Moments later he was begging for his life and, soon after, for his death.

Chapter 9

Charlie was in his element. He would be making calls and ordering advertising all morning. He started with a call to City Hall, where he would register his new nonprofit, Citizens for Beach City LLC, formed only two hours before via an online registration service. Despite having zero new accounts, he was running Beach City destination ads on all local or semi local media that he could find. His father would not approve, so he would make it his business to keep the venture to himself.

Let's see what Anderson Consulting, not to mention City Hall, thinks of that!

"Hello? Yes, who would I speak with about registering a new business locally?"

He held on until the operator connected him.

"Hi there! Quincy Jackson speaking. It's always sunny in Beach City! How may I help you?"

"Hi, Quincy. My name's Charlie ... Bernelli. I'd like to register my nonprofit to do business here in town. While I understand that is not required, I've heard that is the preferred process."

"That's right, Charlie. Registering your business gives you the opportunity for preferred service here in Beach City. I take it this is a second business, since The Bernelli Group is already registered?"

"Oh, you've heard of us. Yes, that's correct."

"So, what is the name, please?"

"The nonprofit is The Citizens for Beach City, and the website is exactly that, dot org." He gave the remaining requested information, was told that a file was now open in his and his nonprofit's name, and that Judge Cheryl Rose would be handling the request within the next two business days.

As soon as he hung up, he called two radio stations, one TV station, and his new friend, Tom Volkov, at *The Beach City Chronicle.*

"Tom? Charles Bernelli here. I will be buying the ads we discussed."

"So, we'll be going ahead with the original order?"

"Yes, well, they're the same ads, but the buyer is not the city; it's a nonprofit called Citizens for Beach City."

"Sounds good to me. Send 'em whenever you're ready, along with the invoice particulars."

He hung up and immediately began dialing again, but then he paused for a moment. He was aware that City Hall would not be pleased with his ad campaign, which meant Christine Pearsall might not approve. And that gave him pause.

He shrugged then went back to dialing. He still had railroad ads, bus stop ads, and postcard printing to arrange before lunch.

• • •

Franny had been driving all morning and had nothing to show for it, except for two speeding tickets and one stop sign violation. The early morning segment of the graveyard shift was an end-of-month suggestion of Captain Cobb's and by suggestion he meant directive. While the morning had entailed no stress, she was bored and sore from hours of sitting in more or less one position. She looked forward to coffee and a fast-food turkey on rye with lettuce and mustard, one of her three go-to lunches.

She stopped for that coffee and sandwich then drove to the station house and made ready to head home for a nap, followed by exercise and an early dinner before her four p.m. regular shift started.

As she passed Brass Hall, the corridor where the department heads' and suits' offices were, a door opened and Captain Cobb poked his head out, crooked a finger at her, and then vanished back inside.

Well, that was ominous, she thought as she followed and found Chief Stalwell behind his expansive, shiny desk and George Cobb standing to one side. Both faced her; neither was smiling. Once she entered the room, they both sat. Protocol indicated she do likewise, and she did.

They all sat for about twenty seconds in silence. Franny wondered if something was expected of her but realized that wondering was exactly what was expected of her. The feeling of being unsure and anxious was the intended effect; she was sure of it. This wasn't her first rodeo.

Finally, Chief Stalwell cleared his throat. "So, Hart, what have you got for us?"

She cleared her throat. When in Rome ... "Well, Chief, I have three moving violations this morning. Um, and, as you know, I've been following up on the city's reports of union reps skimming from pension funds. Though, in the absence of complaints from union leaders or actionable evidence, I'm not sure what we can do. I've also been staking out the high traffic mailboxes, sir, to catch mailbox fishing assholes using double-sided tape or glue or tar or whatever. I've also spoken with the postmaster about making the mailboxes fuck-with-proof."

"And ...?" Cobb asked.

"No response yet. Beyond that, I don't have anything worth reporting, or that will close any outstanding cases."

George Cobb was looking at the chief expectantly. Stalwell sighed.

"Captain Cobb has reports that you're investigating old, closed cases. Are you? And, if so, why?"

She looked from Stalwell to Cobb. "Sir?"

"Come on, Hart," Cobb snapped. "The Wilcox case? And the Volkov tragedy? Haven't Tom and Irene been through enough? Tom Volkov has worked hard to put the loss of his daughter behind him, and his wife ..."

Chief Stalwell looked at her. She could see his reluctance to this meeting in his eyes. This was all Cobb's doing. She and Stalwell had a relationship grounded in trust, the way it should be.

"Why dredge this up?" the chief asked, looking concerned. "Look, you're a good officer. Just tell us what's going on, and we'll help, or point out why it's not appropriate, if that's the case."

"It's not appropriate," Cobb growled, taking a breath to say more.

"George," the chief said, and Cobb looked at him, raised his chin a notch, but remained silent.

Franny shrugged. "I made a few cursory checks based on unsubstantiated intel that happened to come my way referencing an old case that the caller claimed was a murder but may not have been reported as such. There was nothing there. Nothing to worry yourselves about." She looked at Chief Stalwell. "Nothing actionable."

She was determined to keep her investigation hidden yet ongoing until, and unless, she found something that *was* actionable. The department would stand for nothing less. What she was afraid of was that the department heads might not stand for anything more.

"Leave those cases alone, Hart," Cobb chastised.

Chief Stalwell looked at him and nodded, acquiescing, albeit with an air of detached reluctance. "Unless there's something there, then just let us know. My door's always open."

"Yes, sir," was all she said.

• • •

"From what I can tell," Charlie said into his phone, "the power is only out in our building. But it doesn't seem to be on our end—no flipped breakers or shorts that I can see. And I don't smell anything burning." He had walked from the office into the stairwell, where only generator lights were on. He could hear the faint growl of the whole building generator through the walls.

"But the whole building's new!" came his father's exasperated retort, albeit muffled with a dose of static.

"Tell me about it," Charlie said. He was now outside and looking at the adjoining buildings, whose lights were on.

"Call the power company," his father said.

Charlie shut off his phone without informing his father that he had already called the power company and had been told someone would be there within ten minutes. That had been an hour and a half earlier.

Were the utility companies in every beach town this poorly run?

• • •

Franny had finished looking through the police archives and found the information about both the Wilcox and Volkov deaths, but nothing seemed out of the ordinary, other than these were two deaths of little interest to anyone but the immediate friends and families of the deceased. She then looked through all of the old, local newspapers she could find online. Still, nothing piqued her interest.

So, she went to the library and explained to Missy, the young, freshly scrubbed, bespectacled research librarian, that she was hoping to find information about the Wilcox and Volkov deaths that went beyond the police blotter facts of the deaths. Feature stories, perhaps? They needn't be in-depth. Even a mention of the case might suffice.

The young woman had held up a smooth, amber finger, nodded, and then turned her attention to her computer for several minutes before directing Franny to a terminal in the cellar archive, where the librarian said Franny could peruse material without being disturbed.

First, Wilcox. An obit mentioned beloved family vacations in the mountains of Vermont and an even more beloved Irish setter named McCoy. She loved to play the cello and read the poetry of Robert Frost.

Then, Volkov. She found the initial police blotter version of the incident, and another, slightly more in-depth story that stated that Anne Volkov, daughter of *Chronicle* editor, Thomas, and his wife, Irene, had died tragically following a freak accident in the family's home. Franny read that the grieving parents were devastated over the loss of their only child.

As far as Franny could tell, neither story shed any light on the mysterious phone calls referencing a "murder that wasn't a murder." Nor did either connect to any aspect of city business, dirty or otherwise.

She continued reading the second article. Buried at its end were two pieces of information that had not appeared in the official police reports she had perused, nor in the longer, more fleshed-out news story that followed this brief, cursory report. The information was relevant to the case, and Franny could not imagine why, or on whose authority, the information had been removed from later accounts.

She remembered the case and sat for a long moment, thinking, recalling everything she could about the case. She had been in her early teens at the time.

Nothing jumped out at her.

Initially, the new information seemed more of a curiosity than evidence of anything untoward. But, as often happened for her, the answer came once she had all the information and allowed it to percolate for a little while in her subconscious. In this case, it took only a few minutes of sitting quietly in the library, watching patrons go about their business.

She rose to leave and had begun climbing the stairs out of the basement archive when the answer came to her. And the realization was so jarring that she had to grab the banister for support.

• • •

"Hello, Christine. It's Charlie Bernelli."

"Great to hear your voice!"

"Yes! It's good to hear your voice, too! I was hoping to speak with Mayor Mark. We're having the darnedest problems here. Our electricity went out, and we're trying to get it fixed, but the problem doesn't seem to be in our building. Then our water turned brown—rust, I suppose."

"Well, the city is flushing the hydrants."

"Oh? I see. Well, now we also seem to have something wrong with our city tax information."

"Um, can I have the mayor or, better yet, the tax receiver, get back to you? Mark's in a meeting."

"Well, can't you—?"

"Charlie, I've got to run. Sorry."

"Thank you, Christine. I appreciate it. Oh, and we never did have that lunch." He looked at the phone in his hand, but Christine had hung up.

Chapter 10

"Hello!" Officer Franny Hart arrived at the top of the steps and was met by a young woman dressed entirely in black—black turtleneck wool sweater and black jeans — even black eyeliner and eye shadow.

"Can I help you?"

"I was hoping to speak with Tom Volkov."

She nodded. "I'm Sarah, his editor ... and researcher, and typesetter, and ... just a moment." The woman knocked on one of the doors in the little hallway that did double duty as a waiting room.

"Tom? A police officer to see you." She squinted at Franny's name tag. "An Officer Hart."

The door opened, and Tom Volkov stepped back to allow Franny to enter. He glanced only briefly at her. "Sorry. I'm a bit distracted. Deadlines."

"I understand."

He had glanced at an empty chair, an invitation, but she remained standing.

"I'm sorry to have to bring this up, but I was wondering if I might ask you about your daughter, Anne."

He drew back, as though he had been slapped. "Anne? Why?"

"It's about what happened when she was discovered."

"That's all a matter of public record. I'm sure that, given your resources, there's nothing I could add."

"What can you tell me about the cause of her injuries?"

Tom Volkov seemed not to know where to look—anywhere but at Franny. "She hit her head on the headboard of her bed. She must have slipped—a freak accident."

"And was there any investigation into how such an accident might have occurred?"

Tom seemed to find a reserve of strength, to gather himself. He looked her in the eye, his expression one of grim resolve. "There was no need."

"Was there any friction with the responding officer?"

Tom stared at her for a long moment then turned away. "It was a tragedy, and we haven't ... we'll never get over it. There was nothing out of the ordinary in our interaction with the responding officer, and I've ... we've managed all these years by not dwelling very much on any of it—not directly, anyway. We've managed by accepting it—all of it—as facts of life, and done our best to carry on. What choice do we have?"

"How is Irene?"

His expression shuttered. He stood. "Why are you doing this, Officer?"

"Could you answer the question, please?"

"It's all pretty painful, and it's all been covered. So, unless you have a specific point, Officer, I'd like to get on with my work."

Franny nodded, her eyes never leaving Tom Volkov's face. She rose and went to the door, then turned. "Thank you for your time."

She opened the door and was startled to find Sarah hovering just outside, apparently looking for something in a nearby bookcase. She slid her gaze to Franny and smiled faintly.

Once in the car, Franny called Dora. She had no one at the station with whom to share what was becoming a more and more interesting, if potentially dangerous, situation. The call went to voicemail as Franny weighed how much to say over the phone.

"Hi, babe. It's me. I've found out something interesting about that puzzle I've been working on. See you at dinner." She gave two quick kisses, then ended the call.

She had an hour before the end of her shift and felt the constant, covert pressure to bolster the city's revenue by doling out a few more tickets, a pressure that was never mentioned by anyone at any level on the Beach City Police Force, at least, not while on duty. The problem was, when the brass chose to motivate her fellow officers by pointing out who had or had not been successful, the only available criteria for demonstrating who was doing his or her job were tickets, arrests, and closed cases. Such was the nature of the work.

All of this ran through Franny's mind as a subconscious undercurrent while she called dispatch to let them know where she was and what she would be doing.

She cruised along Park Boulevard, which ran from the barrier island on which Beach City was located to the highways that stretched northward. The road was poorly lit, as the few streetlights there were had been shut off to save the county a few dollars. She drove to the eastern border of Beach City. All seemed as it should be. Most of the traffic was heading toward her, from the highways into town, as was usually the case late in the day.

As she prepared to turn onto a side street, she noticed a car pulled over, halfway onto the shoulder. She stopped three car lengths behind the 2017 gold Chevy Impala and was about to check with the National Crime Information Center (NCIC) database to see if the car had been reported stolen or its owner wanted or otherwise red-flagged. Franny realized, however, that she knew this car. She saw it around town frequently. It belonged to Tom and Irene Volkov.

Before calling for assistance, she got out of the car and approached the Impala from the driver's side. She saw that the driver was Irene Volkov and considered calling for backup. Irene Volkov was known to have mental health issues, which could ratchet up her intensity without warning. In a tense situation with a police officer, Irene might become agitated.

Irene was speaking into her cell phone when Franny knocked lightly on the driver's side window, smiled, and waved. Then she motioned for her to roll down the window.

"How are you, Mrs. Volkov?"

"Here's a police officer. I've got to go." Irene hung up her phone, turned, and looked at Franny.

"Is everything all right?" Franny asked.

"Tommy called because he forgot something. I don't like taking calls while I'm driving, so I pulled over to take the call. I pulled over to take the call … to take the call."

Franny paused, taking in Irene's odd speech pattern. "That was smart, Mrs. Volkov. The safe thing to do. So, you're okay?"

"I'm fine. I'm fine. Going to my doctor, my doctor … Well, she's actually a nurse. Been seeing her for twenty years … twenty years. Since, since …" She looked at Franny. "Am I in trouble, Officer … trouble, Officer?"

"No, Mrs. Volkov. I just wanted to be sure you're okay."

"He thought he forgot his keys. Forgot his keys."

"Who did?"

"Tommy. He thought he forgot his keys, but he found them while he was talking to me ... talking to me."

"That's fine, Mrs. Volkov."

"Is it okay for me to get going now? I don't want to be late for my appointment ... my appointment."

"Yes, of course. Be careful now." Franny turned and began walking back to her car. She heard the Impala start and pull away.

She continued walking. A lone pair of headlights shone in her eyes, which she shielded with the palm of one hand. The fool had his brights on! Franny stopped and squinted into the light, waiting for the car to veer to its left, following the bend in the road. When it did not, she waved both arms over her head as the lights grew brighter, heading straight for her. There was no car horn, no slam of brakes or skidding tires. There was only the roar of the car all around her, and then a violent impact that hurled Franny into the air. By the time she landed on the concrete lip of the road, she was, mercifully, already dead.

Chapter 11

The Chronicle and, to a lesser extent, the Long Island and New York papers were dominated by Lieutenant Francesca Hart's obituaries, accomplishments, arrests, and closed cases, along with poignant reminiscences from fellow officers and friends.

Chief Stalwell called her, "one of Beach City's best and bravest."

Captain George Cobb said, "Officer Hart was a model officer, who kept her head down and nose to the grindstone. She will be missed."

Franny's fellow officers were not authorized to speak on the record, but several gave anonymous accounts of her dedication and bravery.

Mayor Mark Morganstern wrote a somber guest editorial in *The Chronicle* about the example Lieutenant Hart had set for service, bravery, and sacrifice; examples that every young person would do well to emulate. He announced that the city was designating March 11th, the day she had died, as Francesca Hart Day and was offering a ten-thousand-dollar reward for information leading to the identity and arrest of the driver of the car that had struck and killed her.

A follow-up story two days later noted that the majority of the traffic at the time of this hit-and-run was heading westbound in the opposite direction. Several westbound motorists believed to have witnessed the accident thought the car in question might have been a blue sports car, possibly a Ford Mustang or Dodge Charger. No license plate information was available.

Chief Stalwell and Captain Cobb spearheaded the investigation, interviewing motorists, bicyclists, joggers, and anyone they could locate who was known to have harbored a grudge against Lieutenant Hart.

Within a few weeks, when the investigations yielded no actionable results, and as the city council election drew closer, news headlines began to shift in that direction. *The Chronicle* endorsed Jeremy Anderson, who had "helped to grow Beach City's profile into one of the most sought-after destinations on Long Island and in the New York metro area."

Stories surrounding Lieutenant Francesca Hart's death were buried deeper and deeper in *The Chronicle* and soon disappeared entirely.

• • •

"Yes, I think you'll be pleasantly surprised," Charlie said into the phone. "We are all about Beach City—our tourism and the success of not only our beaches but our citizens, our businesses, and their owners." He listened for a moment. "That's wonderful. And welcome aboard, Mr. Carson!"

He hung up and sat back, hands behind his head. "Carson's Fish Market. Fourth *yes* today!" he called.

Charlie Sr. appeared in the doorway and leaned against the jamb, steaming coffee mug in hand, which Charlie Jr. knew was spiked with brandy. Or was the brandy spiked with coffee? "I have to say, pretty good for one of your crazy ideas."

"Oh? It wasn't *your* idea?"

"To quote C3, 'as if.'" His father grinned then took a long pull from his "coffee."

Charlie Jr. sat forward, energized. "As I predicted, businesses want to get on board with a Beach City P.R. effort, whatever the council or mayor might think. Supporting tourism and the city in general does look good to pretty much everyone."

His father nodded. "Pretty much."

"I wonder what Jeremy Anderson thinks of our campaign."

"He's a local business, so—"

"He's our competition, he's the city's choice for council, and he was going to steal the idea for himself, with the city's blessing. I saw the damn comps when I was there. He may yet steal it and do a competing campaign, likely with the city's blessing and on their behalf."

"I know," Charlie Sr. said quietly. "Kudos, son, for the idea, and for the execution. I just hope it doesn't bite us in the ass. City Hall has a rep of being a vindictive bunch of assholes."

Charlie Jr. was thoughtful for a moment. Then he began scrolling through the contacts on his phone, found the one he wanted, and pressed the number. "I'm calling Luis Martinez and bringing him on full-time, contract basis ...

"Luis? Charlie Bernelli!"

"How are you, sir?"

"Don't give me that *sir* crap. That's my father, who's sitting right, here, by the way. You don't want him yelling at you."

"Oh, please tell him I say *hi.*"

He cupped the phone. "He says *hello.*"

His father nodded.

"Dad says *hi* and asks how you've been …"

"Well, you know. Not bad."

"Good. Hey, listen. I'd like to hire you as a full-time temp while we work on the tourism campaign you had started on. Got clients jumping on, and we need additional ads and some TV."

"When do I start?"

"When works for you?"

"How is Monday? I have a tenant now, which allows me to take full-time or part-time work. More flexibility."

"Really? A tenant? So, you're a landlord now?"

"I am."

"Is your family okay?"

"My—Oh, yeah, they're fine. No worries."

"Well, I thought maybe you needed the money."

"Um, it's not exactly a legal tenant, so keep it quiet downtown."

"Trust me; I'm the last person who would tell City Hall." He hung up the phone, chuckling, delighted.

"He'll start Monday."

"We keep this up," Charlie Sr. said, "and we'll lose our electricity permanently."

• • •

Dora had been crying nonstop for what felt like a week, though it was more like eight or nine hours. She hadn't eaten and had no desire to. The pain of losing Franny was like a knife in her chest, twisting and tearing, and giving her shattered heart no peace.

Felix had been by her side throughout, allowing Dora to bury her face in his soft mane as her body shook with grief. Unlike some cats, Felix was demonstrably affectionate, a loyal friend. To Dora, loyalty was everything.

Beethoven's "Moonlight Sonata" had been running through her head since she had received the call. Dora long thought of the piece as being dirge-like and had teased Franny about being too serious when Franny had played it. Now she imagined her sweet Franny playing it just for her and thought of the piece as giving Franny life.

The funeral would be run by the Beach City Police Force with Chief Stilwell and, possibly, Mayor Mark, as the primary speakers. Lieutenant Francesca Hart was to be buried with full honors. Chief Stalwell had offered Dora the opportunity to speak, and Dora had accepted, though she had no idea how she would manage it. She had a fear of public speaking and hoped she would be able to pull herself together enough to do her beloved Franny credit.

She thought of Franny's strong yet delicate fingers rubbing her shoulders, and Dora sobbed as Felix licked her face.

Chapter 12

She had entirely forgotten about her Thursday night fight, a step up in her MMA career, against a BJJ team in Rockland Township, featuring women who were superior athletes and deeply schooled in the technical submissions that had made the Brazilian version of the art the sensation it had become.

Dora was so shaken by Franny's death that she found herself looking at her opponent across the mat without knowing quite how she had come to be there. She had attended the funeral on autopilot, barely. She had given her speech in a sort of blackout and accepted condolences with rote, polite appreciation and a plastered-on, insincere smile that had reached nowhere near her eyes.

She had taken the week off from work, which had not been a problem. In fact, she had been politely advised not to be seen anywhere near City Hall or her route, a tongue in cheek instruction delivered via Christine Pearsall, though it certainly came from upstairs.

The woman hit her, a back fist to her right deltoid, and she awoke from her daze. The punch, which was really a scrape, tore away the skin.

She smiled, returning to the moment.

She had been thinking of Franny, daydreaming of vacations that they had taken, concerts they had attended together, and other good times, and feeling a bit sorry for herself. Not a great idea during an MMA fight.

Her mind reached back to a time far before she had known Franny, a time that she thought of as a formative period, when she had become the woman she was now proud to be. A period when she had to endure the unendurable and tolerate the intolerable. She had been witness to and was on the receiving end of abuse that had fueled a lifetime of rage, abuse that she could not have described had she been asked. Abuse against which her mind had formed a shield, a protective memory barrier.

While she could not access the memories, she could access the feelings when the need arose. And she could access whatever instructions her cognitive mind chose as a response.

Apparently, her reputation had preceded her, as she could see the fear on the woman's face. So, she smiled again. The smiles were emotional strikes, of sorts. They caused the woman, her opponent, to flinch.

The woman quickly changed levels, going to the ground, and Dora was happy to accommodate, confident in her strength and knowledge, despite her inexperience. She turned back two of the woman's lightning-fast submission attempts and had no chance to respond with anything besides a cobbled-together sprawl defense, followed by what Shay called a "sweat escape."

It seemed her opponent's name was Claro, and while she was not nearly as strong as Dora, she was fast and knew her submissions. No sooner was Dora out of the second attempt than she tried, and nearly succeeded with, a third. This time, Dora was able to reverse their positions and was on top, in Claro's guard, and attempting the first punch of what she hoped would be a brief ground-and-pound.

Claro slipped that punch, which grazed her left cheek, stunning her. Before Dora could follow up, Claro had wrapped her left arm around Dora's right arm, pulling Dora down, then raised her left leg to meet her arm and slid her left knee over her arm and up toward Dora's neck. She then brought her right leg up, completing a triangle choke, and began to squeeze.

Dora couldn't help but admire the woman's skill and speed.

She had several options, none legal in MMA but workable on the street. Her left arm had some range of motion, though none that would afford her a direct escape from a triangle choke. Instead, Dora moved her left hand to the underside of Claro's upper thigh, grasped a half inch or so of skin between her thumb and forefinger, using her middle finger as added leverage, and pinched *hard*. At first, Claro grunted in Dora's ear, and so she squeezed harder.

"I'll tear this right the fuck off," Dora growled.

"Urraawwrr!" Claro yelled and tapped Dora's arm.

The fight was over.

Claro glared. Dora smiled and shrugged.

Claro looked at Dora, then at the ref, then back at Dora. Finally, she walked away, shaking her head.

Dora understood her unwillingness to share what had happened with her teammates or coach, especially if no one else had seen it. The adult Dora was well aware that pinching was illegal, but the abused, violated little girl who was in Dora didn't care.

She wanted to say, "That was only option one." Instead, Dora smiled at her opponent. "Claro," she said, which she knew meant "of course."

• • •

Charlie literally had one foot out the door when his cell phone rang. He hesitated, wanting to head to his appointment without taking the call, but saw the caller's ID and took the call.

"C?"

"Dad."

He unbuttoned his coat and sat down, knowing he would be late. "You're paroled." It was a statement, not a question.

"Just wanted you to know I'm okay."

"Where are you staying?"

"Halfway house over on Raymond Street. It's okay. Well, not really, but…"

"Are people there using?"

"I don't think so, and I'm making meetings."

"How often?"

"Every day. A few kinds actually. I'm … I'm learning a lot."

"I hope so. You do what they tell you, whether they call it *suggestions* or not."

"Give me a week or so to get my bearings, okay?"

On the way to the restaurant, he sighed, thinking of his son. Charlie the third, affectionately known as Charlie 3 or C3, had been an exuberant child, always excited and engaged, always discovering something new about the world around him, and forever wanting to shout the news to whomever was around. How he had adored that little boy! And how painful watching him grow up had been, watching him buffeted and beaten by circumstances or, more accurately, by his own naiveté. He had badly wanted to protect his son but knew that was impossible. So, instead, his fears had turned to anger.

He tried to refocus, forcing himself to remember eight-year-old C3 playing third base in little league, winning a championship and eating red, white, and blue cake and vanilla ice cream afterward.

God, he needed a drink.

He left his car with the valet, walked into the restaurant, and was shown to a table.

At that moment, he forgot all about his son.

The woman at the table, a woman he had not seen since she had been his lover fifteen years prior, rose to greet him.

He smiled, took her proffered hand, leaned in, and kissed her cheek. "Hello, Christine. You look as beautiful as ever."

Chapter 13

Dora had thought she was over the worst of it. She was wrong. What had she been thinking? That she could turn back toward life, get back on the truck, and tip garbage all day, then come home to an empty apartment that was still immersed in *l'odeur de* Franny?

After a single day at work, a day that seemed to go on forever, Dora had come home, put on some music that she knew Franny would have hated—disco—and tried to dance around the apartment. The idea made sense, and she had tried, she really had, but after less than two minutes, she had flung herself down on the bed and tried to cry. However, she had no tears left, so she went to the fridge, got herself a beer, and drank it in two long pulls. She followed the beer with two more, followed by a shot of bourbon. And another. And another. But her grief remained, distorted and magnified by alcohol.

She took a paring knife and gouged a furrow in her thigh. The pain centered her, making her feel a bit better. She started another gouge, thinking to carve an "F" when her cell rang.

As she dug in her coat for the phone, she spotted Felix staring from the doorway.

"So?"

He kept staring.

"It's called self-pity. I'm entitled!"

He sauntered away.

She answered the phone. "Yeah?"

"Hello, Dora." The voice had an odd, metallic ring and was pitched in a way that didn't sound quite real.

"Who's this?"

"Don't hang up. I'd been calling Lieutenant Hart, but I can't do that anymore, can I?"

"Who the fuck is this?"

"She didn't tell you? About the murder information? I thought you girls shared everything."

"Wait, wait, wait!"

"So, she did tell you. What did she say?"

"She said she was getting some weird calls about a cold murder case from, like, twenty years ago, and that it was connected with the city somehow. Corruption, she thought."

"That's right. It was a murder that wasn't a murder. And I told her the truth was tied up with the city's business, bad-smelling business. And she was making progress, too much progress for someone. So, she was on the right track. Don't you want to see her avenged?"

"Avenged? You got her killed!"

"I steered her in the right direction."

"Why didn't you just tell her who committed this murder that wasn't a murder, instead of sending her to her fucking death?"

"I didn't get her killed. Her skill at her job got her killed. Investigating a murder can be dangerous. And it's not just a murder. Beach City's infested with corruption. It's all connected—the murder that isn't one and bad-smelling city business—and now a coverup."

Dial tone.

Felix was back in the doorway.

"Fuck," she said to her cat.

• • •

"Hi, it's Dora."

"Dora?" Charlie was momentarily confused.

"I modeled for the tourism ad?"

"Oh. Deborah Ellison—Dora. Yes. How are you? I heard … I'm sorry for your loss."

"I appreciate that. Do you have time to meet to discuss something?"

"Well, actually, I was about to drive over to the office. Why don't we meet in the lobby?"

"I remember. Can you meet me now? If not, it's fine. Tomorrow would —"

"As I said, I was on my over there. Fifteen minutes?"

• • •

"Let me put some lights on in here." Charlie went to a corner of the room and, suddenly, the darkened lobby was bright, even cheerful. The colorful geometric panels had a calming effect.

Charlie sat, leaning back, his legs crossed. Dora remained standing.

"So, what's up?" he asked. "Hey, how 'bout I make us some coffee?" He started to get up.

"No. Please" She paused, not sure where to start. "So, you know about my Franny?"

Charlie sat down again, nodding sadly.

Dora continued, "Well, she was investigating something. A murder."

"All I really know is that she was a police officer and, rumor had it, you two were together."

"A murder, but it wasn't really a murder."

"I'm not following."

"She didn't say much about it, except that she was being fed information. And now I've been fed information."

"By whom? What does that mean?"

"Phone calls, talking about a murder that isn't a murder, and which is tied up with some sort of dirty city business, which I assume means corruption."

"And what does *that* mean? And, why come to me?" He appraised Dora, who he saw as a unique city employee, about whom he knew little personally. She had suffered a horrific loss, a loss that might be tied up with a murder ... that wasn't a murder. He wondered if the loss, Officer Hart's death, might itself have been a murder.

Dora was at the no-going-back point in the conversation. Once Charlie was included in her little circle of information, he was in. But could she trust him? She had known him only briefly, yet she had found an odd intimacy in the work they had done. Perhaps it was less to do with modeling than with the way she and Charlie had interacted. In any case, she believed she could trust him.

"Tell me something," she began, "what happened to the ad campaign we worked on?"

Charlie looked confused. "What happened to it? It's going forward."

"Really? You were hired by the city."

"Not true."

"Well, that's how it started."

"Yes, that's how it started."

"And how did it end?"

"What's your point?"

"You asked why I came to you. You're a highly competent outsider who has been wronged by the city."

They sat in silence for a moment.

Charlie spoke first. "So, you think I'm motivated—"

"I believe the caller. I can't speak to the murder the caller mentioned, but I believe my Franny was murdered, and that other things, very wrong things, have been going on here, possibly for a very long time."

"Hmm ... Is this caller male?"

"I think so, but his voice is disguised, electronically, so ... I don't know."

Charlie sat back, tapping a finger against his lip. "Perhaps because you'd recognize that voice."

Dora sat down on a couch opposite Charlie. "Do you mind if I ask ...? Take me through the way your business with the city was cancelled."

He shrugged. "It never really started, so I'm not sure *cancelled* is the right word. The mayor told me we had the business, and when it came time to get the ball rolling, the city said there was no work. Essentially, the business didn't materialize, despite what the mayor said. While it's probably not what your caller meant, to me, *that's* dirty city business. Lack of decency, though perhaps I'm naïve."

"So, he changed his mind?"

"Or someone changed it for him."

"Who told you there was no business?"

Charlie looked at her, tilting his head, his eyes questioning. "Christine Pearsall."

"The city clerk. Well, she would know."

"Yes and ... she's a longtime friend."

"So I've heard." She saw his curious look. "I work for the city. Whatever else is going on, it's a gossip mill, probably like most cities."

"I see."

"So, if you have Christine's trust, maybe you—both of you—could find out what's going on."

"Mmm ..." Charlie was thinking. "Could be someone with an axe to grind, and no more substance than that."

Dora agreed. "Trust me; City Hall is filled with grinding axes."

"Christine is a very principled woman. Even if she'll talk about city business, which is a long shot, she's not likely to know much about something as vaguely defined as a murder that isn't really a murder. That's less inside information than a puzzle."

"Mmm ... I like puzzles."

Charlie nodded. "I grew up in Beach City. Christine and I were together for a while back then, but I got in a bit of trouble and left; moved to Manhattan. We're getting reacquainted now."

Dora sat forward. "I've been thinking about the caller's choice of words. Could be that we're supposed to look for inconsistencies in the way the city does business. Dirty business, so to speak. The phrase the caller used was *bad-smelling business.*"

"Interesting phrase to use when talking to a person who collects garbage."

She nodded then started to speak when a firetruck went by, its siren and engine drowning her out. The lobby was briefly bathed in blue and red strobe.

"The caller used the same phrase with Franny. Hard to believe the choice of words is a coincidence. How would I go about tracking down city business and looking for things that smell bad, so to speak?"

"I can think of a few places. Christine is a possibility, though I think her loyalty to her job might keep her from saying much. I'll say this, she's mentioned that City Hall is not a particularly functional place. The people in charge, especially the higher-ups, do what's best for *them*, as opposed to what's best for the residents. And there's the newspaper, *The Chronicle.*"

"That'd be Tom—"

"Volkov."

"Right. And ...?"

"The Beach City library."

Chapter 14

While it was a Tuesday evening, Rudy's was more than half full. The patrons were all seated or standing along the bar; some drinking on their own or in pairs, others listening to Rudy regale them with some story or other and laughing along with him. The man had a big, belly laugh that befitted his size and girth, and it filled the room, inviting anyone within earshot to laugh along with him.

Agatha Raines sat opposite her husband, in the center of the bar, but she wasn't laughing. All around her was activity, yet she was still, watching the door. She beckoned to her husband.

"Excuse me," Rudy said to his audience. "The boss calls."

He stepped close to Agatha and leaned across the bar. "What is it, Ags?"

She didn't answer but looked at her husband, energy radiating from her eyes.

"What?"

Still, she didn't answer, but she held his eyes with hers, unblinking.

"Rudy," she said then waited.

"Yes ...?" he drawled.

"Rude, we did it!"

"We did ...? Wait—what? You mean ...? Whoa-ho-ho!"

She nodded. "I'm telling you at the bar so you don't make a scene. Don't be yelling nothing out now. It's just another day, and tomorrow will be another day."

He stared at her. "You need to see your doctor; make sure you don't—"

"Already done. He says I'm as good as I'm gonna get."

He nodded, leaned farther over the bar, and kissed her gently. "I love you, baby."

"I know it."

He went back to his audience and his stories, sending occasional worried glances in his wife's direction. But she was no longer paying attention to Rudy. She had gone back to watching the door, and when Dora came in, Agatha caught her eye and nodded toward an empty table.

Once they were both seated with drinks, Agatha waited.

Dora began, "I've paid attention to your accusations about city corruption, and Julienne."

"Oh, they're not accusations. They're facts."

"Good. Look, I work for the city, but I'm with you. So, I have more information, more facts, possibly tied to a long-ago murder, to local corruption and to the death of Lieutenant Hart."

Agatha nodded.

Dora continued, "I didn't know who to talk to. I learned some things from a cop, and now she's dead." She realized what she was saying. "Shit, I don't want to put you in danger."

"Talk to me," Agatha encouraged.

Dora explained the phone calls, the hint of murder, and Franny's apparent discovery of a piece of "the puzzle" that she had been working on.

When she finished, Agatha stared at her for a long moment, digesting what she had just heard. Then she bent her head close to Dora's. "Don't let Rudy know we're talking about this. He'll be afraid the city might come down on the bar or, worse, on me. And he'd be right."

"Aren't you afraid of that, too?"

Agatha smiled. "I hope they do come down on us. Not on the bar, but let 'em come after me, please."

Dora smiled back at her. "Really?"

"Mmhmm." Agatha leaned closer to Dora, her lips pressed firmly together. "Now let me tell you what *I* know, leaving out, for now, the details of who's who. I don't know about the murder that isn't a murder part, but your caller is right about corruption in the city. Anyone, and I mean anyone, who causes the city to look bad from the public's perspective, gets punished. There are people high up in City Hall, people the public knows nothing about, whose job it is to keep the city's public image clean."

Dora squinted. "Isn't that what P.R. is for?"

Agatha nodded. "Yup. Imagine P.R. run by enforcers, in organized crime."

Dora sat back. "That's crazy."

"Now," Agatha continued, "what does any of the corruption in Beach City have to do with a murder ... or pseudo murder? We don't have many murders around here, pseudo or otherwise. I suppose, if you looked into the few we've had, you might find a judge's decision or some police activity that might raise an eyebrow. Then what?"

Dora shrugged. "I don't know. What?"

"The question is"—Agatha looked her in the eye—"how are local corruption and this questionable murder related?"

Dora didn't have an answer.

"Okay, I've got another question," Agatha said, leaning close to Dora again.

Dora waited.

"Did the officer have a personal computer, or maybe a cell phone she didn't use for work?"

· · ·

Carl Matoli, Beach City's Civil Service manager, was playing solitaire on his phone when he received another text. He rarely received texts. He was a year and a half from retirement, with a full pension and a bronze plaque for his den wall, and was not from any of the texting generations. Nevertheless, he clicked on the message.

The following is a list of individuals who are to fail the
upcoming Civil Service exams:

Brian Zino
Robert Tams
Jessica Owens

- J.H.

Carl sighed, copied the names into a password-protected file, and then went back to his game.

Chapter 15

Charlie leaned back in his office chair and gazed out the window, his feet up on his desk, a half-empty glass of Screaming Eagle Bordeaux in his hand. He sipped, shut his eyes, and let go a soft moan of pleasure.

He was having a wonderful time. He had always been able to charm business out of a ghost town, and Beach City was certainly not that. Retailers had begun clamoring to join Citizens for Beach City; some insisting that their names be included at the bottom of the ads. So far, he had bought three months of news spots on TV, three on news radio, bus stations, sides of buses, the train station, and ads in train cars.

He had mixed feelings about Christine. Their chemistry was impossible to ignore. It was, in fact, driving him crazy, and he knew she felt it, too, but she seemed determined to keep him at arm's length. Their recent dinner had been more like a business lunch than a lovers' reunion. Whenever he steered the conversation in the direction of romance or shared nostalgia, Christine changed the subject. Perhaps, with time, that would evolve.

That C3 was no longer a guest of the state and was now responsible for his own wellbeing concerned Charlie. The boy needed structure, discipline. He did not need time to think, muse, or ruminate. C3's thinking had never been a positive. Someone else had to think for him, at least in the short-term.

Now that he was on parole, what was to stop him from finding life a little too challenging, requiring, God forbid, that four letter word—work? What was to stop the boy, now a young man, from finding a new bunch of knuckleheads, armed knuckleheads, and robbing another liquor store?

"Don't you want me to succeed?" C3 had demanded to know. The answer was yes. And success demanded discipline and structure, not firearms. C3's track record did not inspire confidence.

Charlie's thoughts turned back to Christine. Maybe, with persistence

...

He sipped his wine then reached for his phone.

"Christine? I just wanted to let you know how lovely our dinner was and how I'd like to do it again, whenever you're ready, and only when you're ready."

"What a nice thing to say!"

"No, I mean it. Dinner, and only dinner."

"Well, maybe next week?"

"Why not tomorrow?"

"Church Sunday morning."

"Well then, I'll tell you what; I will accompany you to mass."

"Right."

"Yes, right."

"Well, I'm glad I'm sitting down."

"Well, I'm glad you're sitting down, too."

"You'll come to church? You really will?"

"I really will.

"You swear?"

"Christine, I think it's unbecoming of you to ask me to swear." He hung up, chuckling, pleased with himself.

• • •

At dinner the following night, they talked about their lives over his lasagna and her eggplant rollatini. She ordered wine; he ordered scotch, ignoring the still small voice in his head that suggested he refrain.

A few minutes later, Christine watched as Charlie finished his scotch and signaled for another round.

"Not me, thanks. I'm driving." She waved the offer away.

Charlie motioned to the waiter that he, but not Christine, would have the next drink. After ordering, he gave her an emphatic look.

Christine smiled. "My refraining from a second drink isn't a dig at you, Charles; it's just me refraining from a second drink."

He threw back his head and laughed. "Tou-fucking-ché."

She shook her head, clucking her tongue at his language.

"How cool is it that I'm sitting here, having dinner with sweet Christine Pearsall?"

She patted his hand. "Don't get yourself too excited. Sitting here is all you'll be doing. And we'll see if you're this happy about your evening with me once the scotch wears off."

"Why not let me accompany you so we can find out together?"

She shook her head again. "What will you be saying next?"

He waggled his eyebrows.

"You've had too much to drink."

"I disagree." His drink arrived, and Charlie sipped it. "So, I've never asked how you like being the gatekeeper at City Hall."

She didn't answer right away but went back to her dinner.

Charlie watched her eat, saying, "I, for one, am loving being back in Beach City, running the company I always knew I'd run."

"It's going well?" she asked. "The work?"

He sighed. "New clients are coming slowly. I think local businesses want to have the city's blessing before they do business with me. And it seems just about everyone's in bed with Jeremy Anderson." He watched to see her reaction.

Christine nodded. "He's popular, both as a businessman and a politician. Has roots here."

"So do I."

"So, use them."

"You know me. The business is coming ... slowly." He smiled and leaned toward her, covering her hand with his. "That's what I'm doing now. Using my roots."

She drew back and gave him a sharp look. "Charles! You're having dinner with me to get a foothold with the city and local businesses?"

"It's not *just* that!"

She began to laugh, and he joined her.

She looked down at her food, her smile gone. "My work is ... complicated. It's a good job, really. Great benefits, pays well ... but I'm sometimes expected to do things I don't agree with."

"Things you don't agree with? Like, sexual things?"

"No, no. I mean"—she searched for the right words—"using laws and ordinances to punish people and businesses who are not in the city's good graces."

"Like our electricity last week?"

"Like your electricity last week, though that wasn't me. Putting the city in a bad light isn't tolerated." Now she covered his hand with hers. "You can't say anything to *anyone*. They'd fire me, or worse."

"What would be worse?"

She looked him in the eye. "Some kind of humiliation—public humiliation."

"And who is behind forcing you to use city policies as a weapon? Wouldn't it be the mayor? Doesn't the buck stop—"

"The city is run in layers. I deal with department heads, directors ... sometimes assistant directors, who can be pretty vicious. And there's a lawyer, a buffer between the department directors and the mayor. He's one cold guy, not that I've ever met him. You don't do what these people say, you're not only out, you're the main course in a feast of shame."

"How mature," Charlie remarked, shaking his head. "Why can't they run the city in a way that makes sense for the citizens? You know, goods, services ...?"

"Because the citizens aren't running things, except maybe one day a year, are they?" She leaned closer to Charlie, her voice low, her words coming fast. "These people, who are running things, what's in it for them is what it's all about. And they collect information about everyone who works there, and they sift through it. And when they want something from you, they threaten to use it. Sometimes, they do."

Charlie sat back and crossed his legs. He had finished his dinner. "Dessert?"

Christine shook her head. "Not for me, thanks."

"You're immune, right?"

She gave him a hard look.

He was incredulous. "What could they possibly have on you? You're the most moral person I know—a church going girl!"

She couldn't help but smile. "I'll say this for the city, they have me going to church more. Mass three days a week, plus Sunday."

"How about I go with you again?"

"You enjoyed it, did you?"

"Well, I wouldn't ... Yes, I did, in fact."

She laughed. "You're so full of it!"

"I enjoy sitting with you ... anywhere."

"I'm not sure I believe that. We'll see, okay? If there are no strings. And as for the city, Charles, it doesn't matter if I've done something wrong or not. They're masters at making it look like I, or anyone, did something wrong and making them pay through humiliation. If there's nothing there, they make something up. And there's always someone on the team to back up the accusations."

Charlie shook his head. "How the hell do you work there?"

Christine looked away. "Oh, it's not just me they do this to. With me, they don't really have to. I do pretty much whatever they say. That's the problem I'm having—I do what I'm told. I'm a good girl, but a lot of it is wrong. The things I do often hurt people. It isn't right, and I'm party to it."

"I'm sorry." He edged his hand toward hers. "Why don't you have another drink with me, at my place? I could use a ride home after that second scotch." He looked her in the eyes for a long moment. "I'd like to hear more about this and be there for you."

She slapped the table. "Charles Bernelli, you had another drink just so you could get me to drive you home!"

He nodded. "And I'll need to get back here tomorrow for my car."

She slid her chair back and stood up. "Well, I'll give you a ride, but I'm not getting out of my car, and you can walk to get your car tomorrow."

Chapter 16

The campaign for the open council spot was in full swing, as the election drew close. *The Chronicle* featured campaign ads and stories about the candidates, along with residents' letters to the editor expressing their preferences. Officially, *The Chronicle*'s editorial board, aka Tom Volkov, endorsed Jeremy Anderson, citing, "his decades of hands-on enrichment of Beach City's growth and prosperity." The editorial went on: "Agatha Raines displays an admirable focus on justice for all citizens, but we are concerned that she lacks positive plans and programs to implement her ideas, while neglecting the requisite positive energy for Beach City's vibrant tourism economy."

Both candidates went door-to-door with small entourages, answering questions and leaving door hangers when homeowners were unavailable.

Fundraisers were held in advance of the final, pre-election push, at Rudy's for Agatha Raines and Townes Steak House for Jeremy Anderson. Each candidate accused the other of duplicity. Agatha Raines reiterated her accusations about Julienne's supposed illegal dumping of waste "effluents" into the channel and reminded the public of Jeremy Anderson's stake in and support of the company. She also answered *The Chronicle*'s accusation by explaining that cleaning up corruption was indeed a positive plan that would lead to fresh leadership in multiple city departments; leadership that would bring its own innovations and programs.

Jeremy Anderson called attention to the city's prosperity and the role he claimed to have had in it, promising further growth and abundance in the future, specifically condo and coop construction projects along the boardwalk, projects which Agatha Raines condemned as eyesores that would ruin the city's ambience and lead to traffic and parking nightmares.

Beach City residents took to Facebook, commenting, accusing, fomenting, and fulminating as Election Day approached.

Election Day itself was quiet, a calm before the storm. As the day wore on into evening, residents obsessively visited and refreshed *The Beach City Chronicle*'s web page, where the Board of Elections would post results. And when Agatha Raines was announced as the winner by a mere two hundred and seventy-five votes, the Anderson campaign called the results "fraudulent" and vowed to "uncover thousands of uncounted Anderson votes."

• • •

Bernard Trager had a horrific headache. He was the director of the Beach City Board of Elections and had just received a text from J.H., instructing him to install Jeremy Anderson as the new Beach City Council Councilman.

Four cups of black coffee and an hour of vacillating later, he made his decision.

The day after the election, the Beach City Board of Elections announced, via email, robocall and a lead in *The Chronicle*, that two hundred and eighty-seven additional, uncounted Anderson votes, hidden by computer error, had indeed been found. Jeremy Anderson was declared the winner of the election and would be the new councilman.

Nearly a week of outrage manifested as letters to *The Chronicle* and a raucous crowd of picketers outside City Hall made their feelings vociferously known. During the second week, the letters and picketers dwindled. By the third week, they had ceased altogether.

• • •

City budget "rollouts," as they were called in Beach City, were traditionally made known the week following election day. The intervening days were filled with flurries of activity, as each director and his or her assistants jockeyed for position with Lance Feeversham, the city's budget director and, of course, the mayor himself, though Mayor Mark strove to maintain, as he put it, "equal relationships with all," by distancing himself from the daily struggles of each department in favor of those of the city's residents.

Some of this year's shenanigans included:

Judge Cheryl Rose made sure that her coffee maker broke down a few days after the election, as opposed to any other time. She claimed to need a larger unit, as both her bailiffs were major caffeine addicts.

On the Sunday evening, following the election, Sally Freschetti, the Beach City Director of Animal Control, typed up an anonymous letter addressed to the council, complaining of the Fire Department's poor response time to several fires during recent weeks. This was the fourth such letter that she had written in the last quarter, each referencing gaps, errors, and negligence on the part of different city departments. She knew that these letters were put into files and brought out as justification, blame and humiliation of department directors and their assistants in the days following budget rollouts.

The WOS, or "Wall of Shame" newsletter, was the in-house city newsletter issue that accompanied the budget rollouts, carrying budget news while shaming those whose work fell short and lauding the exemplary few. One did not want to be labeled a "WOS."

Harry Livingston, the director of the Beach City Water and Sewer Department, was proud that this past fiscal year, his water—well, the city's water—had been the purest in the county by five percent. Unfortunately, Sally Freschetti complained that two of her cats had died as a result of contaminated water which, of course, came from the city's supply. She asked that Mr. Livingston not be blamed, though the latter request was made to divert suspicion away from her.

Harry Livingston had arranged, months earlier, with Judge Rose, to jointly complain about both the noise and the smell coming from the city kennels. Only one of those complaints went through, as Judge Rose did not complain about the kennels, but instead sent a private note to Jon Hagen "reluctantly calling attention to the apparent vendetta" that Harry was waging against Ms. Freschetti and Animal Control.

Glenn Euclid, the city union's shop steward, complained confidentially to Jon Hagen that Carl Matoli, the city's Civil Service manager, was doling out Civil Service patronage "passes," allowing friends and family to occupy plum positions in the city's union, positions that would deliver benefits, including retirement pay for life.

And so went the ongoing, internecine strife between Beach City departments directors and managers.

• • •

Dora had tried and failed to gain access to Franny's computer and phone. The fact that Franny had a personal computer and phone was encouraging, but useless without access. She had called Agatha, who came over to help and offer moral support.

"What did Franny think about the way City Hall ran?" Agatha wanted to know.

Agatha's views on the subject were so jaded that even Dora, who considered herself properly cynical, was having difficulty believing all Agatha claimed, though Agatha claimed every word was true. Was absolutely nothing done appropriately at City Hall? And how would Agatha know?

"With these men, it's all about dick size," Agatha explained. "Everything's a pissing contest."

"But they're not all men," Dora pointed out.

"It's dick size with the women at City Hall, too. They've been infected with corrupt testosterone." She tapped the piece of paper on which she was taking notes. "So, let's write down everything that was important to Franny —movies, songs, lyrics ... And we'll start looking for passwords."

"Why don't we get something to eat?" Dora suggested. "I can focus better while I eat."

Agatha nodded slowly. "Petrocelli's?"

"Takeout?"

An hour later, they were back with the food.

"So, are you into gossip?" Agatha asked as she speared a crouton.

"I'm as into gossip as anyone, but same as anyone, I'll never admit it."

"How 'bout that couple at—"

"At the table in the back." Dora nodded. "Charlie Bernelli, the new ad guy. Competition for Anderson Consulting. I worked with him recently."

"I know. And the city clerk, Christine Pearsall. Particularly interesting, given his—well, your—ad campaign competes with Anderson's official city ad campaign, and she has some influence over contracts."

"It is interesting," Dora agreed.

"Between you and me — she's my source."

"Source? For what?"

"Christine. For my inside information about City Hall. In-house dirty work's part of her job, and she hates it. She has principles." Agatha tipped her head from side to side, equivocating. "And yet, she's also a loyal and compliant employee."

"How loyal can she be if she's sharing secrets with you?"

Agatha shrugged while she chewed. "There are different kinds of loyalty. She sees a lot through the prism of religion."

A half-hour later, the computer and phone were unlocked. Password? *Felix521*. The cat's birthday was May 21st.

"Not the most secure password," Agatha mused.

Dora nodded. "My honey wore her heart, and I guess her password, on her sleeve."

They scoured the computer first and, within another forty minutes, had stumbled across Franny's important notes, cryptically labeled *"Important Notes."*

"How'd she ever get to be a cop?" Agatha wanted to know.

Dora looked sad. "She was smart and tough, and never looked like she was trying. She got criminals to confess, and they didn't even know they were confessing. They thought they were confiding in her."

Dora double-clicked the file. A message appeared, requesting a password.

After trying unsuccessfully to open the file for twenty minutes, Dora and Agatha gave up and turned their full focus to their dinner containers.

• • •

Charlie and Christine reminisced about their time together over drinks and cocktail shrimp. He snapped his napkin open and tucked it into his belt when the waiter brought their dinners, which was a delicious penne a la vodka for Charlie and a linguini primavera for Christine. It was early, so they were able to sit at a family-sized table in the near-empty restaurant. They ordered a bottle of house Merlot to go with their dinners. All wonderful, but the most delicious aspect of the meal, for Charlie, was being with Christine again.

He had forgotten how much he enjoyed her company—her combination of earnestness and dry wit, her subtly sexy-without-trying-to-be personality. Sexiest of all was her modesty.

He had forgotten about all these things. Probably, on some level, he had intended to.

She raised her glass, her third. "You're just trying to get me drunk."

He raised his and touched it to hers. "Oh, such a struggle."

They each sipped then put their glasses down.

She gave him a mock-stern look. "Behave. This is only our second date."

"Um, it's more like our twenty-first."

She twirled her linguini around her fork. "Actually, it's our second second date," she insisted. "Or is it our third second date, or our first second date?"

Charlie laughed. "I have no idea." He was admiring her neck. When she put her hair up, as it was tonight, her oh-so-graceful neck was exposed. It was all he could do to keep from kissing it, right here in Petrocelli's.

"You once told me how uncomfortable doing the city's dirty work was for you."

"Yes, it is. It always has been."

"And you told me about the different department directors stabbing one another in the back."

She smiled sadly. "Which never ends."

"So, tell me, why wouldn't they band together against you? You're in a position of power there, far as I can tell. And if backstabbing is second nature to them, wouldn't they backstab you? Wouldn't they want you compromised?"

She nodded. "They would, but you said it yourself—I'm in a position of power. They're all afraid of me."

Charlie chuckled, covering his mouth with his napkin. "Of you? Scary lady!"

"I have the higherups' ears, and I know just about everything about everyone. I can say whatever I want to whomever I want with impunity, and they all assume I will. But, do you know what the most intimidating thing about me is? I'm honest. And honesty scares the crap out of them."

Her expression changed, becoming more directly empathetic. "How's C3?"

Charlie sighed. "We just spoke. First time in a while. He's on parole, moving into a halfway house. But, to honestly answer your question, I really have no idea."

She covered his hand with hers. "To answer my question, you love your son."

"Well, sometimes tough love is best. I'm trying to do what's best for him."

"He's your son."

"He's my son."

Christine paused, thoughtful. "I remember he wore his heart on his sleeve."

"I'm sure he still does."

"I remember he had a good heart. Do you think jail ...?"

Charlie didn't answer but went back to eating his last bit of dinner. After a few minutes, he stopped and looked at Christine, holding her gaze. "I don't have the luxury of thinking about his heart or his feelings. I just want to keep him alive and help him stay clean and sober."

She nodded. "And your dad?'

Charlie smiled. "He's good. Slowed down some. Still drinking bourbon in his coffee, or vice versa. And more golf than work nowadays, but he's excited about the new incarnation of Bernelli."

"And how's that going? Is he involved?"

"It's going okay, and no, he's not involved, except as an observer and supporter, and as my father. Still have a handful of old clients, and a few new ones." He gave a half-smile. "No thanks to City Hall." He had hoped to bring the subject up, wondering what Christine knew about the sudden reticence of the city to work with his company. "What happened to the great start the mayor and I made?"

She looked away. "Who knows? The city is the city. Doesn't run on logic. Runs on … politics, the whims of assholes." She dabbed at the side of her mouth with her napkin. "Let's not talk work."

Charlie smiled. "I agree. And you don't have to worry about me finding a way to get you to come to my place. I've given up on that … for now."

She gave a wary smile. "Oh?"

"We'll go to your place."

"You'll take a raincheck, is what you'll do."

"Exactly. I was about to say that. I'll take a raincheck, is what I'll do. But we should discuss the raincheck at your place."

Chapter 17

Dora made a point of never watching the news. She learned what she needed via texts and by talking to Mo, Esteban, and everyone at work. So, she was caught by surprise when she received the text from Mo and a work email about the Covid-19 virus. Her gym had closed, and she and her co-workers had been deemed "essential," which meant that they would carry on with their jobs, despite this bizarre pandemic. She had noticed people wearing masks over their noses and mouths but hadn't given them any thought, other than to shake her head at their silliness.

In the past, she had seen pictures on the news of people who wore masks as they went about their business. She had the impression that they were in Asia, and that they wore the masks primarily when flying.

Within days of the first work notification, employees were advised to maintain something called "social distancing." Everyone was supposed to stay six feet away from anyone else. Within days, City Hall was closed entirely.

It was like a sci-fi movie, where everyone gets sick and zombies take over, or Martians, or … but this was real. People were getting sick. Some were dying.

Her awareness of the situation was that it began as a minor story, something she heard was going on in China. A flu or something like one. The stories did not concern her.

She noticed when the stories told of a more serious, ongoing situation —the virus had spread to parts of Europe, particularly Italy and Spain, where the demonstrative love people showed one another—their tendency to hug and kiss—was proving dangerous.

And then it came to America and spread. Fast. Especially in New York.

Now everyone was "sheltering in place," a term that meant people were purposely staying home and isolating, avoiding one another and places where groups of people tended to congregate. Toilet paper and paper towels were suddenly in short supply. There was a fear that food might be hard to get, though that had not yet proven true.

So, Dora was home, with Felix, practically bored to tears.

• • •

Is the Beach City Police Force actively investigating Franny's death?
Dora wondered. If so, was Captain George Cobb in charge of the
investigation? Would he also investigate the "dirty" aspects of city business
that the caller had referenced?

While the city viewed Franny's death as a hit and run, Dora believed it
was more; that Franny had made a discovery that had led someone to
decide she had to be killed.

But killing a cop? What could possibly lead to such a thing? Money?

The caller had said this was something to do with city *business*. That
had to mean money. Fixed parking tickets, denied or fast-tracked building
permits, or liquor licenses? Dora didn't think so. Something much bigger.
This was big money.

But what city business involved large enough sums of money—
contracts! City contracts. And all she could think of was construction.

While she thought, she began doing pushups to shed stress and allow
her mind to relax enough to focus. Whether it was her job or MMA,
physical exertion and pain helped her focus.

Who, specifically, benefited from change or access to power at City
Hall?

She knew nothing about construction contracts. Wasn't most of the
construction private? Nothing to do with the city, except for permits? Or
was city construction performed by city employees? She didn't know and
was unsure how to find out.

Other "dirty" city businesses ...? She thought of the work she had
done with Charlie on the new ad campaign, which was meant to undermine
the city's.

So, what had happened? Despite Mayor Mark's apparent blessing, the
city had given the campaign to Anderson Consulting. Jeremy Anderson.
Who had that kind of power besides the mayor? Purchasing? Dora wasn't
sure.

Agatha had made mention of some lawyer, a power broker of sorts, but
she didn't know who that would be. Someone unofficial, which made no

sense because the power all lay with the council and the mayor, though the policies certainly were carried out by others.

Her mind was running in circles.

Anderson's biggest client was Julienne Inc. who, according to Agatha, was dumping effluents into the channel on the bay side and about a mile offshore on the beach side. Who benefited?

Well, Julienne benefitted from Anderson's relationship with City Hall and certainly Jeremy Anderson himself benefited.

Illegal dumping would probably save Julienne a lot of money and do an end run around regulators. Would someone at Julienne, or perhaps even Jeremy Anderson, kill a cop if that cop found out about illegal dumping?

• • •

"I don't know how I let you talk me into this," Christine said, and Charlie looked to see if she was kidding. She looked serious, but there was a hint of humor in her eyes.

"Look," he said, joining her on the couch. They were in his apartment, which he had spent the entire afternoon cleaning and rearranging. Christine had that effect on him. "We've both been lucky enough to get Covid tests, and we're both negative. So, that should put you at least somewhat at ease."

"Somewhat," she agreed. "But we're not going in that bedroom, Charles. Nor are we 'doing it out here,' which I know you were about to say."

He laughed and shook his finger at her. "You! You know me well." He leaned close suddenly and kissed her on the lips. It was a soft, gentle kiss, with no urgency to turn into anything more.

She kissed him back. Then, when he pulled away, he saw that she felt as he did, so he kissed her again, with more passion this time, but still with no push to do anything more. It was a kiss that said it was just fine remaining a kiss. It was a kiss that asked politely, with love, for more kissing. So, they kissed some more, with hands caressing one another's face. Like teenagers, for whom kissing was a new discovery.

After a few minutes, he sat back and saw that she was looking at him, her walls coming down. She smiled a sweet, self-conscious smile and looked down.

"I have church in the morning, at ten," she whispered.

"No, I don't think you do."

"I do. Oh, wait. I don't. This virus—"

He smiled. "I could get used to this virus."

She frowned. "Don't say that. Real people are sick with this thing!"

He shook his head, still smiling. "You are such a good girl."

She smiled back. "Sure you don't mean a nice girl?"

"I guess we'll see ... no church." He smiled, a mischievous glint in his eye. "But seriously, I am now a gentleman."

He saw her dubious look. "I know how you are Charles."

"I've changed since we were together before, but don't take my word for it—spend time with me. I'll be ever the gentleman, and if it doesn't work for you, stop. I won't push you to do anything you don't want to do."

Now she leaned over and kissed him lightly then passionately. When they stopped, she watched his expression, which was one of curiosity.

"Have you given any more thought to what I asked?"

She turned to him. "What did you ask?"

"About a possible murder sometime in the past, about these weird phone calls that Officer Hart and then Dora Ellison were getting, and how any of that might be tied to the goings on at City Hall, and to Hart's death. If anyone would know about that part of it, you would."

She folded one leg beneath her, swinging the other gently, grazing the floor. "The dysfunction at City Hall is so thick you could cut it with a knife. But what you've described sounds more like a focused conspiracy that's somehow covering up a murder, probably two murders. I'm not sure you'd get enough people at City Hall who are on the same page to be involved in something like that, not unless we were talking about a very small coverup. Everyone is at everyone else's throats. Very little of the teamwork needed for a conspiracy."

Charlie considered what she said. "Hmm ... You know what is needed?"

"What?"

He took her chin in his hands and pulled her to him. "More kissing."
She could not disagree.

Chapter 18

Frank Patella, or Cranky Franky, as he was known by those he spent most of his time with, was late for work. He had been late for work, or had been a no show, most days for the past nineteen years. This was his own private joke, since he had been technically and happily employed by the same employer in a capacity that was never mentioned, except on his original work form, and was wholly unrelated to his actual job—except in name. He was a messenger. He was The Messenger.

Franky also spent nearly an hour every day watering and feeding his beloved flowers. They graced the windowsills and the tables arranged in front of each of his windows. There were orchids and petunias, zinnias and geraniums, begonias and nasturtiums—all surrounded by ivy and heather. He planned to add bonsai trees and self-contained hydroponic gardens.

These were his babies. His family. He did not go to work until he gave them some love.

The city had originally hired Franky as a messenger, to deliver envelopes between departments. That he had, in fact, become a different sort of messenger was probably an attempt at humor by someone somewhere. Perhaps not a coincidence. Franky didn't believe in coincidences, and he didn't give any of this much thought, except to smile now and then to himself about this private joke, and to look up and nod to his Uncle Sal, wherever he was—probably not up, if he gave it any thought, which he did not.

If he were to be honest, also unlikely, he would have had to admit that his job did not always entail sending a message. At times, it did. But, at times, his job was to clean up a mess, to make it go away. Maybe he should then be called a janitor or a cleaner, or maybe a magician, since the mess often simply disappeared.

He sang softly to his orchids, pouring just a little bit of lukewarm water into each of their containers. Today, he was doing both jobs—he was sending a message, which also involved a cleanup. Rare, but it happened.

He added water to his annuals and to their miniature ground cover, smiling and singing softly. *"I see trees so green, red roses, too. I see them bloom for me and you. And I think to myself what a wonderful world ..."*

In the past, he'd had to be careful about keeping track of the routes he took to his destinations and who might have seen him on the way. But now, because of this corona virus pandemic, he wore a face mask, covering the lower half of his face. It was, in fact, a bandana, and at any other point in his life, he could only have worn a bandana over his face if it were Halloween, or if he were robbing a bank, something he had never done ... yet. He was always open to new experiences.

Today, people all over were wearing masks, as medical authorities suggested. This virus was no joke. The only fools who weren't wearing masks were those who were okay with infecting their fellow citizens or risking infections themselves. The low that people sank to amazed him. What was the world coming to?

Yes, today, he would be late for his job. His aftercare required him to be at a twelve-step meeting, and today, it had been Narcotics Anonymous, and it had been his turn to share.

So, he had told a story—*the* story. Why he had become an addict, though he could not be sure he would not have become an addict, anyway. Maybe it was genetic. He explained why he had become violent, though he could not say for sure he would not have become violent, anyway. He had once cared for someone, and she had cared for him. He had once trusted someone, and she had been trustworthy. He had once loved someone, or perhaps he loved her in hindsight. No, he *had* loved her. He had given himself to her. And because his life had been such a dangerous jungle, their love had been like the sun coming out after a terrible storm.

No matter how he looked at it, she had been special. They had been so young, barely more than kids, yet he remembered their love as fully grown love. And she had been beautiful. She had the pick of many boys, yet she had chosen him, at least for a time. Until—

Yes, today, he would be late for delivering his message, because he was first delivering another message—about the dangerous interplay between love and addiction. The story of Frank and Anne.

• • •

The medical facility, which housed the groups that C3 was mandated to attend, was actually a complex of three low, brick buildings that had been built in the 1960s. The complex now housed two dentists, an obstetrician, an ophthalmologist and optometrist husband/wife practice, a freight forwarder, a candy manufacturer's corporate office, and the Rockplace Counseling Center, which offered mental health and addiction-related services, social work and, after hours, twelve-step meetings of various kinds.

C3's parole conditions required that he participate in group counseling twice a week, one-on-one at least once a week, and daily twelve step meetings, with at least four of these being Alcoholics Anonymous or Narcotics Anonymous meetings.

He had asked his father if he could move back home. He hated the halfway house, where there was some camaraderie and mutual support, but also a feeling that reminded him a little of prison. He wasn't really free. His father responded that he needed structure, and C3 agreed, saying his father would be better able to keep an eye on him if he were living at home. Surprised, his father had relented.

The ongoing Covid virus situation had migrated all of these to a video chat platform. Today was the first day of in-person meetings, which were limited to the first ten attendees to show up, all of whom were to be masked and practice social distancing. The rest would attend online or by phone. Today was Adult Children of Alcoholics—ACOA.

"Hi, everyone. I'm Terence, and I'm an adult child."

"Hi, Terrence," the group said in unison.

"Today's topic is Step One," Terence continued. He was in his fifties, wore silver, wire-rimmed glasses, had thinning grey hair, and a slight paunch that spilled over his belt. "I'm powerless over the family disease and my life is unmanageable."

Most of those in the room nodded. C3 was looking at a young woman with dark hair and a single, thin, auburn braid. She wore a too-tight lilac blouse with ruffles fringing a plunging neckline.

"I grew up in a crazy situation," Terence went on, "with an alcoholic mom and a father who gambled and ran with some bad people. It wasn't my fault, and I couldn't cope with the dysfunction. I didn't cause it, I couldn't control it, and I certainly couldn't cure it. So, it came out the side of my neck, so to speak. I acted out, caused trouble, broke windows, got high, got in fights. Anyone identify? Tracy?"

The young woman with the lilac ruffles had sensed C3's interest and was looking pointedly in the opposite direction, but her energy remained focused on him. He could feel it—a spark between them. She was startled by the question. "Hmm ...?"

"Can you identify?"

"With ... oh, um, kind of, I guess ..."

"How so?"

"I-I'm not sure I'm comfortable enough to share this. It can take me a while to feel safe." She turned toward Terrance, focused now on the question. "Um, I did have a pretty abusive stepfather and stepbrother. And you don't want to know about my boyfriends."

Terrance nodded sadly. "I understand. It's important that you feel safe. Franky?"

Franky was tall and lanky, with hair that was a color somewhere between blond and grey and floppy bangs that covered his eyes. He looked out from a perpetual squint. "Me? Heh, I feel safe. I always feel safe." He laughed, and some of the less secure members of the group laughed uneasily. "I just don't like people. I like plants." His tone was defiant, as though daring anyone to challenge him.

Terrance waited, but Franky did not elaborate.

"Can you identify?"

Franky shook his head and pouted out his lower lip. "Identify? You mean, like tell you who I am? You run the group. You should already know." He looked around for signs of approval.

Terrance was patient, speaking calmly. "I mean, have you ever had an experience similar to what I described? Or, would you like to tell us a little about your past, how you came to join us?"

"I could," Franky said, "but then I'd have to kill you."

The same two or three people giggled.

Franky did not. He had expected fear from these people as he did from everyone and found ... *compassion?*

"What about you, Charles?" Terrance asked, looking at C3.

C3 shrugged. "I don't know what happened. I guess I trusted the wrong people and woke up one day wearing orange."

• • •

The Bay Constable employed four men during the day and two, Constables Mitch Schoen and Tony Aldretti, at night to keep an eye on the city park docks and local bay waters, as well as some of the larger local construction sites, from both land and water vantage points. Their primary tasks were to make sure that boaters and jet skiers were not too inebriated or reckless to threaten public safety, and to make sure that those who fished had the appropriate licenses, and the fish they caught were within the legal limits of the season. They were also tasked to be on the lookout for vandalism and to ensure that nothing illegal or inappropriate was dumped into the water. The constables were armed but had rarely needed to use their firearms and were strongly discouraged from doing so.

Mitch and Tony played music over one of their phones, set softly to *speaker* during their shift so they would also hear any alerts that came over the radio. Typically, their shift was quiet until school ended and the summer parties began. This year, with Covid-19, it was different. Quieter, and much stranger.

Mitch loved classic rock, just about anything from the early 50s through the 80s, up to and emphatically not including disco. Tony preferred classical music—symphonies. Tonight was Tony's night, so they were listening to Antonín Dvořák. Mitch was surprised to admit he liked the music.

Just after three a.m., Mitch tapped Tony on the shoulder. "On the dock, seven o'clock."

"Hmm?" Tony had been dozing. "Yeah?"

"Shh! Couple of guys. Dark clothes. No boat. No lights."

Patrolling the docks from the water, they kept the engine in gear, just above idle. They had just passed the spot Mitch was indicating, on the dock, to their left.

Tony shifted into reverse while Mitch flipped on the microphone.

"Police. Stay where you are. Police. We need to see your hands."

The two dark shapes had been bent over a low, dark shape, possibly a garbage can or a small dumpster, between them.

Mitch trained the boat's searchlight on the pair. Two young men; one tall and lean, Caucasian with longish hair, and the other possibly Latino, stockier, with short hair.

Tony maneuvered the boat to the dock and, once they were close, Mitch secured the boat with towline.

"See some ID?" Mitch said. He was just over six feet from the two. Tony remained on the boat, having moved from the bridge to the searchlight.

Neither man moved.

"Got names?" Mitch asked, louder and more forcefully.

Both men reached into their rear pockets.

"Do it slowly," Mitch said.

One, the shorter, darker complected of the two, fumbled with what looked like ID, but Mitch had no time to learn more, as the taller, leaner man had whipped a short, cylindrical object from his pocket, flicked his wrist, and the object, which was a specially made baton, telescoped to nearly two feet in length.

An instant later, Mitch was writhing on the ground, blood pouring from the side of his head.

"Whoa!" was all Tony managed to yell before Franky Patella was on the boat, the baton shut and flipped around to its other end, from which a thin, steel blade protruded.

Tony, Franky knew, had seen him, so he thrust the blade at the constable's gut then pulled hard upward, slitting the man's stomach then drawing the blade quickly across the constable's throat. He then leaped back to the dock where Berto, his partner, was struggling to tip the nearly full dumpster onto its side so they could resume their task.

"Fuckin' hell," Berto breathed. "Did ya have ta do that?"

Franky giggled, loving the terror in Berto's eyes. He couldn't help himself. "Nope," he said, giggling again. Then, together, they went back to pouring the contents of the last of the barrels into the bay.

This had been their first try at using this site for dumping. There was simply too much waste product to dump at the factory, which left this

Clean Acres construction site and city dockage. Both were patrolled by Bay Constables. They would pass word along so that, next time, their reception would be friendlier.

Chapter 19

When Dora was a teenager, her parents took her to a family therapist. The session had consisted of her parents describing a litany of Dora's misdeeds, all of them true, though her perspective on each was somewhat different from her parents'. At the end of the session, the therapist explained that normal children develop a healthy sense of themselves which, as they grow up, develops into self-confidence—a healthy perspective of who one is and how to connect with the world outside oneself.

In Dora's case, the therapist explained, she had not developed that self-confidence, so she overcompensated with violence and rage. Dora had waited for them to get to *why* she had not developed that self-confidence and talk about the violence her father had visited upon her and about her mother's inability to protect her. Wasn't that what therapist's did? Secrets were uncovered and clients healed.

But her parents denied anything like this ever happened and insisted that their daughter was delusional, on drugs, or was mentally ill. As the session ended, and both her parents expressed their sadness at Dora's emotional disability, the therapist asked for her thoughts.

Dora's response was to put into play what would become one of two primary coping mechanisms—silence. She didn't answer. She kept her opinion to herself, since her experience was that allowing others to know what she thought was to open herself up to criticism and ridicule. Vulnerability was dangerous, so she shrugged and remained silent.

She was on her way out to the library when she remembered that it was time to feed Felix. She poured a bit of room temperature, bottled water into his water dish. Felix only drank bottled, never tap. He was particular, refined, Franny used to say. Dora then mixed tuna from a can with cooked chicken breast and set the food dish with the thick green capital "*F*" on the floor next to the water dish. Felix ate only people food, select people food.

"Who's a good boy!" Dora said in her special Felix voice. "Who's a good boy? Gonna have some dinner; some tuna and chicken. Where's my Feelie?" She made kissing sounds, stopped, and listened. By now, Felix should have been sauntering into the room, rubbing her side, or meowing at the door.

She used her baby voice—her Elmer Fudd. "Is my Feewie pwaying hawd to get? Come awn, babe. White meat onwy!" She stood up, her hands on her hips. She should have at least heard his low, distinctive *rowll* by now.

She went to the front door and opened it. "Who's a good boy? Who's gonna have some dinner?" She knew she sounded frustrated and knew Felix would know, but she didn't care. She was worried.

She walked around the side of her building, where the alcove housing the hose faucet was. She peered around the building's back corner, into the parking lot and the bit of dirt and grass beyond that functioned as a backyard of sorts. She then went back the other way, passed the dumpster, toward the front, keeping her eyes on the ground, especially under the bushes.

"Come on out, Feelie …" She stopped, thought a moment, then went back to the side of the building and looked under and around the dumpster, where Felix loved scrounging for scraps.

"Where's my Feelie? Who's a good boy?" She turned, and something in the dumpster caught her eye. Later, she would realize it had been a familiar bit of fur. She took a closer look, then recoiled, both hands clasped over her belly. Then she spun around, her body convulsing and lurching— dry heaves.

Felix's twisted body lay on the pile of garbage in the half full dumpster … in two pieces. He had been decapitated. Much of his once luscious, thick fur mane was matted with black blood.

"Huuhhhhh," she moaned, bent double, gasping. "Ugghhhh." She fell to her knees, gasping. Then Dora put into play the other of her two coping skills.

Her extremities went cold, her sinuses flared, and her muscles filled with blood as she let her own private beast out of its cage.

• • •

Franky was sitting alone in a back booth of Cobbs' Diner, watching a table of high school girls laughing and talking and peering at their phones. None of them wore masks. Two were hot. Franky wore a mask, though not so much to keep from getting Covid as to minimize the possibility of being recognized. He thought the virus was a good thing. He could wear the sort of mask he would wear on a burglary all the time, in places of business. Every time he thought about it, he started to laugh. He was *supposed* to wear the mask. Just when you thought life was shit, a crazy cool gift like that came along.

Franky watched Horace instructing the waitress, Carolyn, and wondered why he was afraid of Horace. After thinking about it for a moment, he realized that it was really George he was afraid of, and George reminded him of Horace. Horace was a little bit bigger, but you could talk to Horace. George could be one vicious cop. Franky knew this from experience.

Horace came over to his table and sat down. Franky said nothing. He did not so much as look at Horace, who stared at him until Franky finally met his eyes and smiled.

"Well?" Horace said.

Franky met his eyes. "Message sent."

"Cleanup?"

"Nah, I left the message. This way, she knows; she gets the message. Much stronger message to have her find it than to have it disappear." He looked at Horace but was thinking of George, which made him a little nervous, as though he were confessing a crime to a cop. "I had that leeway, right?"

Horace said nothing.

• • •

Dora brushed the mud from her hands and laid Felix's remains at the bottom of the hole that she had dug behind her apartment's parking lot. The rain had been coming down steadily for more than an hour, and she knew the hole would start to fill with mud soon, so she gently lay a photo of herself and Franny on top of his body then filled the hole with dirt.

"We'll always be with you, Feelie. Forever," she said as she finished.

She then recited *Kaddish* and stood for a long moment, staring at the little mound of dirt, remembering how full her life had been with Franny and Felix.

Once back in her apartment, she washed and changed her clothes then dialed the library. She knew that the person who did this wanted to dissuade her from making exactly this kind of inquiry. *Well, fuck them.*

"Hi. Yes, my name is Dora Ellison. I live here in Beach City. "

"Hi, Dora. This is Missy. I'm a reference librarian. How can I help you?"

Dora paused, thinking about how to answer the question. "I'm interested in some local history."

"Okay," Missy said. "Please describe what you are looking for."

Dora did her best to explain that she was hoping to look over records of local city and county court decisions, along with newspaper articles about those decisions. She was particularly interested in the enforcement of policy and ordinances where there was conflict. She requested that her query remain absolutely private.

"Well, that's potentially a lot of information, but okay. Is there a particular start and end date you'd like the information to cover?"

"The last twenty years."

Missy paused. "Oh, that could take a while. Are you looking for information related to a particular event or circumstance?"

"I don't know. Or, actually, I do believe I am looking for information related to a particular event—a murder or, at least, a death."

"Okay. So public policy or enforcement, where there's conflict and where there may have been a related, suspicious death. I do have access through the library's portal to a database of news articles. Can you narrow down the timeframe or give me further detail?"

Dora tried to collect her thoughts, which seemed to be racing more than they should have been. "Well, one potentially related murder is much more recent. Franny … Lieutenant Francesca Hart, of the Beach City Police Department?"

"Okay. You said one murder, so was there another?"

"The other would have occurred much longer ago ... I think. So, that and controversial city business over the twenty-year period. The murder would have been around the beginning of that time. At least, I think that's the case."

"Well, murders do tend to attract the attention of newspapers and the police. Who was the victim?"

"I'm not sure. It's been referred to as a murder that isn't a murder."

"Referred to by whom? And what does that mean?"

Dora was silent. "I ... honestly don't know."

"Oh."

"I'm sorry I don't have more information. I know ... the murder ... the information I have is vague, as are the policy issues and controversies that might be related to it." She sighed. "It's an I'll-know-it-when-I-see-it situation."

"I do like puzzles." Missy was silent a moment. "When is a murder not a murder?"

"I like puzzles, too. And I ... don't know."

"Well, I'll have to give it some thought. So ... Dora, right?"

"Yes, Dora ... Actually, Deborah Ellison, but everyone calls me Dora."

"Then so will I. I'll tell you what, Dora. Let me give you a couple of web addresses to start with. We are just beginning to open the library on a limited basis, to small numbers of people at a time, provided they wear masks and social distance. Once you've looked over what I give you, let's find a time that's good for us both, and we'll discuss it."

• • •

"Today, we'll be talking about our favorite slogans." Terence nodded toward the cards lined up on the floor in the center of the circle, each of which contained a phrase written in a different color marker.

"I'll start," Terence said. "Mine is 'Let Go and Let God,' because when it comes down to it, there's very little I can personally control. I have a tendency to get frustrated with life, and there was a time that I drank alcohol and used drugs to cope. So, now that I don't do those things, it might make sense for me to stop trying to control outcomes, to just let go and let God."

Franky shook his head. "Easy for you to say. You're running this group and getting paid. We're stuck having to be here and getting nothing for it."

Terence didn't answer; he just nodded, waited a moment, then said, "Franky, why don't you go next?"

"Because I'd rather not."

"Okay," Terence said. "You don't have to, but why not? I mean, really. There's nothing to be afraid of."

"I'm not afraid of anything. And don't give me any of that reverse psychology crap. It won't work. Besides, it's a no-brainer. I like chillin', so 'Easy Does It' is my favorite."

Terence gave a little smile. "Great. I get that. We don't want to get wrapped too tight."

A pear-shaped woman in a black sweatsuit and red hoop earrings raised her hand.

"Lucy?"

"I like 'Keep The Focus on Yourself' because whenever I visit my mom, she's really critical … and not always with words. Sometimes with the way she looks at me or pauses after I say something. Then she'll say *Reeaaaalllly?* like she's trying to get me to doubt myself or get me to feel guilty."

"Okay," Terence said. "So, how does the slogan apply?"

"I, like, don't have to buy into her whole side of the conversation. I don't have to respond to her. I can just let her stew, or I can politely respond to whatever she says on face value. I don't have to interpret her, or blame, or whatever. I can keep the focus on me and let her worry about her. Takes some of the pressure off."

"That's right," Terence agreed. "Pressure we might otherwise respond to with drugs. Good!" He turned to Charlie.

Charlie smiled. "I like 'Keep Coming Back.' It was really nice when I got here, and people wanted me to come back. I'm not used to that. I'm more used to *get the fuck outta here*."

"Well, we want you here," Terence told him. "Another slogan is 'A Day at a Time.' Your needs are met for today. In fact, we probably are doing better in this moment than we think. So, why don't we think about that and consider what we might have to be grateful for?"

Charlie shook his head. "That's another thing. You guys are always talking about gratitude. What is that? Like a church thing?"

Terence looked around the circle. A dark complected, balding man with a sleeve of faded green tattoos raised an enormous hand. Terence nodded at him. "Big Mike."

"Yeah, I'm Mike. It means to be glad we have a thing, not to take it for granted. For me, it helps if I imagine I didn't have whatever it is, then, now I have it. Or I imagine I never heard of it, then I suddenly have it. Like a place to sleep or food in my refrigerator, or the use of my arms and legs."

Terence looked at Charlie. "Or your father and whatever he adds to your life."

Charlie sighed and shrugged. "Yeah, well ..."

After the meeting, as Charlie was leaving the building, he heard Franky call to him.

"Know what my favorite slogan really is?"

Charlie waited.

"Take no shit."

Charlie didn't answer.

Franky went on. "When I was in, that's how I got by. I was ready to fight all the time. Even if I lost, which was like never, I won. You know?"

Charlie nodded. "Same. Every discussion was a confrontation. First day, three guys tried some shit. I hit the biggest one."

"And they left you alone, right?"

"They did ... after I got my ass kicked."

Franky pointed at him. "But everyone knew you took no shit."

Charlie had to agree.

• • •

It was still raining; it had been for days. The walk from Dora's building to her car, which was along the south wall of the parking lot—maybe twelve feet, if that—had left her drenched. What makeup she wore had run down the front of her blouse. Why had she worn makeup, anyway? She never wore makeup.

As the torrents drummed steadily against her car's roof, she realized she was anxious. Why would she be anxious? Maybe because she was a step closer to finding out what had happened to Franny and what the phone calls were all about. Maybe.

She had not really even known where to look. She had first googled Franny's murder and made herself miserable reading about it. Then she had googled "*Beach City Business*," which had brought up every business located in the city. Then she had looked around on the city's website and the site of the local police department. Nothing of interest. Next, she had googled "*Murder, Beach City*." Still nothing. After that, she'd had another crying jag, so she had called the library again and asked for Missy. Now, here she was, waiting for Missy to get off work so they could talk, masked up, in her car.

A small, dark shape scampered toward the car. Dora saw that it was Missy, holding a poncho over her head. Dora unlocked the doors so Missy could climb into the back seat.

"Sorry to sit back here. Social distancing." She shrugged and grinned an *oh well* grin. "What smells so good?"

"A pint of vegetable lo mein."

"Really?"

"I got you one, too. And chop sticks, napkins, and I wore gloves, so I never touched any of this."

"I'd turn it down, but I'm starved! So, thank you."

Dora beamed.

• • •

Franky's usually stoic expression took on a poignance that Charlie had never seen before.

"Let me tell you something. Life freakin' hurt. Man, I was a happy little kid. But everything hurt. Good stuff hurt. Joy hurt. I had this girlfriend years ago; that hurt. So, I took a step back. I stopped participating in relationships. I stopped being so involved, and it still hurt,

139

but not as bad. Then I got into plants. Plants and flowers, man. And they helped. I mean, when's the last time a plant gave you shit?" He looked around the circle, as if daring anyone to disagree.

Several heads nodded.

Charlie knew just what he meant.

"People told me what a bad guy I was. What a piece of garbage. So, you know what? I lived up to it."

"Who?" Terence asked. "Who told you what a bad guy you were?"

"*Who?*" Franky scoffed. "Who *didn't* tell me? Everyone—my family, the neighbors, the cops, the judge, society. You!"

Terence shook his head. "I never—"

"Not you, like you. You, like everybody you. The freakin' world."

"That must have sucked, Frank."

"Franky. My name's Franky."

"Franky. My apologies." Terence looked around the room. "Who wants to share next?"

C3 raised his hand and launched into sharing without waiting to be acknowledged. "Hey, I'm Charlie. And I know what he means. With me, they used the word '*difficult.*' I was a difficult kid. My father told the rest of the family that—my aunts and uncles, the neighbors. I had people come up to me just recently and ask me why I'm so difficult. Shit, I don't know. I don't think I'm difficult. I think the world's difficult. These people are difficult.

"My old man was hammered just about every night when I was a kid. He ran an ad agency, and he took clients out. Wined 'em and dined 'em. He'd come home, get upset if he didn't get the contract, and he'd drink, and there would be this silence in the house. And freakin' angry silence. He always thought everything should be better than it was. And after my mom left … not good. He drove her away with his silence. Not good. I'm difficult? *That* was difficult. The *world's* difficult. I just want to get the hell off it."

"And hence, the drugs," Terence said.

"Yeah, hence, the drugs."

"So, Charlie," Terence said softly, "do you want to stop?"

"Drugs? Using? I have stopped," Charlie answered emphatically. "I go to my meetings. I mean, like, here I am."

"Yes," Terence answered. "But having that desire to stop is paramount. That's the only requirement for stopping—desire."

• • •

The first thing Dora learned, with Missy's help, was that the city, county, and police department websites contained only static information about the services provided—the people in charge, and so forth. Missy located the Beach City page of the website *NewYorkincarcerationsite.com* that listed local outstanding warrants and arrests, but it only went back six years and yielded nothing that caught Dora's attention.

"A murder that isn't a murder," Missy repeated several times. "You know, if the person who is calling you has, or had, some connection to the victim, he could mean a murder that was never prosecuted, or where no arrest was made. In other words, a murder that is not yet *officially* a murder."

Dora brightened. "That could be. It makes sense!" Then her expression fell. "But how do you search that?"

"Well, maybe it was publicized, but not as a murder."

"Maybe," Dora agreed. "Remember, we're also looking for inconsistencies in city business, or controversies that could be what he called *dirty business.*"

"You know ... didn't he say *bad-smelling business*?"

"That's right."

"Maybe he's referencing your job—garbage."

Dora shook her head. "Why? How could that be? Is he saying something about me? Does he think *I'm* involved? Or that there's corruption at Sanitation? There probably is. Could be about where the body is buried, I suppose. But I think it's more a coincidence in the use of the phrase *bad-smelling*, as in underhanded dealings, dirty business. I don't see how it's my department—Sanitation."

"Okay," Missy agreed. "Let's focus on that."

They spent ten minutes happily eating lo mein and brainstorming.

"It says here"—Missy was looking at her phone, clicking links and reading—"that the city clerk maintains records of all council meetings, ordinances, regulations, laws, and public transactions. I know Christine Pearsall, the clerk. We've been at city events that involved the library. I could FOIA the information we're looking for."

"What's that?" Dora wanted to know.

"It's an official, legal request under the Freedom Of Information Act. The only thing is that it will still be a whole lot of information, since we don't know what we're looking for." She waved a chopstick. "Sometimes, you've got to let the information percolate, and the idea will come. You know?"

Dora smiled. "Happens all the time when I'm on the truck."

"We can cross-reference coverage of council meetings that were controversial in *The Chronicle's* archives with social media comments to see what people thought of the city's decisions."

"You can do that?" Dora had finished eating and was stuffing her empty carton, plastic fork, and Coke can back into the takeout bag. "How do you find related social media comments?"

"It would mostly be Facebook. We search the case info, the name of the plaintiff, and anyone involved. Keywords really, in both Google and in Facebook's search field."

"Sounds good to me. Just one thing."

"What's that?"

"Do we have to do all this in my car?"

• • •

Charlie liked hanging around with Franky, who reminded him of the friends that he'd had before going to prison; friends who understood the way he thought, because they thought the same way. He knew Franky was what his father would call "trouble" and that he would not have done some of the things he was starting to realize Franky had done, except that he understood that beneath those crimes was pain.

That Franky was more than a decade older than him, with much more street experience, added to the allure of his friendship. Like Franky,

Charlie felt more at home with others whom society called outcasts than he did with the "good influences" his father wanted him to befriend. He did not understand those people. The so-called good influences behaved as though they were better than he was. How could you be friends with people who thought and acted like they were better than you?

He knew that many people, his father included, thought there was something wrong with him, that he was no good on some level, and the good influences seemed to think so, too. The way he saw it, there were people like the good influences and his father, who looked down on him, through no fault of his own, and then there were people who understood him and who he understood. People like Franky.

Charlie was pretty sure that Franky—who enjoyed his nickname, Cranky Franky—had felt sad and lonely just about every day of his life. Well, except for those days on which he was too high to feel much of anything. And except when he was caring for his flowers. Franky sang to his flowers.

Charlie thought he understood. Being high didn't hurt anyone. Yes, it got in the way of being the person he was expected to be—a productive member of society—but he believed that being high was a whole lot better than reality.

When he wasn't high, he tended to be sad, or hurt, to feel like the rest of the world was over there somewhere, doing what they did, feeling the way they felt, and giving him a hard time for being the way he was, which was different.

Franky got that, and he got Franky.

Some days, he compensated by doing whatever made him feel good. For C3, that might be playing a little guitar. He wasn't good at it, but he could hear when notes fit together and led to other notes. And he could hear, understand, and play chords.

Or it might be looking at birds. He liked looking at birds and had an app in his phone that knew where you were in the world, what birds lived there, and what they looked and sounded like. He thought birds were beautiful. The patterns made by their colors and feathers were some of the most beautiful art he had ever seen.

Franky had his flowers; C3 had his birds. Both were better than most people.

Neither he nor Franky took much interest in people, though C3 looked forward to the day when he would have the courage to approach a woman. That was a ways away, though. Franky didn't seem to have it in him to like, or even notice, most other people. He was too messed up. Prison had messed him up. Life had messed him up. Some girl from his past had messed him up.

Franky said it was good to know someone on the outside who knew what it was like, meaning being in prison. To be on the outside ... of prison, of life. To have to look at most people, the good influences, like looking in from the cold through a window into everyone else's warm living room. To know you didn't belong because you didn't understand, whereas they didn't understand you. They judged.

He also understood Franky did some really bad things. Franky talked around those things; he didn't speak them aloud, specifically. But Charlie knew ... and knew not to ask.

He was not outside at the level Franky was outside, a level where you actually hated the rest of life, which rejected and hurt you so much that you preferred prison, where life was wicked and brutal ... but understandable. In prison, you didn't have to understand much of anything, except how to take care of yourself. Everything else was taken care of. You didn't have to worry about figuring out how to get a job, or money, or insurance, or a vehicle. Everything and everyone knew their place and was accepted. It was all taken care of.

Charlie understood that Franky was further outside society than he was. He knew that Franky hurt more, was more damaged than he was. He also understood something he had heard in meetings.

Hurt people hurt people.

• • •

Missy had taken an interest in Dora's murder-that-wasn't-a-murder puzzle and thought the best way forward was to meet—socially distanced and wearing masks—at Missy's apartment, which was in what had once been a high school and was now an apartment building in the center of town. Dora's apartment was also in the center of town, but several blocks south, a block from the ocean. They lived barely half a mile from one another.

The first thing Dora noticed about Missy's apartment was the plants—hanging plants, potted plants, and crawling plants, flowering plants, vegetables—everyplace there was a window, and some places there wasn't. There were spider plants, and cacti, and tiny, ancient looking bonsai trees, and many plants that Dora could not name. The plants told Dora that Missy was compassionate and meticulous.

Dora also noticed Missy's dog, a tiny, chocolate terrier mix that was oddly silent for a terrier. Dora had never liked dogs, especially small dogs, which she thought of as loud and intrusive, yappy and overbearing, never as elegant as cats. The dog eyed Dora, and Dora eyed the dog.

"That's Comfort," Missy said from behind a blue mask.

"Hey, Comfort," Dora greeted, scratching behind the dog's ear.

Missy led Dora into a living room, which connected to a dining room. The living room was painted blue and had framed Picasso prints from various eras on its walls. The dining room was brighter, painted sunshine yellow, with Van Gogh and Monet prints on its walls. The effect was welcoming, calming.

Missy carried a laptop and two notepads into the dining area and motioned for Dora to sit. "Let's work in here, where the light's best."

Dora sat down opposite Missy, who put down the computer and pads and took a step toward the kitchen. "Tea? Ice water?"

"I'm good," Dora said.

Missy came back, sat down, opened the computer and one pad, and slid the other toward Dora. Comfort trotted around the table, sniffing Dora's ankles and looking up at her with curious eyes that were alive with interest.

"I don't usually like dogs, but this guy's kind of cool."

"Comfort is way cool. So, let's start with what you've got."

"Okay. Let me log in to the city website."

Missy slid the computer across to Dora then pulled it back. "Why don't you sit here"—she patted the chair next to her—"by me so we can look together? Should be okay, long as we wear masks."

They looked at the city's website, with Dora pointing out information about taxes and local ordinances that may have been enforced, as Agatha suggested, in less than equitable ways.

"Interesting," Missy said, "but this is all general information. Nothing about specific instances of conflict, nor about a focused vendetta."

Dora agreed.

"So, let's take a deeper dive," Missy suggested.

They looked through archived issues of *The Chronicle*, bookmarking city-related stories that seemed to be worth a closer look.

"I took the liberty of making FOIA requests for city records and was given complete access to the clerk's database." Missy's tone was matter-of-fact.

"Really!" Dora said, impressed. "I'm surprised the city was so open. I've worked there most of my life, and open is not how I'd describe them."

"I don't think my access reflects openness," Missy explained. She was seated on the floor and her legs had been crossed, but now she folded them beneath her and to one side. "I think it reflects laziness. They didn't want to go through the files, sifting what was deemed useful or acceptable for me. Too much work. And what did they think I was going to find, anyway? I'm just a librarian. Do I look like a threat?"

Dora laughed. "But who is more of a threat than someone who knows how to dig for information?" She could not see Missy's expression behind her mask, but she was pretty sure the librarian was grinning. She had smiling eyes, pretty eyes, framed by dark curls that swirled into shoulder-length, blue-black hair. Her skin was a warm, light brown. If Dora had to guess, she would have said that Missy was from somewhere in the South Pacific—south Asia or Indonesia.

Stop thinking about what she looks like, Dora told herself. *She's a source of information; a librarian who is here to help find out who killed Franny.*

She saw that Missy was looking at her and turned away, pretending to look at a blemish on her arm.

Sitting with another live human, outside of work, was refreshing for Dora, who had been getting stir-crazy during this Covid-19 lockdown. She had been wandering her apartment, drinking beer, blasting music, and talking to both Franny and Felix, occasionally breaking plates out of rage and getting upset with herself when she had to sweep up the shards.

At Missy's suggestion, they sifted through city council meeting minutes, cross-referencing their findings with *Chronicle* articles or, more often, letters to the editor from disgruntled plaintiffs. In some cases, businesses seemed to have received permits and renewals, despite significant numbers of complaints; not in itself reason for a permit to be denied, but there was a great deal of that, and it was something to be considered.

Permits where there should not be permits.

And there was the opposite, as well—permits that should have been granted by all appearances yet had been denied. These were harder to weed out, but they were there and were a target of people with axes to grind toward City Hall. Permits that were denied were followed by greater groundswells of social media activity. The denied parties fulminated on Facebook and were supported by friends. Permits that were granted, despite complaints, were also followed by angry Facebook comments, usually by people living in proximity to the liquor store, tobacco or vape shop, bar in question, as these were the types of businesses that had received the questionable permits.

"Here's something interesting." Missy nodded at her computer screen and moved away to give Dora room to look.

"Anne Volkov ... Tom Volkov's daughter. A teenager. What a tragedy. Franny mentioned it. She didn't draw any conclusions, but she was aware of it."

"Maybe it's more than a tragedy." Missy was looking at Dora, a light in her eyes. "How do we find out more?"

"How 'bout I go see Tom Volkov and ask him?"

Missy's eyes went wide. "Really? You'd do that?"

"Why the hell not? But let's finish this."

They returned to their search. While they had no way of judging the validity of the city's objections to residents' complaints, here, too, there was a pattern. In many cases, they found with some digging, the city often had a prior disagreement with the applicant, not so much with the permitting decision or lack thereof, but something seemingly unrelated and … almost personal. One council member, Agatha Raines, had accused the city of waging "vendettas." Then the city had found health code violations at Rudy's.

Were these necessarily related to Agatha's criticism of the city? Did Rudy's deserve the violations?

Ultimately, only the city and, perhaps, Rudy, knew the answers to those questions.

Plumbing and building permits, liquor licenses, residents with large numbers of parking tickets, many of these interactions with the council and, to a lesser extent, the mayor, were rife with conflict that sounded personal. Of course, the majority of that conflict flowed naturally from the circumstances—people were not happy with paying summonses or being denied permits, despite believing they had dotted the i's and crossed the t's.

After another hour on Google, scrolling through old Facebook content and the local newspaper archives, they had found circumstantial evidence of quite a lot of possible petty corruption—fixed parking tickets, zoning irregularities, all of which alluded to but not proven in social media flare-ups and letters to the editor in *The Chronicle*.

Dora looked at her notepad and the lists of city-related conflicts. *Were any of these connected to a murder?*

She stretched her legs, beginning with her hamstrings, while letting the information float freely in her thoughts. She swung a leg up on the black, faux marble countertop and grabbed her foot, stretching her torso toward her toes. She stretched the other leg, then her calves, with the heel of each foot on the floor and a toe against the wall. She breathed in, stretched, breathed out. Repeat. Other foot.

It came to her that the person in charge of enforcing these aspects of city business when the conflict turned "dirty" would ultimately be Terry Stalwell, the police chief. To all appearances, he was a good guy, which meant nothing, of course. All sorts of people who appeared honest and decent were not.

But day-to-day enforcement might not rise to his level of attention. No, the person in charge of enforcement on a day-to-day basis would likely be someone lower in the hierarchy. And they might not know what they were a part of.

I was only following orders.

Dora recalled the caller's wording, the phrase "bad-smelling city business." She had wondered if this had somehow referred to her job, but now remembered one of the city's ongoing and public controversies—the alleged dumping of Julienne's liquid waste into the channel. If the city were looking the other way and allowing this dumping, would this not qualify as "bad-smelling city business?"

Chapter 20

The Corona virus—Covid-19—had been slowed by New York's aggressive approach. The state was opening in phases, which made sense to Dora. Her own job had been deemed essential, and she continued to work right along, albeit in a mask. She, Mo, Estéban, and the other crews already wore heavy gloves.

People had begun ordering food from some of the local restaurants, which then either delivered or allowed customers a short way into the premises to pick up. Outdoor dining was said to be allowed soon. Supermarkets had drawn or taped arrows on their floors, indicating the direction one was to walk in, to keep customers out of one another's breathing spaces.

People were expected to wear masks in any circumstance in which they were not able to remain at least six feet from anyone else. Some scientists claimed that six feet was not enough distance; the virus's droplets could stay in the air longer and travel farther than was originally thought. Others claimed the virus was little more than a virulent flu. Dora didn't agree; she had been friendly with Herman, who had worked at the food pantry and was one of the sweetest people she had ever known. Herman had gotten sick early in the pandemic and had died almost immediately.

Dora wondered what would happen to larger retail outlets, which had been closed for months, and malls, which were all but empty. Whole sectors of the economy must have been negatively impacted, Dora realized —all of those who maintained the malls, who worked in and cleaned the stores, who supplied them with products. Many of those people must be struggling or out of work. News reports confirmed her conclusions.

She tended to think more deeply about these things after three or four beers and a few shots, when the trauma of losing Franny and Felix was sufficiently anesthetized for her mind to peek out from its bunker and roam free, if only for a little while.

The rest of the time, especially when not collecting garbage or working out, she was obsessed with bringing to justice whomever had killed Franny and Felix. A wellspring of rage percolated just below the surface. She knew that doing something, even if it was something useless, was better than nothing.

The MMA gyms were shut down and would likely be one of the last types of physical exercise facilities to open, because one was literally on top of one's opponent. Professional MMA was just starting to come back, with everyone involved tested and isolated on a remote, as yet unnamed, island. Gyms did not have the ability to bankroll such procedures and restrictions, especially when they still had rent to pay, along with a dwindling customer base. The gym owners, Dora suspected, were busy trying to stay alive, to eat and pay their rent or mortgages.

She thought fondly about fighting, especially when she was drinking. She wished she could attack someone, somewhere—or, better yet, that someone would attack her.

Oh, to have that kind of outlet.

She settled for research, and after the research, she sought a means of validating her research.

She felt she had imposed enough on Missy, at least for a while. They were becoming friends, she thought, and did not want to hurt that vulnerable sapling of a relationship. So, she called Charlie Bernelli.

"How's your isolation going?"

"Isolation? Liquor stores are delivering." She could almost hear his smile.

"What do you make of these people who refuse to wear masks?" She thought of Charlie as relatively macho and wondered what he thought. This bizarre macho behavior had taken hold around the country, with men, and some women, who refused to wear masks or social distance. They held enormous, mask-free parties; sometimes inviting someone with the virus then betting on who would get sick.

"I have every right to not wear a mask? What the fuck is that?" came Charlie's answer. "Do I have every right to set your house on fire or run your kid over with my car? They're either idiots or assholes. Even if they don't get sick, they could be carriers who get others, especially older people, sick."

"Are we on speaker?"

"No one else is here. I'm quartering a chicken."

"How's your dad?"

"Sad. He spent an afternoon a while back walking with a friend of his, and the friend got sick and died."

"From the virus?"

"Yeah. And now Dad's quarantining. With his friend, Johnny ... Johnny Walker."

"What day's he on?"

"Ten. He'll be okay. Johnny's flushing out his system. The virus will run from him. He sees this as an occasion to up his game."

"Ah," Dora said. "So, I've been researching anyone with an axe to grind with the city."

"How?"

"From council meeting minutes, cross-referenced with police reports and newspaper articles. And some Facebook raves."

"Smart," Charlie commented. "You thought of this?"

"A librarian is helping me."

Charlie didn't answer for a moment. "Huh." He paused again. "And ...?"

"There's smoke, for sure, and probably fire, but is it the right fire? I mean, this sort of shit goes on everywhere—conflict between residents and the powers that be. I mean, this could be a lot of Agatha Raines' stuff ..."

Charlie sighed. "I get it. What's typical municipal conflict, and what's more nefarious that might be a murder, and that might have led to Franny's —"

"And Felix!"

"Um, who's Felix?"

"My cat."

"Your cat?"

"Fuck, yeah. Someone murdered my cat. Chopped his fucking head off. And they did it because of this shit I'm looking into, and because I'm getting too close to who killed Franny, and that happened because she was getting too close to the truth about this murder."

"The murder that wasn't a murder. You or Franny had two possible candidates for that, right?"

She was panting, her anger building. She took two cleansing breaths. "Yes. Sort of. Deaths that could possibly fit the bill."

There was a silence. "Fuck, I'm really sorry about your cat."

"Charlie ... you're a smart guy, and you don't seem to be tied into the city."

"Ha! Far from it!"

"Help me here. How do I figure out where the connection to the city business is?"

"So, nothing in the newspapers or council minutes jumps out?"

"Oh, a lot jumps out. Nothing narrows it down."

"Okay ... Can you give me a day or two to think about it?"

"Sure."

Charlie hung up, turned, and saw C3 standing and staring from the doorway.

"How long have you been there?"

"Not long," C3 said, coming in and sitting on a stool at the counter.

"You like listening to my conversations?" Annoyed, Charlie poured himself another scotch—his fifth this afternoon. He would probably have another two or three before dinner, but they were short scotches, or so he told himself.

"I wasn't ..."

"Really?"

C3 searched his father's face. "Your friend's cat was killed?"

Charlie set his glass down, carefully laid the knife on the counter, then turned to his son. "Yes. Why?"

C3 didn't answer; he was thinking *hard*.

• • •

Tom Volkov watched Dora walk up the path from the sidewalk to his front door. When she knocked, she was out of his range of vision, but he was pretty sure she had seen him.

He glanced toward the stairway, wondering if he should go up and warn Irene to stay up there, but he knew she would want to know why, and then he would have to decide if he should tell her why, and if he didn't— and he wouldn't—she would want to know why he wasn't telling her.

The rabbit holes had gotten too deep for him, so he sighed and went to the door. If Irene happened to come down while Dora was here, he would take the path of least resistance and ignore her as best he could.

Many locals knew that Anne's death had taken a toll on her, and many thought her—quite correctly—to be mentally ill. That she seemed to have slipped into schizophrenia or psychosis was not for him to say, though privately, he thought she had.

He opened the door and greeted his guest with a wan smile. He realized she was wearing a mask, which reminded him that he ought to be wearing one, as well. The paranoia surrounding the virus had subsided somewhat, but other states, particularly in the south and west, were now seeing significant spikes, and the news was reporting the possibility of a mutation that, while no more deadly than the original virus, was significantly more contagious.

He pulled a mask out of his pants pocket. What had the world come to that people were walking around with spare surgical masks in their pockets? Then he glanced back toward the stairs. What, indeed?

"Come in." He held the door open and stepped back.

With a glance that forced him back a step, she walked past him into the living room. There, she sat down on the far end of the sofa.

"You know who I am?" she asked.

Tom sat down in an armchair at right angles to her and nodded. "Dora Ellison. You work for the city, and you were in Charlie Bernelli's tourist campaign, which ran in my paper." He started to rise. "I'm sorry. Can I get you something to drink?"

"No, thank you." She laughed self-consciously. "I guess you saw the ads. Caused a bit of a splash."

"They did, at that. Very innovative idea, and very good for the city, in my opinion, whatever the official word."

"Yes. Thanks. I'm here to ask about the police investigation into— forgive me for bringing this up—your daughter, Anne's, death."

Tom's expression didn't change. "It's all a matter of public record."

"I know. I was just wondering if you and Mrs. Volkov were satisfied with the findings."

Tom squinted at her. "What is your connection to my daughter's death, and why bring it up now, after all these years?"

Dora pressed her lips together. If she was going to do this, she was going to have to go all the way. She had never been one for subtleties. "You know Fran—Officer—Lieutenant Hart—and I were close." She started to choke up and paused to regain her composure.

"I ... didn't. I'm so sorry. But again, what does that tragedy—your tragedy—have to do with mine?"

She shrugged. "I don't know that it does, but I wanted to ask your opinion."

Tom shook his head and pushed his glasses farther up the bridge of his nose. He held his hands out, palms up, an "I don't know" gesture. "Why would anyone think there was a connection?"

Dora took a deep breath. "Because Franny was getting phone calls ... about a murder, a murder she was told wasn't a murder."

He sat back and crossed one leg over the thigh of the other. "I'm sorry, you've lost me. Does that allude to my daughter? Someone thinks she was murdered?"

Dora clasped her hands together and leaned forward. "Franny was getting calls, and since her death, I've been getting them."

"Well, when Fran—Officer Hart—was getting calls, what were they saying?" His voice had taken on the beginning of an angry edge.

Dora nodded. "The questionable death—the caller didn't mention Anne specifically—had something to do with some kind of dirty business of the city's."

Tom seemed to consider this then shook his head. "That all sounds kind of vague. I've—we've—never had any reason to suspect that Anne was murdered."

Dora nodded, pointedly holding his gaze. "I do. And Franny did. I know this is difficult, Mr. Volkov—Tom—but can you tell me anything about that evening?"

Tom shrugged then shook his head. "We were out to dinner—Irene and I—and we came home, and we found Anne. She had hit her head on a night table. She slipped, or … I don't know." He was getting agitated. "We called 911, of course, but it was too late. There was no one else here, and no evidence of anyone else having been here."

"And you don't have any reason to doubt the police reports?"

He was looking at her with more intensity now. "Look, Dora, I'm humoring you, and that's because you've had a terrible shock and a loss of your own, and I'm sorry for that. No one … no one understands that more than I do … than Irene and I do."

"Is she here?" Dora glanced toward the stairs.

"She is, but my wife has not been well. I'm sure you understand." He stood, signaling the visit was over.

"Thank you, Mr. Volkov."

"Tom, please. Trust me; my daughter was not murdered."

"I'm sorry to dredge this all up." She opened the door and stepped outside as Tom held the door. She got as far as the first step then turned.

"As a newspaper editor, you must see a lot of local stories involving the city cross your desk."

Tom nodded. "Certainly."

"Can you think of anything that just smells like something crooked?"

"You mean on the city's part? Corruption?"

Dora glanced quickly in either direction then nodded.

Tom scratched the back of his head. He leaned against the doorjamb, letting the door half shut against his back. "I guess the closest I can come to anything that goes beyond your typical low-grade, one-hand-washing-the-other crap would be Julienne's relationship with Jeremy Anderson and the accusations about their allegedly dumping waste into the bay. You might want to talk to Agatha Raines. That's her tune, and I'm not saying she's wrong, but you've got to wade through some thick politics. There are all sorts of local, and not so local, businesses that might be tempted to save disposal costs by dumping their waste into our waters. We have local fishermen—business, charter, sport—and polluted waters are no good for anyone. But she comes off as"—he searched for the word—"strident. Besides, our water doesn't stay local; it flows all over. And the oversight of our waterways … well, that responsibility can be as hard to pin down as the water itself. The health of our waters transcends boundaries—

156

hyperlocal, county, state, and federal. And when there's resistance from business interests, you get intentional distraction, and it turns into a bit of a maze."

Dora nodded, smiling. "I don't expect you to do the cops' job, but if anything jumps out at you, would you point me in that direction?"

He looked her in the eye. "While I would probably know by now, if anything comes to light that points blame at someone for what happened to my Annie, I'll be all over it."

• • •

C3 walked into his father's house, slipped out of his sandals, draped his soaked poncho over the back of a chair, and then plopped down on the couch. He was beat. Another morning filled with therapy, drug testing, twelve-step and family groups, with barely time between each for a smoke, let alone lunch or coffee. The walk there was nearly two miles, which wasn't too bad, except it had been pouring since early last night, and the dirty puddles were four inches deep in the downtown area, where sewers had not been cleaned of leaves from the previous fall.

He felt disrespected without a car. Who his age didn't have a car or, at least, the use of one? He knew it was his own fault, at least to a degree—he really did—but that didn't make his feet any drier.

He walked quickly into the kitchen and opened the freezer, just as he had planned. The vodka was there, as he expected. Two bottles, twice as good. These thoughts had been there, waiting to be freed, waiting for the moment when he would be there, standing in front of the bottles.

He stared at the bottles, waiting for them to take over his mind, as he knew they would.

He had looked forward to this moment.

But it didn't happen.

There was nothing. The vodka, or the thought of it, had no effect.

Puzzled, he walked in a circle around the kitchen, leaving the refrigerator open, until he again stood in front of the freezer.

Nothing.

Nor was there a negative. He had no dislike of the vodka or the idea of the vodka.

It was neutral in his mind. It was nothing.

He hurried to his bedroom, where he had stashed a bit of weed and half a gram of coke.

They were still there, in the false compartment under his desk.

Nothing there, either.

They held no interest.

He sat down on his bed, feeling a bit like a man who had finally convinced the girl of his dreams to accompany him to a hotel, only to find he had lost interest.

What was he going to do?

He picked up his phone and punched in a number he had never called before.

"It's always sunny in Beach City. How may I direct your call?"

"City Clerk, please."

He waited.

"City Clerk's office. This is Christine."

"Hi, Christine. It's C3."

"C! Hi."

"How are you? How is your job? Is the city opening up?"

"In a modified way, yes. Permitting papers, taxes, even traffic tickets can be dropped in a special yellow mailbox in front of City Hall. Everyone, including the mayor, is in the loop, sometimes in the building, sometimes virtually. Since the office is mostly virtual, I am, too. The mayor wants us to be virtual as much as possible. Safer that way."

"That makes sense."

"Was there something I can help you with, Charlie?"

"Maybe. You know, I go to a few different kinds of meetings, right?"

"I do."

"What if I heard something there, about a crime that might have been committed?"

"What did you hear?"

"Something about a murder, sort of."

"What's a murder, sort of?"

"Sort of, as in, not a murder of a person."

"Meaning?"

"Of a cat."

Chapter 21

Tom Volkov walked through the door of Cobb's Diner, ignoring the sign that said, "*Takeout Only,*" and sat down in the booth nearest the cash register, from behind which Horace Cobb watched him warily, saying nothing.

Eventually, Cobb turned toward the kitchen and called, "Carolyn, two coffees." Then he walked over to the booth and sat down opposite Tom, who leaned forward, whispering fiercely, "Not here. I don't want to be seen talking to you unless you're at the register."

Carolyn arrived with the coffees.

Horace said, "What? I need a shower?"

"You heard me," Tom said. "We need to talk."

"You gonna eat?"

"I might."

"Okay, when you're done. My car, the white Escalade, is in the back lot. Tinted windows. I'll see you coming, pop the locks."

Tom shook his head. "Not good enough."

Horace sighed. "Okay. When you're done eating, walk through the lot so I see you, then two blocks south on Flower Street. I'll pick you up in the Escalade."

Tom had the meatloaf, which he had to admit was pretty good. Louie, Horace's cook, had been a chef in the Navy, but that had been twenty years ago. He had been working for Horace since.

Once in the car, Tom talked while Horace drove around the neighborhood.

"That garbage lady, Dora, came to see me."

Horace kept driving. "And ...?"

"She's connecting what happened to the lady cop and her cat to ... you know, the bigger picture."

Horace didn't answer.

Tom was about to repeat himself when Horace said, "I heard you. She was supposed to do that. It's what we want. We want her to get the picture ... the real lay of the land."

Tom digested this. "And if she doesn't listen?"

"Not your problem. She'll be handled."

"Of course it's my problem! This could blow back on me."

"It hasn't yet." Horace briefly looked at Tom without expression. "Twenty years. Hasn't yet."

"But she didn't listen when it was her girlfriend the cop. She didn't listen when it was her cat. What will she listen to?"

Horace thought about this. "That's … actually a good question." He paused and smiled. "And I'm sure there's a good answer."

• • •

Dora was mystified. Glenn Euclid, the shop steward, had sent for her. Euclid never sent for anyone unless there was trouble on the horizon. Famous for his rages, which played against type, as Euclid was five-foot-six, weighed in the neighborhood of one hundred and twenty-five pounds, and wore glasses so thick that his eyes looked enormous and distorted behind them. And yet, most of the tippers, drivers, and other union members were so afraid of Euclid that, if they needed to speak of him, they whispered.

Dora was merely curious. Did he really get so angry that white foam collected at the right side of his mouth, and only the right side?

She was disappointed when she found him calm, even reasonable, if stern.

"The police union says you've got to lay off."

She stared at the little man and had to keep herself from laughing. "Huh?"

He was reading something on an iPad and now raised an eye toward her. His voice had an edge to it, a barely hidden threat. "Don't give me *huh*, just stop whatever it is they're talking about."

She put both fists on her hips and leaned back slightly. "How 'bout you tell me what they're talking about?"

"I really have to do that?"

She waited.

He sat up, facing her directly. "How 'bout this? I'll look into it, but you owe me a day's overtime for doing it."

Dora squinted. "I have to pay you for doing your job?" She was bothered that Euclid wore no mask, technically a violation of City Hall rules, though he worked with his door shut so no one would see him without the mask. Everyone was aware of his, and a few others', defiance. Dora felt one could make the argument that working without a mask in a closed room was more dangerous than doing so in other circumstances— the virus was trapped in the room and could multiply, thereby increasing the virus's "load" exponentially.

"Unnecessary work. You know what they're talking about, okay? They're the police union. They don't pussyfoot around. Whatever you're doing that they don't like, stop doing it. We need to maintain our"—his tone became delicate, even dainty—"spirit of cooperation."

"C'mon, Euclid. You can't dock my pay."

"That's Mr. Euclid. And I believe I can." He paused. "Try me."

They stared at one another for a full ten seconds before Euclid blinked.

"I'll give you a hint. Do the words *rogue investigation* bring anything to mind?" He paused, but Dora did not answer. After a few moments, Euclid nodded. "Tell you what; think about it for a day. Just for a day. In two days, you and I will visit Captain Cobb to see what he and his union have in mind."

Dora took a deep breath then exhaled a sigh. "I'll get back to you." She turned and left the room, muttering as she crossed the threshold, "Fuck you."

"What was that?" Euclid called.

She held up a gloved middle finger as she entered the elevator. "Wear a fucking mask, dickweed."

• • •

C3 and Franky were sitting several feet apart on a bench outside the counseling center. C3 was smoking a Marlboro Light; Franky was smoking a Camel. Franky had been doing most of the talking.

"They don't understand … and there's only so much I can say in there. They could call the cops or cut off my meds, or who fuckin' knows?"

C3 nodded, took a drag on his cigarette, and scanned the street for attractive women. The counseling center was across the street from the train station. During the summer, the trains were filled with young women heading to the beach, having bought a day beach package, which included both beach pass and roundtrip train ticket.

"I hear ya," C3 said, which was literally true, though he wasn't really listening.

"Everywhere I look, I see assholes," Franky said, squinting into the distance.

"So, what're you gonna do?"

"Something ... soon," Franky muttered between teeth clenched around his Camel.

Franky's tone gave C3 pause. He had heard a similar tone just before Franky had slammed someone's hand in a door ... repeatedly. The incident had happened at the counseling center, after group one day, and had gone unreported.

"Easy, man," C3 said in as soothing a voice as he could muster.

Franky flicked his cigarette into the street. "Later. I'm outta here."

• • •

Forty minutes later, Franky pulled his blue Mustang into the driveway of a townhouse in a gated community on Long Island's North Shore. The uniformed guard at the front gate had called ahead. Franky was expected, but he rang the buzzer on the intercom.

"Yes?" someone asked.

"Franky Patella," he answered.

A buzzer sounded, and he entered.

Beyond the brightly lit foyer, with its blue slate floor, was a living room, painted in royal blue with matching twin sectionals, each festooned with pillows.

On the couches sat the Cobb brothers, Mo Levinson, and Tom Volkov. Standing more or less in the center of the group was a tall, lean, ebony-skinned man in an impeccably tailored royal blue suit, shirt, and tie.

Twinkling from his wrists were sapphire cufflinks, which matched his tie pin. Franky had never seen him before.

The man smiled faintly but only with his mouth. His eyes were cold, detached, and watchful.

George Cobb rose and shook Franky's hand. Then he motioned him to a spot on a sectional.

"Franky, this is Jonathan Hagen, a lawyer who works for the city. He's called us here to address a growing problem the city has."

Franky looked from Cobb to Tom Volkov, then to Mo Levinson, and finally to Hagen who, he saw, was watching him carefully.

"You have a question, young man?"

Franky shrugged and raised an eyebrow. For some strange reason, he could not bring himself to look Hagen in the eye.

"He doesn't work for the city." He jutted his chin in the Volkov's direction.

"No," Hagen said, "he doesn't."

Franky looked at Mo. "He's a garbage man."

Mo smiled. "Good to see you, too, Franky."

Franky shrugged again. *Never show weakness.*

"You're here," Hagen continued, "because we're letting you take the gloves off." He watched Franky's reaction, which was like a child on Christmas morning, as a smile blossomed on his face.

"Really? How far off?"

"I have only two caveats."

"What are—"

"Two conditions. Don't get caught and—"

"We don't want to know," Horace Cobb finished for him.

"Okay by me. I'm always careful. I cover my bases."

There was a pause. Hagen continued to smile, which was starting to bother Franky. "That's why you just did three to five."

"Hey!" Franky started to rise.

Cobb stood up with him, giving him a warning look. Franky sat.

Hagen continued, "We will be pursuing multiple fronts; one of which will be spearheaded by Tom and *The Chronicle*."

"What about the chief?" Cobb asked. "He's a hands-on guy. He'll have questions, at the very least."

Hagen smiled. "Don't you worry about Chief Stalwell."

Chapter 22

Dora's job demanded that she be up five days a week before three a.m. That was down to four now, because recycling had been suspended since the advent of Covid-19. Without Felix to feed and clean up after, she could now get up at four.

Today, she was sitting at her dining room table, eating Cocoa Puffs and raisins in almond milk. She did her best to estimate the perfect amount of each so there would be little or no cereal or milk left when she finished. The task was nearly impossible and required zen-like focus. But today, she was less interested in that outcome than in the stories surrounding the weekend's MMA bouts. When she finished reading several articles about the fights and watching highlights on YouTube, Dora turned to *The Chronicle* for local news.

The enormous, bold headline instantly caught her attention:

INSURRECTION!

The article read, in part:

> The Chronicle *has uncovered a series of activities, sources claim, are connected to a "shadow" effort to undermine Beach City policy. A multi-front investigation has uncovered several intertwined stories that will be pursued separately and independently. The first is a series of crimes, including vandalism and attempted arson at a major local business. The second is alleged corruption by a politically connected "actor" which is said to have been ongoing for many years. The third involves a forthcoming libel lawsuit.*

> *While each of these is important in its own right,* The Chronicle *has learned that they are related incidents that are part of a concerted effort by local community activists to bring down and supersede the current Beach City administration.*

> *In a related story, police sources claim that detectives have found links to a local individual possibly responsible*

*for the death of police officer, Francesca Hart. More
information will be made available as it comes to light.*

"Whoa!" Dora looked at her watch, but it was still too early to call Tom Volkov to find out more about the identity of Franny's murderer.

She navigated to her Facebook feed and saw, in the local Beach City group, posts with the hashtag *#FindBeachShadow*, echoing *The Chronicle* article, promising justice for whomever was targeting the city's business and whomever was responsible for Lieutenant Hart's death.

Her adrenaline level was already too high to do much of anything besides stretching and working out, but the Facebook posts had enraged her, and she knew she had to do something physical. So, for several hours, Dora stretched and performed a circuit of exercises that she knew would at once exhaust, invigorate, and distract her. She then showered in near scalding water and meditated until she was much closer to her target numbers—blood pressure, pulse, and mental state.

She had an awareness that her meditation was within a few minutes of her ending bell when the phone rang. She decided to answer.

"Dora, Charlie. I'm at Rudy's."

"I can hear."

"A bunch of cops were just here, led by George Cobb, looking for Agatha. Whatever's going on, it's serious. This was not a c'mon-down-to-the-courthouse-for-a-chat vibe."

"I take it she wasn't there."

"No. Do you know where she is?"

"Why would I?"

"I didn't mean—"

"Have you read *The Chronicle*?"

"No, but I heard. A little far-fetched, don't you think?"

"Maybe so, but people might believe it. People respond to blame."

Charlie didn't answer at first then asked, "What do you want to do?"

"I know one way we might be able to find out where these stories are coming from."

"Volkov," they said together.

• • •

They met outside, put on their masks, and climbed the stairs to *The Chronicle's* hallway office. Charlie knocked on the doorjamb at the top of the stairs.

Sarah looked up from her computer, smiled at Charlie, nodded at Dora, and then put on her mask.

"Is Tom here?" Charlie asked.

"Hold on," came Tom's voice from the other side of the wall. Then he appeared in the doorway, grinning. Then realization dawned, and he drew a white mask sporting a blue *Chronicle* logo from his pocket.

He looked at Charlie. "I keep forgetting my mask. So, are you here"—he looked at Dora—"with your model, to discuss a new ad? The original ad's still running and doing well, but there's always room for improvement."

"We'd like to hear more about these stories you've been running."

Tom looked confused. "Which stories would those be? We've got quite a bit of content."

"The stories you've just started running, about this shadow conspiracy to undermine Beach City policies, about whatever's going on with Agatha —"

"And," Dora interrupted, "about Lieutenant Hart's murderer."

"Murder? Who said anything about murder? What we wrote about was getting to the bottom of who was responsible. We never wrote anything about murder, but someone was driving that car, right?"

"So ...?" Charlie said.

Tom sighed. "Charlie, we have a great relationship. You're a valued client, but we never reveal sources."

"Well," Charlie said, "that's part of what I'm getting at. And, as a valued client, maybe you can cut me a little slack by helping us understand. This young lady"—he indicated Dora—"lost a beloved friend —"

"More than a friend," Dora corrected.

"So I understand," Tom said, "and I'm sorry for your loss, but the stories will have to speak for themselves. I cannot reveal sources, and I cannot say more until I have more information and until the appropriate time to publish that information."

"What about Agatha?" Charlie asked.

"What we published is a police matter. I'm not the right—"

"I don't think *The Chronicle* wrote anything about her having anything to do with the police," Dora said.

"See? I just gave you some otherwise unavailable information. I'm trying to help here, but my hands are tied." He shrugged and held out his hands, palms up. "Best I can do."

"I see," Charlie said. "Well, thanks for your help." He turned then proceeded down the narrow stairway, with Dora right behind him.

"Stonewalling," Charlie stated once they were outside.

His phone rang.

"Yeah?"

He turned to Dora, whispering, "Sarah, from Tom's ..."

He turned back. "I do." He listened. "I see. Oh. Oh ... Thank you." He hung up and put away his phone.

"We shouldn't have come here."

"What does that mean?" Dora wanted to know.

● ● ●

An hour later, Dora was seated at a table at Rudy's. Drinking while seated at the bar was now against a Covid-related law. One had to sit six feet from the nearest patron unless a physical divider was present, and one had to order food. So, she sat alone at a table, in front of a plate of steaming chicken wings, a container of bleu cheese, and a pint of Guinness. She'd had a long pull of the Guinness and half of one wing when Agatha Raines pulled up a chair and leaned in.

"Rudy told me you were here."

"Okay." She dipped the second half of the wing in the bleu cheese and ate it whole, bone included, then licked the tips of her fingers.

"We are building a case, and we need to work together."

"Uh-huh," Dora said. She did not like being approached so directly, even by Agatha. Engagement with just about anyone for any reason was a risk since Franny's death and since Covid.

"Uh-huh is right. There's some bad shit goin' down. You read the paper?"

"I did. Fucked up."

"You see this?" Agatha placed a postcard on the table in front of Dora. On it were many of the accusations she had seen in *The Chronicle.* "The shit is hitting the fan around here. Know why?"

Dora reluctantly turned from her chicken wings. "I guess you're gonna tell me."

"Because of you."

Dora just looked at Agatha.

"Truth," Agatha said. "Because of the shit you stirred up. 'Cause of what they did to your girl."

What Dora was feeling was tired—tired and hungry. "You make it sound like it's my fault."

"No! I'm here to help. Let me tell you how." She grinned. "You know what Clean Acres is, right?"

"In a general sense."

"And you know what I've been saying about the pollution in the bay?"

"Same answer."

"Well, the water in the bay has tested positive for the effluents that are the waste products at Julienne's facility. That's fact. Same stuff. And no one contests that. But equally true, no one's been able to find the smoking gun to prove Julienne's been dumping their shit in our bay. Proving it came from them is a whole other story, and their game is making it the *required* story."

"I get it," Dora said. "Want one?" She offered Agatha a wing.

She shook her head. "My fridge is filled with these. I can hardly look at them."

"You know," Dora started, pleased to not have to give up the wing, "we should do this at your place." She looked around. "Less scrutiny, more wings."

"Well ... Anyway, so Clean Acres, a state-of-the-art co-op development. Clean Seniors, a 55-and-over, and Clean Living, an assisted living facility. They're all on one fourteen-acre lot overlooking the bay. Their marketing was all done by Anderson Consulting. That"—Agatha stabbed the table with a finger—"is where they're dumping the poison."

"Can you prove it?" Dora took another pull from her Guinness. She caught Rudy's eye and pointed to the empty glass. "Smoking gun."

"I thought you'd never ask. I obtained soil samples from Clean Acres, and guess what chemicals turned up near the pilings of their bulkhead?" She looked knowingly at Dora, raising an eyebrow. "Not so clean. And here's the best part. The whole place is owned by a shell company that Julienne and Anderson Consulting both have a piece of."

Dora had taken another wing and now waved it at Agatha. "Will this hold up in court?"

Agatha leaned close. "Fuck court."

Chapter 23

Monday mornings were the best of times and the worst of times. Normally, Monday was garbage day, and in the spring, that meant not only weekend garbage but baseball weekend garbage, which was, admittedly, not quite as bad as football weekend garbage, but worse than basketball or hockey weekend garbage, with the dark horse—MMA weekend garbage—gaining steadily. This year, of course, was different. There was no baseball. There were no major American sports.

But while there was not the usual enormous spring Monday garbage haul, there had been a noticeable increase in takeout garbage—pizza boxes, clamshell burger boxes, paper and plastic bags, and cutlery—along, of course, with the remnants of the food that had been in those containers, mixed with napkins, cigarette butts, beer cans, bottles and suds, and other food items. All this meant that Mondays were hard work, but Dora relished hard work, punishing her body, especially in ways that whipped her into shape, that strengthened her and increased her endurance. These were all positives, the gifts of Mondays. And this Monday was the third day of hard rain, so much of the garbage was sodden and soggy. Garbage DNA blended by the elements.

Estéban drove slowly and steadily, a pace Dora and Mo could maintain.

Their sentences were intermittent, broken up by them each stepping to the curb, grabbing the cans, tubs, crates, tied packs of garbage, then tipping, sliding, or dragging everything to the truck and into the hopper.

"Don't know how I'm ever gonna fish if this rain don't stop."

"What? You can't fish in the rain?"

"Your name came up by the lockers yesterday."

"Yeah?"

"You're trying to find out what happened to Franny. People are talking about it."

Dora didn't answer right away. She just kept working.

"No big deal," Mo said. "Thought you'd want to know."

"Why the fuck wouldn't I? We were close. And why are you bringing it up? I know what I'm doing."

Mo held up his hands, palms out, in a "hey, I didn't mean anything by it" gesture.

They worked a while longer.

Dora broke the silence. "You think I'm making waves? Like, bad waves?"

Mo shrugged. "Not for me to say."

"Well," she said, "I've seen the postcards."

After another half-block, he asked, "You learn anything?"

Dora stopped, turned, and looked at Mo. "Why would you ask me that?"

"Because I know you cared about her."

"So?"

"No big deal. I just hope, if it was an on-purpose thing, they catch the ones who did it."

"Uh-huh," Dora said then thought, *Good to know.*

• • •

City Hall's slow opening was continuing apace. Christine Pearsall made sure she was there every day, on time as always, since much of the city's business ran through her office. She stopped at the Starbucks drive-thru, as she always did. She ordered and received her mocha soy latte, vente, and then headed for City Hall.

John was not at the front desk in the lobby, which was not unusual, so after putting on her mask, she headed for one of the two elevators at the far end of the lobby. It was early and the elevator was empty, but she pushed the "*close doors*" and "*3*" buttons with her elbow. From the elevator, she went to the time clock to punch in for the day. Not finding her card, she went back to the elevator, went up to "*5*," using her elbow again to push the buttons.

The Beach City Personnel office was run by three women; two of whom were on duty at all times. Rachel, a hard-working, thirty-something, single mom of twins, was at the counter. Her expression was hard to read, given the mask covering the bottom half of her face.

"Hey, Rach. Could you make me up a new punch card? Mine's not out there."

Rachel stared back. "Sorry, Chris, no can do."

"Printer busted again?"

That was when she felt the gentle touch at her elbow and turned to see John.

"You need to go, Chris."

"Go?" What was he talking about? It wasn't even nine a.m.

"I need to escort you from the building."

"Huh? What's this about? Let's go see Mayor Mark. He'll clear it right up."

"Trust me, Chris; you need to go."

And all at once, she knew. It was a feeling rather than knowledge. As though she were in an elevator shaft and, suddenly, there was no elevator. As though she dropped through the floor.

She allowed John to walk her to the front door, but he didn't stop there. He walked her to the sidewalk and gestured with his head that she was to leave the property. Despite his face covering, Christine thought she could see the sadness in his eyes as he left her at the edge of the sidewalk.

Aisha's Halal food truck, her favorite street food, was parked a short distance away. She walked over, but Aisha had that same look. "Sorry. Can't serve you."

"What's that supposed to mean?" Now she was mad. "I'm pretty sure that's illegal."

"It's my private business. I can serve, or not serve, whoever I want. I'm sorry."

"But, Aisha, you know me." She stomped her foot then realized how silly that must look, but she didn't care. "It's me. C'mon!"

Aisha shrugged with what appeared to be real regret. "Call a cop."

There was something about the look in her eyes. *Call a cop?* Was she saying that George Cobb had something to do with this? She wished she had her work computer.

She went to her car, determined to find someone she could trust to talk to. As she hit the button on her key fob, she saw the long scratch that ran the length of her doors. She closed her eyes, took a deep breath, got in the car, and drove to Charlie's house.

She let herself in. She and Charlie had exchanged keys and stopped knocking nearly two weeks prior. As she entered, she heard tense voices and found Charlie at the dining room table, in front of an iPad, a messy plate of what had been some sort of eggs and toast and a half empty mug of coffee. Sitting at right angles to him was C3.

"Hey, Charlies," she said as she took a seat.

Both Charlies glanced at her, but only briefly.

"You okay with Christine hearing this?" Charlie Junior asked.

C3 nodded, pressing his lips together. "The thing is, he didn't actually say he was working for the city. He just said downtown. *They trust me downtown* is the way he put it."

"But you're sure," Charlie Junior started, "that he was talking about official city business?"

"Dad, he was talking about the city!"

"I'm just looking for clarity here, C."

Christine reached out and touched C3's hand. He twitched and pulled his hand away.

"How can I help?" she asked.

C3 exhaled and took a sip from a glass of water that had been in front of him. "I heard one of the guys at my program talking about doing some bad shit."

"Some *violent* bad shit," Charlie Junior corrected. "Some very bad shit."

"And this is something that already happened, or that will happen?" Christine asked.

Charlie Junior interrupted, "This is violence on behalf of the city."

C3 whipped his head toward his father. "How 'bout letting me tell it?"

"Please do," Christine told him.

C3 nodded. "Yeah. Like he said. Thing is, I like this guy. The only guy in my group I get along with." He stood up suddenly and began pacing. "If there's no proof, there's nothing anyone can do, right? It's like when a wife reports her husband is threatening her. Until he's done something, the cops can't do a thing."

Charlie Junior nodded. "I'm not a lawyer, but there's some truth in that."

Christine looked resolute. "We should tell Stalwell."

C3 looked at her. "So, rat on my only friend, who hasn't even done anything yet?"

"Or wait until someone's killed," Charlie Jr. pointed out. "Tell me something; why did you come to me?"

"Because, Dad, this guy's batshit."

"And ... you like him?" Christine asked.

C3 nodded. "He's the kind of batshit I sort of understand."

Charlie's phone buzzed, and he picked it up. "Bernelli Group. Charlie speaking." He glanced at each of them while he listened, his glances moving faster the more he listened. "What? Why?" A pause. "Well, they have to tell her what she's accused of!" Another pause. "Okay, calm down. It's going to be okay. You need to hang up and call your lawyer. Whatever's going on, they have to follow the law, at least—" He was cut off. "No, don't talk like that. They do!" A pause. "Okay. Good." He hung up.

"That was Rudy. Agatha's been arrested. *Detained* is the word they used."

"For what?" Christine asked.

"Agatha Raines?" C3 asked.

Charlie nodded. "Misusing public funds and vandalism."

"Vandalism? Agatha Raines?" Christine said. "Come on!"

"Yeah," Charlie said. "Come on is right."

"What did she vandalize?" C3 asked.

"They're not telling her."

"They *have* to tell her," Christine insisted.

Charlie nodded. "I suspect they will, eventually ... after letting her stew in a cell for a while."

His phone buzzed again, and he answered. "Bernelli—" He was cut off. "Oh, hey, Dad. What's—" He listened, frowning, then stood up and yelled, "Are you fucking kidding me?" A pause. "No, I'm sorry. Relax. Just ... don't say another word. I'm on my way."

"What was that all …" Christine had started to ask, but it was too late. Charlie was already out the door.

Chapter 24

Mo sliced the fresh clam meat into strips then slipped two of the strips onto his fluke hook. The docks were emptier than usual, owing, he assumed, to the virus, but some of the usual crowd were there.

He cast his baited hook a short way then began jigging the weighted, baited line up off the bottom in short, even tugs. He liked to imagine the fish, swimming along the bottom and being attracted to his bait. He had the notion that imagining this would help it to occur, so he was so absorbed in the life of his imagined fish that he did not hear the person approach.

"Bitin'?"

Mo turned, saw it was Franky Patella, and shook his head. "Not yet." Mo continued jigging his line, recasting several times in different directions.

"The lady you work with ..." Franky started.

Mo didn't answer. He was imagining what the bottom of the bay looked like where he had cast his line. Were there obstructions? Was it shallow? He could tell from the wet pilings that the tide was going out.

"... on your route," Franky continued. He wasn't going away. "Rumor has it, she's into MMA."

Mo turned and looked at Franky, nodding. "She is. She's good, too."

"Yeah, well, she's a woman."

Mo could feel the intensity of Franky's look. "What?"

"You know about MMA?" Franky asked.

"I like watching it. It's the only fuckin' sport around now." MMA had made tentative inroads into the largely banned world of televised sports. A private island was being utilized by the UFC promotion, and fights were held in an empty arena. Watching the sport, which Mo had long enjoyed, was now a surreal experience.

"Actually, I'd like to hear about it. About how she fights, I mean."

"What? You mean, like, technical shit?"

"Well"—Franky lit a cigarette—"yeah. I'd like to hear about how she fights. It interests me."

• • •

Charlie Bernelli Sr. lived in an over-fifty-five townhouse development in Laredo Beach, a half mile east of Beach City, where residents had the option of adding medical services to their monthly maintenance—services with escalating tiers of care and cost, up to and including in-home hospice services. As usual, Charlie's father's front door was not only unlocked, it was wide open.

"Pop! Pop!"

He found his father at the kitchen, thumbing through his mail and nursing a coffee, which he knew had probably been spiked.

He waved a postcard at his son. "Have you seen these postcards? Did you get one?"

"I did. Pop—"

"What the hell are they talking about? Conspiracy theories? Are they eighth grade girls?

"Pop—"

"I have neighbors who believe this crap. They think there's a conspiracy somewhere, trying to damage Beach City! Who? Where? What conspiracy?" He bent over, looking under the table. "Under there? Nope. Oh, I know. They're in the bathroom, with the rest of the shit."

"Pop," Charlie Jr. started, "some people do believe these postcards and the social media, where some people are saying much the same thing. They're counting on that. Now, Pop—"

"But, why? What's the purpose of spreading bullshit? To be popular? To be cool?"

Charlie Jr. sat down adjacent to his father. "Yes, in a real sense, it is. They're doing it to hold onto power. The purpose is control. Controlling people's perceptions about what goes on in and around Beach City and casting blame."

"But who's doing it? Who wants to hold onto power?"

Charlie raised an eyebrow in thought. "I don't really know. Who's *in* power?"

His father shrugged. "Who? The mayor?"

Charlie nodded toward the card. "You think the mayor's behind that? I can't see it. He's an old, grandfather type of guy. I don't think he's behind very much the city does."

"Watch it with the old grandfather stuff. Maybe people on the council. In any case"—he waved the postcard again—"this is a cousin of the business we've been in since I was C3's age."

"Yeah, someone's working hard to control perceptions around here."

His father nodded. "How is the boy?"

"Pop, I'm here to talk about how you are."

"Me? Oh, I'm fine. Or, actually, I'm not sure how I am. I was feeling poorly about three days ago, so I took myself to the urgent care, and they ran some tests."

Charlie Jr. slapped the table. "Why didn't you tell me?"

"Because you'd get all riled up"—he chuckled—"like you are now. Now, if you'd shut up, I'll tell you the rest of it." He paused. "So, I called my doctor, which is where they were supposed to send the results, but I can't get him on the phone."

"He's a doctor. What else is new?"

Charlie Sr. waved a finger. "Don't be so quick to say that. I've never had trouble getting Dr. Krieger on the phone. Anyway, listen to this. Craziest damn thing you ever heard."

"I doubt that." Charlie Jr. shook his head. "Some crazy shit going around."

"I finally got through, and they refuse to give me the results."

"Your own test results? Is that legal? And why wouldn't they?"

His father held up a hand. "Just wait. It gets better. It took me three days and getting Robbie Bishop involved—"

"You had to get a lawyer involved to get your test results?"

"And here's the holdup. The police—get this—suspect me of selling opioids." He chuckled, and the chuckle grew into a laugh, which went on until Charlie Sr. was shaking and gasping for breath. He held up a saltshaker for his son to see, sprinkled some salt onto the table, and then sat back with a grin. "Have some cocaine!"

"Dealing opioids?" Charlie Jr. asked. "The police are saying that about you? About *you?*"

Charlie Sr. nodded. "Ever since this virus hit, the world has gotten nuttier and nuttier."

• • •

Dora was at the police station, trying to find out what had happened with Agatha's arrest. She hadn't learned much, only that Agatha had, with Rudy's help, made bail and was no longer in jail. The desk sergeant wouldn't tell her what the specific charges were, but she suspected they had something to do with Agatha's long-running feud with the city. In this case, with the city's stand-in—Julienne Inc. She knew that Agatha had been on Julienne property and on the Clean Acres property, which was part-owned by Julienne, collecting soil samples, so she suspected that trespassing was part of whatever crime she might have been charged with. Of course, Dora knew, there was probably more to the story, on both sides.

So, Dora did what she often did when faced with a confusing, challenging situation—she took the bull by the horns. She walked around the block, from the police station to City Hall, put on her mask, and strode past the unmanned front desk, to the elevators. She pushed "6," the penthouse: Mayor Mark's office. She knew the mayor to be a decent, compassionate man, though he often seemed a little out of it, who would cut through the BS to whatever was at the heart of the issue.

Outside the elevator doors was a walk-through scanner next to several small bowls on a table, behind which sat a uniformed police officer with a computer tablet. Dora emptied her pockets into a bowl.

"Name?" the officer asked.

"Dora Ellison."

The officer scanned the pad. "Don't see you here. Got an appointment?"

"Nope, but it's important. The mayor likes to say—"

"Save it. Hang on." He spoke quietly into a microphone on a cord around his neck then nodded toward a couple of chairs. "Have a seat."

After her possessions had passed through the scanner, Dora took them, sat, and waited.

Several minutes later, a young, female police officer came in through the same entrance that Dora had. Dora realized that this woman was probably Franny's replacement. Franny had frequently pointed out, with both pride and frustration, that she was the lone female officer on the BCPD. Behind the female officer, George Cobb walked in, smiling.

"Officer Trask," Cobb said, "this is a Beach City celebrity, Dora Ellison, the face of the Beach City independent tourism ad campaign and a model city employee." He opened an unmarked door and stepped to one side. "Dora, why don't you come on in and make yourself at home? You can stay as socially distanced as you want. It's a pretty big room."

Dora glanced at the larger door bearing the plaque reading, "*Mayor Mark Morganstern*," then did as she was asked, wearing her mask and sitting in the chair farthest from Cobb, who leaned forward on his forearms, smiling as though delighted she had come, though she did not believe that for a minute. And, as she explained why she was there, he continued to smile while squinting, focused on her words.

"First of all," he said when she had finished her tale, "let me tell you how sorry I was to hear about Officer Hart. She was one of our best. I know you were close." He rose and exhaled. "We do have a pretty good idea about who is behind her accident, which was anything but."

Dora exhaled. "Well, I was hoping to speak to the mayor—"

"No need," George Cobb interrupted. "On this, trust me, I speak for him."

The female officer stood quietly, just inside the doorway.

Cobb went to the door, which the officer opened for him, and beckoned for Dora to follow. "Come on; let's go around the block. They'll need a statement at the precinct." He paused to make a brief, quiet phone call then opened the stairwell door. "Why don't you take the elevator? Meet you outside so we're distanced. Then we can go in together."

Once downstairs, they walked together to the precinct.

Cobb nodded at the sergeant behind the window in the lobby. "I'm here with Dora Ellison," he said.

The clerk nodded, and then Cobb led Dora to a room, inside of which were a table and three chairs.

It was at that point that the female officer approached Dora, holding out a hand. Her first instinct was to grab the hand and pull hard, which would yank the woman off balance. She reminded herself that she had no need to fight with every person who approached her, and then she reached for the officer's hand, realizing she was simply shaking hands, just as her mind registered that no one shook hands during a pandemic. As that thought landed, the officer snapped a cuff around Dora's wrist, and the other cuff around her own.

"You have the right to remain silent—"

Dora turned to Cobb. "What the hell?"

"I told you we had a suspect in Officer Hart's murder, though the actual charge may be reduced to manslaughter. We'll see." His grin, which had never left his face, broadened. "I hope it won't be. Anyway, we now have that suspect in custody. Oh, and you're under arrest for the murder of Lieutenant Francesca Hart."

. . .

As Chief Stalwell listened to Charlie Jr., with the occasional comment from C3. He frowned, squinted, and leaned forward, with an expression of focused skepticism. He did not wear a mask, though Charlie assumed that the size of the desk between them would adequately serve that function. As Charlie spoke, the chief leaned back, folded his arms over his ample belly, and listened.

When Charlie finished, the chief was silent for a long moment then glanced at the door. His voice was deep, his tone authoritative. "Let me get this straight. Your son knows someone who commits violent crimes—"

"He has"—C3 nodded—"and he's about to again."

"—on behalf Beach City?" The chief looked at C3 and his father.

Both nodded.

"Well, that's quite an accusation. And, you say, you can't tell me who this is, though you know the person's identity, and you can't tell me who's behind this, pulling the strings?"

C3 nodded again. "I heard about it at a twelve-step meeting. He's anonymous."

The chief looked at C3 for a long moment. "If what you say is true, this is a murder we're talking about."

"I think my son might have some concerns about his own safety."

C3 shook his head. "I guess I can tell you. I don't care. We're talking about Frank Patella. He works for the city, I believe."

Chief Stalwell nodded. "I know Frank, and I'll look into it. I have some other questions, which we'll get back to. Now, about your father, Charles Bernelli Sr.; I can look into what the holdup is with his records at urgent care." He shook his head. "I haven't heard anything about your father and opiates, a drug investigation, or anything like that. Not sure you have your facts straight, but I'll look into that, too. But I think maybe someone's pulling your leg."

Charlie Jr. and C3 looked at one another. Charlie stood up, his son following suit. They turned to go.

"There is one thing, though," the chief said, as though it had slipped his mind. "Your father's name came up in reference to this conspiracy controversy."

"My father," Charlie Jr. said. It was a question but came out as a statement.

Stalwell nodded. "Yours, too."

"So, if you're not the man to ask, who is?"

Stalwell nodded in the direction of City Hall then rose to walk them to the door.

As they left the chief's office and moved into the clerical area that was on the official side of the counter, just inside the public entrance, George Cobb walked in, turned, and held the door for a policewoman and, trailing her in handcuffs, Dora Ellison.

Chapter 25

The next morning, Dora was released, given her possessions, and walked to the exit of the police station and jail, where she was surprised to find Missy, the librarian, waiting for her, wearing jeans, a red knitted sweater, and a matching red mask. Puzzled, Dora looked around but saw no one else.

"You're here for *me*?"

"Mmhmm …"

"Why?"

"You needed bailing out. I've been working from home part-time, so I'm around."

Dora squinted. "But … why?"

Missy shrugged. "Why not?" She turned and began walking toward the parking lot. "Coming?"

Once they were driving, Dora quickly realized they were not heading toward her house. "My house is the other way."

"Right."

"So … turn around."

Missy gave her a quick look and a smile. "Bringing you to my place."

"I'm … not understanding."

"Too much heat at your place. It'll be easier for you. Anyway, this lockdown's making me nuts."

They arrived at the apartment and, as Missy opened the door, there was a scrabbling sound, and then Comfort skittered around the corner into view, stopped, took one look at Dora, and began to howl.

"He's happy to see you again!" Missy said. She picked him up in her arms, petting his head. Comfort pressed his head back against her hand. "Dora will be with us for a little while, Comfort."

"I don't know," Dora said. "I enjoy his company, but truthfully, I'm allergic, and I'm a cat person."

Missy smiled. "Comfort doesn't seem worried." She walked out of the room then peeked her head back in. "He has hair, not fur, by the way. Hypoallergenic."

Comfort regarded Dora for a long moment. He looked like, but not exactly like, a Yorkshire terrier. The difference, Dora thought, was the ears, which did not stand up like a Yorkie's, but flopped over, sometimes to the side, sometimes inside out. His eyes were enormous and sad, like those of a basset hound. His fur—or hair—ranged from burnt sienna to grey to silver.

Comfort had apparently taken enough stock of Dora and began to howl anew, this much more forcefully.

"So," Dora said, "you're a dog, and you're a boy. Strike two."

Comfort instantly stopped howling, turned, and sauntered off in the direction Missy had gone. Dora followed.

She had paid little attention to Missy when they had first met, but now she made a few mental notes. Missy was shaped rather the way Dora was, though Missy was softer, rounder, smaller, and with far less muscle. Dora was fond of characterizing herself, somewhat tongue in cheek, as "a slab of beef—filet mignon." Something about Missy struck Dora as sweet, or gentle. Something indefinable yet ever-present.

Missy was at the bar. She turned as Dora entered. "Drink?"

"Beer?"

Missy opened a refrigerator that was set into the bar. In it were bottles and cans of beer, both domestic and foreign.

"What'll you have?"

"Can of Bud?"

Missy obliged, poured single malt scotch over rocks, then held the bottle toward Dora. "Sure you don't want?"

"Why not?" She sat down on one of the chairs, her beer on the table in front on her. Comfort sat quietly near her feet, following her motions with his eyes.

"Ice?"

Dora nodded.

Missy placed the scotch on a napkin in front of Dora then sat down on the couch. "So, where are we at?"

Dora explained about her union pressuring her to stop her investigation, about Agatha's claim that Julienne had been dumping waste at the Clean Acres site, and about Agatha's subsequent arrest.

"Do you think the article and postcards about an anti-city vendetta are a distraction?"

"Wouldn't you say?"

"Music?" Missy asked.

Dora nodded.

"What kind?"

"Rock. Anything."

"Name something."

"Moody Blues."

Missy nodded. "Alexa, play Moody Blues. 'Every Good Boy Deserves Favour.'"

Alexa said, "*Playing Moody Blues. 'Every Good Boy Deserves Favour.'*"

Missy sat down again. "What do we really know about this alleged murder?"

Dora shrugged. "I said I'd ask Tom Volkov, which I did, and it's either nothing or he's stonewalling. If so, he's a pretty good liar. If it's more, I don't know how to find out. He says his daughter hit her head and died. A tragic accident."

Missy nodded. "What might Franny have found out?"

"That this wasn't an accident."

Missy nodded again. "Mmm ..."

Dora nodded. "I don't know what she'd have learned, or how that might be tied in with any local corruption or tensions. The caller implied a connection from day one, between a murder and Agatha Raines and Julienne, and the city. Or at least the council ... How's all that tied in?"

Missy shrugged. "Maybe Tom wrote something that pissed off someone at City Hall, and maybe that got his daughter killed?"

"I don't know. There were cops there—police reports, newspaper articles—in his own paper."

"Or," Missy began, "everyone knows about the accusations about Julienne polluting the bay. Maybe Tom uncovered a smoking gun, and someone tried to shut him up by going after his daughter."

Dora shook her head. "I don't see how. Julienne's only been here six years. Anne died way before that. Other than the phone calls, there's no evidence that what happened to Anne Volkov was murder or that it was connected to anything else."

"No evidence … that we know of. But then, what happened to Franny and your cat? Hey, is Tom still married?"

"He is. His wife's not well. She hasn't been the same since her daughter died. So, maybe Franny found some link. But what?" She sat back and took a long pull at her beer.

Missy agreed. "She was getting too close."

Comfort was rubbing his head against Dora's calf. Unconsciously, she reached down and scratched the back of his neck then, aware of what she was doing, she looked down at him and smiled. Then her smile disappeared.

She looked at Missy. "Who the fuck would kill my cat?"

• • •

"Is there anything else?" the man asked.

Chief Stalwell shook his head. "Isn't that enough?"

The man seated opposite the chief was still. He was good at remaining extremely still and observing others. His eyes seemed larger than they were because he wore thick glasses, held in place by enormous black frames. He was a small man with a big reputation; a reputation for helping whoever asked for his help, regardless of their ability to pay his fee. He had his own set of criteria for taking on clients.

"But is it everything?"

The chief rose. "It's everything I can give you at this time, which is quite a bit more than I am obliged by law to give you."

"Then, thank you."

Robert James Bishop, Esquire stood up. Though both men wore Covid-19 masks, each could see the sincere, mutual agreement in the other's eyes.

Bishop turned to go.

"Bob," the chief began.

"Terry, if I learn anything germane that is not protected, I'll let you know."

The chief nodded. "That's all I can ask."

Bishop left, eschewing the elevator for the stairs and avoiding the banisters. Empty elevators were one thing—he could push the buttons with his elbows—but crowded elevators were something else. And who knew if the air in an elevator—empty or crowded—circulated or was purified?

As he headed down the stairs, he muttered to himself, "The crap that goes on in this town could be a cottage industry."

He made his way to the crimson Lincoln Navigator in the thirty-minute spot, then headed to Rudy's to discuss Agatha's charges with her and her husband.

Rudy's had undergone Covid-related changes, similar to bars all over the state. Since bar patrons frequently ignored mask and distancing restrictions, the state had passed laws to ensure compliance. No one could drink at a bar unless ordering food, and there had to be six feet between that person and any patron not accompanying that person. No more bellying up to the bar to drink. Therefore, Rudy had added more tables and chairs, up to the limit, given the required spacing, which gave him five tables with about six feet between each. He was glad no one ever measured.

When Rudy had brought Agatha back from the police station after bailing her out, they had been welcomed by two tables of friends from the neighborhood—LaChance and Keisha Williams, Delroy and Shanice James, Little Ru and Eunice Paul, Big Ru and Nia Paul, Winnie Chambers and her wife Pearlie, Hakeem and Aliyah Woods, Kelvin and Michelle Franklin, and Willis Thomas, who was with his mother, Betty, who had been a crossing guard near the school for many years and had watched Rudy and Agatha grow up. The other three tables had been occupied by members of the city's construction and police unions, including their leadership.

A passerby wandering in might have taken notice of the racial disparity of the two groups, but both groups had often occupied these tables close by one another, and no issues, racial or otherwise, had ever come between them.

"I don't see color," was Rudy's oft-repeated motto.

Both groups had ordered wings, sliders, and fries. Both groups had been drinking beers and shots, talking and laughing.

When Rudy brought Agatha in, the bar fell silent, but only for a moment. The neighborhood friends erupted in cheers and hoots, and everyone hugged Agatha and welcomed her home.

"Go easy on her," Rudy advised. "She's got little Rudy to see to now."

A cheer went up, and more hugs were offered to Agatha. No one noticed the look that passed between her and her husband, the subtle, sad shaking of her head, or Rudy's stunned expression.

The other group mostly nodded in their direction and looked toward their union leaders. After the initial din died down, one of the union leaders approached Rudy.

Craig Balboni was the president of the largest local construction union, one which supplied Beach City with a majority of its carpentry-related labor. He was slightly overweight, dark-eyed, and balding. His membership called him Baldy. He had been president for nine years, largely because of his reputation for loyalty and fearlessness.

"Rude, can we talk a minute?

"Sure, Craig, sure."

He led Craig into the back then turned. "What's up?"

Craig shook his head and pressed his lips together. "You know I love you and Agatha—"

"But?"

"Aw … it's not like that."

"But?"

"Okay. But—and I'm looking out for you here—maybe it'd be safer for everyone if you brought Agatha home. You're a great cook. Make her a nice meal, watch a movie. I mean, what with the controversy and all."

Rudy nodded slowly and stared down at the smaller, powerful man. "Yeah, I get what you're sayin'. And you know my wife would agree. Keep the peace, get some rest, and we'll all get along better tomorrow kind of thing."

"Exactly!" He slapped Rudy on the shoulder and started past him.

Rudy lay his own massive hand over Craig's, holding it there and stopping Craig short.

"I hate that shit," he said. "And I'm not my wife. See? I get exactly what you're saying." He slowly removed Craig's hand, twisting the man's arm ever so slightly but making clear by the strength of his grip that he could, if he wished, twist much harder.

"Thing is, my wife out there"—he gestured toward the bar—"she's already home."

"Oh, I see. Okay, then." Craig turned and walked back into the bar, shrugging and holding his hands out at his sides in an "I tried" gesture.

The bar remained silent.

Rudy sat down next to Agatha, took her hand in both of his, and stared into her eyes. "We'll try again, baby," he said.

Agatha looked up at him with hope and tears in her eyes.

He smiled an empty smile at his two tables of friends and lifted his beer. "To my beautiful wife."

His friends raised their glasses and, as they drank, a wet, wadded-up napkin bounced on the table in front of Agatha and landed in her lap.

Rudy stood up so fast that his chair was knocked backward.

Craig stood up, also, and held up his hand. "Easy, my friend."

Then he turned to his men. "We are guests in this man's establishment, as we have been many times—"

"Yo, Balds." The way the man said it sounded like "balls."

Craig looked at the man, who had long red hair and was sunburnt. The man's name was Nate.

"The man was just expressing himself," Nate said, his tone that of a wronged, innocent man. "Freedom of speech."

Rudy walked over to Nate. "How 'bout your friend and I settle this … just the two of us?"

He didn't answer.

Rudy nodded. "I thought not." He turned back to his table. He was followed by a hail of wet, wadded-up napkins.

Hakeem, who was closest to the union men, stood up. Delroy, who was next to him, also stood.

Rudy gave them a look that said "wait." Then he turned toward the union men.

"Y'all get out of my place. Go on. Time to go. Don't worry 'bout the bill."

Agatha tugged at her husband's arm. "Rude."

"Yeah, Rude," one of the union men said.

"Kinda Rude," another said.

Hakeem took a step toward the union men, reached back and, in one lightning motion, grabbed his chair by the upper seat back and windmilled it over his head, into the middle of the union group. The table that the chair landed on splintered, the chair broke into pieces, and the man one of the chair's legs had hit, Eugene, grabbed his shoulder and stood.

"What the fuck is wrong with you!"

Hakeem smiled. He had already grabbed another chair. "Just expressing myself. Freedom of expression."

"Yeah, well, express this." He charged Hakeem, tackling him at the waist.

In an instant, fists were flying, chairs were being used as clubs and projectiles, and bottles were broken, as Rudy herded Agatha and the rest of the women, except for Winnie, who loved to fight, into the storage room in the back.

When Rudy returned, he was holding a sawed off 12-gauge, which he cocked.

The fighting slowed, but only so those fighting anyone who looked his way were able to take advantage of the distraction.

He pulled the trigger. The blast and the shower of wood and sawdust was followed by dead silence, and a woman's voice from somewhere above them, saying, "What the fuck?"

The room cleared in a hurry. Inside of a minute, the union men were gone and a lone, white face, framed by enormous black glasses, stood in the doorway.

Agatha went to the diminutive man and hugged him, then turned. "Rude, you remember Rob Bishop?"

The lawyer smiled. "Nice of you to make the place so presentable for me."

Chapter 26

Luis Martinez had been working from home for months. He was in contact with Charlie Bernelli, his employer, and occasionally Ramon, the photographer/videographer, and any number of programmers. He felt blessed that, during this crazy time of Covid-19, he still had a job, and one he could perform from home, via technology. Work-related meetings were held via video chat, with documents exchanged and worked on using Google Drive, often by several people at once in real time. Life was challenging. Leaving his apartment was scary but, for Luis, it could have been so much worse, and he felt blessed to be aware of that.

And there was Linda. He had met Linda by accident. She worked at a fast-food chicken joint in Beach City's west end. She waited on him politely, with a big smile that he came to look forward to. For weeks, Luis was too shy to do anything more than smile back; it was enough. Then, one day, he was excited about a new ad that he had created and which Charlie and a long-time client had raved about. When Linda smiled on that day, he was surprised to hear himself suggest that they have coffee when she got off, which was at four p.m., not necessarily the ideal time for coffee.

They walked on the boardwalk, wearing their masks, neither of them speaking. Now and again as they walked, Linda's hand brushed his. Luis was afraid to do more, afraid to ruin what he thought of as a fragile baby bird of a relationship.

He had his work, his home, a tenant who helped with his mortgage, and now he had Linda.

He was content.

He had taken to getting up early in the morning to watch the sun rise. Most days, his work schedule allowed him the flexibility to work and sleep when it suited him. Rarely were the deadlines sooner than a day or two away, and Luis could work quickly when he needed to.

He liked the mornings. The sky was beautiful, the silence tranquil. He liked to hear the first bird chirp.

He had just finished brushing his teeth, getting dressed, and making his first coffee of the day, when there came a banging on his door.

"Open up! Police!"

His first instinct was to run out the back door. This was not a thought, but an impulse. He was terrified, while knowing he had no reason to be.

He glanced out the back window. Several dark shapes he assumed were police were arrayed out back.

He went to the front door and opened it.

"Luis Martinez?"

He nodded, keeping his hands visible.

"We'd like you to come to the station to answer some questions." The lead police officer was a big man. Not fat, not young or athletic, just big. Big and white and nasty-looking.

Luis fought to keep his wits about him. "Am I under arrest?"

The man shook his head. Something about him was familiar. Then Luis realized that he looked like the owner of one of the two diners in town.

"You're a person of interest, but if you don't come quietly, we may find cause to arrest you."

Luis nodded. "I'll come."

• • •

Franky had gotten the call from Mo, who had heard from George Cobb, just after five fifteen a.m., forty-five minutes before the police had arrived. He had known the call would come, so he had packed a bag with some clothes, toiletries, his baton blade, and a burner phone. He understood that his cell phone had to stay behind.

He would probably not return to the house, so he taped a note to the dining room window, asking Luis to care for his flowers and plants—his babies.

He liked staying where he was well enough; Luis was a decent landlord, who was careful not to make waves that might draw attention to himself or their living situation, which was illegal. That suited Franky fine. He was confident Luis would care for his babies. Luis was a good man.

He was dressed in dark clothes, his possessions in a small backpack. Perhaps it was that the call had come from Mo, who he was pretty sure was relaying instructions from Hagen, but as he hurried down the side streets, he was not worried about being seen or recognized. After all, to whom would he be reported? His mind took him back to memories of the days when Anne was still around, when the three of them were so close and so untouched by the rest of this dangerous world. It had been a wonderful time … while it had lasted. Then a horrific time, though those events had led to his twenty-year stint of work for the city, to health benefits, protection, and a life that was well suited to him.

Survival for them had come at a cost, except for Anne, of course, who had not survived. For the survivors, the cost had been their security in the world, their view of life as being filled with possibility and potential. For him, life was a moat of alligators and a land of tigers. Armor and weapons, and the willingness to fearlessly use them, were the tools he needed to survive and overcome.

He arrived at the cavernous building, quickly found his way inside, and set up camp.

Chapter 27

The broken pieces of the table and chairs had been brought out to the dumpster, the floor was swept and mopped, and Rudy was returning from the sink in the mop closet. He found Agatha waiting for him, looking resolute. He ignored the look on her face and took her in his arms. They rocked silently for several minutes.

"We've got a real problem now, Rude. Those union guys and their friends were the core of our business."

Rudy stopped and tipped his head to one side. "Don't care who they are. Can't come into my place and tell me about my wife. People will come. It will work out. And if it doesn't, like the man said, the birds in the trees get fed, we'll get by. Have faith." He pulled out a chair and sat down. "Anyway, we got to take care of you. You need a doctor?"

She shook her head. "Already saw Robinson. Actually, his nurse, Lola."

He nodded. "You okay?"

She nodded.

"We've got to settle with the police."

Agatha waved him away. "Bishop will see to it. You heard him."

Rudy scowled. "What he said was his opinion. He also said he had to see if there was any substance to the charges, was what he said."

Agatha took her husband's face between her hands. "I know—we know—there's no substance to the charges."

The front door opened, and a uniformed police officer, an older man, and a somewhat younger woman entered. All three wore masks.

"Mr. and Mrs. Raines," the officer began, "this is—"

"I know who they are, Officer. I get to see them every year." He turned to the man and woman. "Howard. Robin. Now, I know we have no inspection today, so why would the Health Department be stopping by? Too early to serve you drinks."

The man, Howard, took out a piece of paper. "This is business, Rudy. And I'm sorry. I like you folks, but I don't get to pick who to shut down."

"You're shutting us down?"

"I am. I have to. It's not up to me." Howard looked away.

Robin had taken a roll of duct tape and scissors from a small bag and begun taping the Health Department notice to the mirror behind the bar. She then went outside and taped another notice to the inside window of the front door and another to the inside of the big, street-facing window.

Agatha had stood up, her hands on her hips. Rudy remained seated, one hand shielding his eyes. He dropped his hand and stood up, towering over everyone.

"What in hell is going on in this town?" He was looking at Howard and Robin, but they saw that Rudy's question was not directed at them. "The whole town's gone crazy. Like, there's crazy pills in the water!"

"Not up to you?" Agatha said to Howard, her anger building. "So, who *is* it up to?" She paused. "You know Rob Bishop will handle this."

Howard gave her a long look. "I'm sorry, Rudy, Agatha. I hope he will. Really, I do."

• • •

Dora had been unable to sleep, so she and Missy agreed upon an alternate plan. They would drink until they passed out. Missy drank scotch; Dora drank shots of bourbon chased with beer.

Dora lay on the floor with Comfort, playing a game where she pretended her hand was a skittering crab, or perhaps a small rodent, though she suspected Comfort knew it was her hand, which Comfort chased and attacked, wrestling and biting it lightly. Now and then, the little dog would be distracted by some small thing, such as one of Missy's socks, and would march off with it clasped triumphantly between his teeth.

The little dog was so sure of himself, with such character and attitude, that Dora forgot why she was there, that she had been bailed out of jail, ostensibly for killing her own beloved Franny.

Eventually, Missy, who was sitting on the couch, glass in hand, asked, "What was your childhood like?"

Dora was on the floor, lying on her back, Comfort's chin on her chest, rising and falling with her breath. She angled her head toward Missy. "Why do you care?"

"I don't. Sorry. Never mind."

They sat in silence a while more.

"It sucked," Dora finally said. "Not for discussion."

"I don't need to know. None of my business."

Dora shifted Comfort's head into her lap and sat up. "Long as you put it that way, it was pretty much characterized by conflict. Lots and lots of fighting. My father beating my mother, my mother pretending it wasn't happening."

"Right," Missy said. "Physical fighting?"

"All kinds of fighting. The words were the worst."

"Even when you were little?"

"Especially when I was little." She shook her head, remembering. "Bad shit happened in that house ... when I was little."

"That had to have sucked."

"Like I said."

Missy put on some music that Dora had never heard before. "What is this?"

"McCoy Tyner."

"Whoa. He can *puh-lay!*"

"That he can."

"I never felt safe," Dora volunteered after several minutes. "And I had good reason."

They traveled the complex melodies, rhythms, and colors of Tyner and his band.

"Do you know how you learn to be safe?" Missy asked.

"I'm guessing your parents teach you."

"Yes, they do. But they don't just say, '*okay, you're safe now.*' Safety is communicated via wordless glances from mother to baby. Often, while nursing."

"Huh?"

"Which releases a sort of love chemical—oxytocin."

"Pretty sure that didn't happen for me." She drank the last of her shots then pointed to her shot glass, which Missy promptly refilled. "That's my oxytocin. My experience? The people you love the most, and who supposedly love you the most, hurt you. Often. Repeatedly. So, you've got to be ready. Always. Love chemical. Huh."

They listened to the rest of the piece then looked at each other when it was done, simultaneously appreciating the pianist's virtuosity.

"What about you?" Dora asked.

"Well, my parents came from Southern China during a bad time, so they didn't feel safe either, because they weren't safe. Have you ever heard of the Cultural Revolution?"

"Mmm ... nope."

"Well, Chinese society got turned upside down, often violently. People knew they weren't safe, so some got out."

"Were you alive then?"

"I was probably conceived then." Missy laughed. "Gotta do something when you're traumatized."

"Ha! Got that right."

"But I was born here."

"And became a librarian?"

"Well, not right away."

"But you needed to somehow learn all this shit."

Missy shrugged. "Some was family lore. And I like to read."

"What's this music?"

"Stanley Clarke."

"I like it."

"So do I. One of the things I learned is that it's better to allow yourself to be vulnerable, to take risks and deal with any pain that shows up."

"Better? What's that mean?" Dora was sitting stock-still, a hand gently on the dog's ribs, which slowly expanded and contracted.

"Maybe not better. More fulfilling? Rewarding?"

"Fuck rewarding," Dora muttered.

"You need to be able to feel your fear, to feel vulnerable, to be able to move past your need for violence to compensate."

"Hmm ... Maybe. After."

"After what?"

Dora smiled. "After ... it's no longer necessary. To get some people to stop behaving in ways that hurt others, you've got to talk to them in language they understand. Your way might be more fulfilling, but if you're taken by surprise, you could be screwed. I might be less fulfilled, but I'll survive. I'll win."

"Try this sometime"—Missy leaned forward—"focus on the inner part of you. Breathe into it. Surround it with white light ..."

"Aw ... come on."

"No, really. Try it!"

Dora looked skeptical. "Is this some Chinese martial arts thing?"

"Um ... no. It's a library thing. Like I told you, I like to read ... about meditation, among other things."

Dora closed her eyes for a few moments then shook her head. "I still don't feel any fuckin' safer."

Missy got up off the couch, knelt next to Dora, and put her arms around her, gently hugging her. Startled, but pleased, Dora turned and kissed Missy on the mouth. Missy's mouth remained closed. She completed the hug, got up, and went back to the couch.

She shrugged. "Just trying to help you feel safe."

"So you ... didn't mean it that way?"

"Um... no. It was very nice, but no."

"Aw ... shit."

• • •

Tom Volkov was sitting on his bed, staring at the television, where he had been attempting to watch a thriller that included murders; good guys who were pulled into bad situations that were not of their own making. He sought out such movies, without being aware of why. They were typically resolved when the good guy heroically turned the tables on the villain and was returned to everyone's good graces.

Movies like this one made him feel good on some visceral level.

He was having trouble focusing. He could hear Irene in Anne's room, talking to their daughter—well, talking to herself. He turned up the volume and focused on the movie as best he could, but disturbing thoughts and images intruded. This was happening more and more often, sometimes waking him up at night, or showing up in dreams in which he struggled with any number of challenging situations or adversaries.

If he could only stop thinking!

He had to stay the course. He didn't like the course. He knew plenty was wrong with the course. But what was the alternative? He had lived a nightmare for decades. Annie was long gone, and his Rene, too, was gone —lost in a mental fog and an emotional landscape too wrecked to overcome. He was trapped. He had fallen into what had been a small, ethical hole so long ago, but the hole had a trap door, which had a trap door, which had ... and he was now at what he hoped was the bottom.

A half-full glass was on the night table. He looked at it for a moment, trying to remember if it was vodka or water. What difference did it make? He laughed, took it, and drank half. Vodka. Good. Maybe it did make a difference.

Rene was getting louder. He could hear her footsteps.

Oh God. What now?

She burst into the room, waving one of those damned postcards. "Tommy, you've got to put a stop to this! These ... these ... these accusations! These innuendoes! These lies! Do you know what they're doing to Annie?"

He closed his eyes, hoping she would disappear. She didn't.

"Rene, no one's doing anything to Annie. They can't touch her. They can't hurt her. No one can. I swear."

Irene's face shook, her complexion darkened, her skin mottled. Then he was surprised to see her eyes clear.

"Well, these and what you're putting in the paper are hurting people. You're a journalist, not a propagandist. You've committed your life to telling the public the truth, no matter what the cost. What happened to that?"

He shook his head. "Rene, will you please go back to Annie's room?"

"She agrees with me!" Irene cried, waving the postcard in his face. "You are spreading this ... this ... this symphony of lies! Fix this, Tommy, or I swear you won't have me around. Fix it, or I will! Is that what you want?"

Symphony ...? Maybe some classical music would help. And more vodka.

"Okay, Rene, okay. Okay, I'll take care of it. I will, I promise."

Muttering, she left the room.

He changed the channel to one that broadcast symphonic music twenty-four-seven. Bach. *Perfect!* He could feel the symmetry of the music's structure starting to reorder the chaos of his mind.

And yet … And yet … Irene's words, and their meaning, persisted.

• • •

As night became early morning, Missy made vegetable and cheese omelets, with some kind of soy bacon substitute. Dora didn't know what to make of the latter. She held up a strip. Looked a bit like bacon. Smelled like bacon … kind of. She broke it in half.

"Come here, Comfort."

Sensing her intent, the little dog trotted over and sat on the floor, waiting by her feet.

"Okay if he has this?"

Missy rolled her eyes. "The dog eats his own shit. There's not much you can't give him, 'cept chocolate, grapes, and raisins. Though, I must say fat, like in cheese or steak, gives him the runs."

Dora held out half her slice of the soy bacon. Comfort took it carefully between his teeth, making sure not to hurt Dora, then rushed off to his bed, which was in a corner of the room. He had a bed in most of Missy's rooms.

"He seems to like it."

"You're a garbage woman? He's the original garbage man. A little dumpster with legs."

"Except it comes out the other end."

"That's right. Sustainable." Missy laughed. "So, you started to tell me last night about your family."

"Well, my father, Freddy, was an alcoholic salesman. He sold medical equipment and made a lot of money, but he was an asshole. He beat my mother, Dorothy, who had bipolar and panic attacks, and couldn't, or wouldn't, do anything about it. In fact, she did worse … with words. Dorothy grew up kind of well off—my grandfather was some kind of door-to-door salesman. Anyway, she lost her fancy life when, upon learning she was pregnant, Freddy left her. Beat her up and walked out. Fucking coward. Disappeared. The courts could not find him."

"You okay?" Missy asked.

Dora nodded. "Me? Oh, I'm good. Be better if I found him, but I'm good. Anyway, my mother struggled with poverty and raising her baby, Deborah —me. She babysat and cleaned homes, and we lived on that and food stamps. She was overwhelmed, and her mental illness made it worse. She sometimes took it out on me. She said later she regretted that, but I never forgot. Think of a puppy who loves you."

Comfort had come over and nestled himself against her leg, making a little circle of himself, his head near his tail.

Dora stroked his back as she spoke. "You can yell at that dog, beat that dog, but at least for a while, that dog will keep coming back to you, expecting love. That's what I did." She looked at Missy. "I wet my bed till I was fourteen." She peered at her glass. "How much did I have that I told you all that?"

Missy shrugged. "More?"

Dora shook her head. "I started having panic attacks in my late teens, along with these … episodes. Rage. Violence. I'd just … break things. If I tried to stifle that, I'd get more panic attacks. My job's really physical, which helps."

"What about seeing someone?"

"A therapist? I have. Four."

"Someone who prescribes?"

"Done that, too. It helped. Still helps. But not with the rage. What helps with the rage is feeding it, and it's one hungry rage."

Missy looked confused. "Doesn't that make it stronger?"

Dora smiled. "It does."

"But wouldn't you heal better if you found a way to forgive your parents?"

Dora didn't answer. "I'm meeting with my lawyer tomorrow, so I'm going to crash. Thanks for everything and … sorry."

Missy rose, smiling. "No worries. I think it was sweet."

Once Missy was gone, Dora listened until she was sure Missy was in the bathroom, washing up. Comfort had remained pressed against her leg and was looking up at her with his enormous green-brown eyes. Dora rearranged herself so she was lying next to him on the couch. Then she pressed her face into his back, feeling his quick, easy breathing. As she drifted off to sleep, she felt Comfort turn toward her and begin to lick her face.

Chapter 28

As Missy was making a late lunch of blueberry pancakes while Dora napped on the couch, the doorbell rang, sending Comfort into a brief frenzy and waking Dora, who watched as Missy went to the door.

Missy turned. "All right if your lawyer comes in?"

Dora nodded then watched as Robert James Bishop, Esquire came in and stood facing her in the foyer, between the front door and the living room. He wore an N95 mask, the cream of the crop.

"Hello, Dora. Is now a good time?"

Dora nodded.

"Coffee?" Missy called.

"Too late in the day. Already past my limit," Bishop said as he sat down on one of the beige armchairs and leaned forward, his hands clasped between his knees.

They sat for a moment in silence.

"So ...?" Dora said.

"How are you?"

Dora gave a quick exhale. "Living the dream."

He nodded. "I'm also representing Agatha Raines. Now, I'm not at liberty to discuss her case in detail—"

"I know she was arrested for some kind of vandalism and libel, right?"

The lawyer looked down at his hands then up at Dora. "The reason I'm bringing it up is that your cases are connected, in my opinion, in a conspiracy of sorts. Not so different from what the city seems to be suggesting others, including both of you, are part of. Except you are the victims, not the perpetrators. The challenge will be proving it. First and foremost, however, is establishing your innocence."

"Agreed," Dora said as Missy came into the room with two mugs of coffee, sat down next to Dora, and placed a mug before each of them.

Dora took a sip of her coffee and closed her eyes. "Mmm ..." She sipped again. "Okay. Now I can focus."

"It's okay to ...?" Bishop looked at Missy.

"Yes," Dora answered.

"So, we have two witnesses," Bishop said. "One who overheard you and Officer Hart fighting in your home, just prior to … to what happened, and the other who says she saw you in the car that hit her."

"Both are bullshit," Dora said.

"Well, we have to prove that."

"Do we?" Missy asked. "But isn't the burden of proof on the prosecution? Isn't Dora presumed innocent?"

Bishop nodded. "Yes, and the lawyer for the city, whose name is Hagen, is attempting to prove his case. Our job is to prove them wrong, thereby invalidating their efforts."

Dora put down her coffee and sat back. "Well, for one thing, we didn't have an argument just prior to the event. We never argued. This thing happened late in the day. We weren't even together. We weren't together all day, so how could we have had an argument just prior? Define just prior."

Bishop nodded. "As far as I know, just prior means just that—minutes, not hours—and that's good."

"I was home at the time, and for quite a while before. I wasn't in my car. I did get a call from her. Maybe we can prove that with phone records." She and Missy looked at one another, brightening.

"Hmm …" Bishop said. "Is there any possibility that what their witness heard was a fight over the phone?"

"No, it is not," Dora insisted. "How 'bout we pick up on this later? I've got somewhere to be."

Missy looked at her.

"I'm going to wash up and change before going. Is that okay, Mr. Bishop? I do appreciate your help. Can I give you some money? A check? I really have to be somewhere."

Bishop shook his head. "No need." He rose to leave. "And everything else we need to discuss can wait. Thank you for your time. I'll let you know once I have more information."

· · ·

When Dora walked through the door, she heard that intense, familiar rustling, followed by someone yelling, "Tap, tap, tap!"

Dora stepped into the gym and bowed.

"You didn't feel my tap?" Shay was asking Wire.

"I guess I was so psyched to get an arm bar on you that I kinda—"

"You gotta acknowledge the tap," Shay said, as she shook her head. "If you don't—"

"Hey, kids!" Dora was grinning.

The two turned then lit up. "Hey, kid!" Shay rushed to Dora and hugged her. Wire was right behind her.

"How ya been? What's this shit I read?"

Dora shrugged. "Ain't nothing. I'll deal. But I need to train. Been too long. Gonna stretch, then how 'bout we go?" She turned to Wire. "That okay?"

"Hell, yeah," Wire said. "Already kicked her ass."

"Heard the tap," Dora said, and Shay laughed.

Ten minutes later, Shay had put on her gloves and headgear and was in the ring.

As Dora stepped through the ropes, she waved a glove at Shay. "Don't go easy on me now just 'cause I've been—"

In two quick, leaping strides, Shay had crossed the ring and hurled a front leg roundhouse kick at the side of Dora's head, which Dora managed to partially block with her opposing forearm. Still, the force of the blow rocked her.

Dora grinned as she advanced toward Shay. Her mind was clear and focused. She was ready for controlled violence.

She was home.

• • •

The air was saturated with fear, driving everyone to talk at once—yelling, arguing, talking over one another, with barely restrained intensity. Violence was in the air.

Jonathan Hagen sat at the head of the table and watched for a few moments before he rose slowly, leaning forward on his palms, which rested on the table. A position of power.

"These issues, the controversy, your concerns are going to go away soon. And we'll all go back to our lives, and everything will return to normal. Now, I'll hear what each of you has to say, but one at a time."

He nodded to Tom Volkov.

Volkov looked at each of the people at the table. His tone was pleading. "I run a newspaper. The public perception of the news is all I have so, arguably, I have more to lose than anyone here."

"Public perception is not all you have," Horace Cobb said. "You have advertising."

"Covid's been destroying my advertising revenue."

"Well, I run a restaurant, and people are afraid to come in, and we have renewed state restrictions. I rely on physical, paying customers, not virtual. Without the good will of the public, I have nothing. Nothing!"

Volkov shook his head. "But your customers are not at risk. You're not sticking your neck out!"

Mo's face was rigid, as though injected with Botox. The actual ingredient, though, was terror. "My job is literally all I have. My future. My benefits. My 401k. My pension."

"But your job's safe," Volkov countered. "Your job's essential."

"Enough!" George Cobb banged a fist on the table. "I have to maintain order and public safety, while keeping the chief's eyes away from us. He's not stupid; he has suspicions. The longer we wait, the more dangerous this is for us all. But, you know, the vendettas are not what's hurting us. What's hurting us is fear! Do you think the public will stop doing business with any of us—*any* of us—because of this controversy?"

"Listen to me!" Tom Volkov's tone turned shrill. "We've got to back off. I deal with public reaction every day. I know how to read the public. Trust me; they're tired of all the fighting and bitterness. It's dividing the town!"

"With all due respect," Hagen said, his voice low, his tone reasonable, "division isn't the problem. It was our goal, and we've achieved it. People don't know what to think, which is better than them thinking the wrong things. We *are* controlling what they think. In any case, it's temporary. All of your concerns are being addressed."

He turned to Tom Volkov, who recoiled at the empty depth of Hagen's eyes. "Tom, you can say what you've always said, what journalists have said for, oh … a century or two—you've gotta protect your sources. And then, you do it."

"Well, I don't know how long I can hold them off," Volkov countered.

"Do like they do in AA—hold them off a day at a time." He smiled. "You don't have to say much of anything. The information we wanted out there *is* out there. Relax. No more offense. Now, it's all about defense. Just don't respond. Or, say little. Or, use non sequiturs."

The Cobb brothers exchanged concerned looks.

"I have RJ Bishop breathing down my back," George Cobb said. "And Stalwell's been asking me questions. He knows he's in the deep end of the pool, though there's no evidence linking anyone to anything."

Hagen chuckled, a strange sound, devoid of any humor, like some unnamed creature might make in the woods at night. "All of them— Stalwell, Bishop—they'll all tie themselves in knots trying to figure this out, to see the logic, when the logic—our intent—is to tie them in knots." He looked them all in the face, one by one. "The poison's working. Just let it work. All we're doing is pouring gas on a rumor mill, which Tom, it is your duty to report, just as you have been. You don't have to report any of this as fact. Report that people are talking, and what they're saying. Nothing's on you. The public's obsession is news. And a lot of the news is speculation about what might happen, or some talking head's perception of what might, or might not, happen."

Tom Volkov thought a moment. "Maybe I can get a quote from the mayor about how these rumors have crossed his desk and how concerned he is for the welfare of the city, and that we're all in this together. That sort of thing. Jon?"

Hagen smiled and pointed at Volkov. "Good. Do it." He snapped his fingers. "Oh, I know! Let's put out a quote that there's a list. A list of people—local people—who are working together to undermine the public good. We can say it comes from the mayor, so George"—he turned to George Cobb—"you won't have to answer to Stalwell. I'll make up a list, so we will, in fact, have one. Stalwell will read about it and go to the mayor, who will have deniability and will refer him to me. Mayor Mark knows that when there's even a whiff of political dirt, and the dogs are at the door, I'm the answer. He comes to me every time. And I'll say—" He laughed with sheer joy. "I'll say, I'm so sorry, but I cannot talk about this, though I truly want to. Attorney/client privilege! Mmm ...?" He looked at each of them for a long second.

Smiles broke out all around.

"That'll work," Horace Cobb said.

His brother nodded, as did Tom Volkov.

"We'll all have plausible deniability," he continued.

"What about me?" Mo wanted to know.

"No one's connecting you to anything," Hagen said, pausing and looking around. "Okay, then."

Everyone rose to leave.

He looked at Mo. "Stick around. We need to talk."

• • •

In the days that followed *The Chronicle* articles and postcard campaign, the Beach City Facebook groups were inundated with questions, theories, and accusations. Multiple new groups were formed around rumors and counter-rumors. There were Beach City Police Supporters, Beach City Cheerleaders, a Black Beach City group, Beach City or Bust, along with a BC Tourism Support Network that grew out of The Bernelli Group's tourism ad campaign and the groundswell it generated.

The city responded with an online chat appearance by Chief Terry Stalwell and Captain George Cobb, ostensibly intended to quell the confusion and unrest but, arguably, the effect was the opposite, since their messages were more than a little contradictory and appeared not to have been coordinated. Chief Stalwell called for calm and expressed confidence that the articles were simply reporting rumors and beliefs held by a percentage of residents. Captain Cobb, on the other hand, referenced a list of citizens—a cabal was the word he used—who were working to upend the city's decision-making apparatus and who opposed the "will of the people." He vowed to uncover the truth and the identities of those on the list "by whatever means necessary."

More than a few people expressed their concern over the lack of any public statement from the mayor.

Chapter 29

As Cobb's broadcast was ending, Dora was putting on her denim jacket.

"Where're you off to?" Missy asked.

"Taking a walk. I get so little cardio, you know—"

"Take a mask, please."

Dora pulled a surgical mask out of her pants pocket and waved it in Missy's direction. "Okay, but I won't be near anyone."

She went directly to the parking lot behind the building from which the broadcast had originated, which also housed *The Chronicle* offices. She parked at the rear of the lot then walked around for a few moments to identify the best vantage point, given that the light was coming from a spotlight mounted on the building. Once she was sure, she pressed the "*video*" button in her camera app and leaned the phone on the rubber beneath the window of an SUV in the first line of cars in the lot.

She waited just over ten minutes, ducking down when she saw George Cobb exit the building.

"Great broadcast, Captain."

Cobb turned toward her, but Dora remained in the shadows of the parked cars. He shielded his eyes.

"Thanks … Who's that?" He took a few steps toward the sound of her voice as Dora slipped silently behind two cars and stepped into the lit open space behind the police officer.

"George!" she yelled.

As Cobb spun, Dora leaped onto the back bumper of a nearby truck that was slightly off to one side. Using it as a springboard, she flew through the air and landed just to Cobb's right. With her right thumb and forefinger, she unlatched Cobb's service weapon, slid it out from its holster, and then tossed it to one side.

Cobb had already begun his reflex swing—his right arm clubbing straight down toward her back—but Dora slid to her left at a slight angle and blocked her right arm upward, catching his arm at the outermost point of his elbow with a force at least equal to his own. There was a crack, and Cobb screamed, his arm broken.

He fell to the ground, clutching his arm, then quickly scrambled to one knee, which Dora kicked out from under him. He fell again, writhing against the pain as he tried to rise. One of his hands gripped his broken elbow. Dora pounced on the other hand, sliding her grip along his wrist until she had a hold of his thumb.

"Tell me, Cap; who's behind these postcards and the news articles?"

Cobb's face was a mask of rage. "You crazy bitch. I'll have you back in jail in ten minutes, without bail!"

"I don't think so." She nodded toward the camera. "I'll post video showing everyone in town that you were whupped by a little girl, who made you whimper like a baby."

Cobb's eyes flicked toward her phone. "Fuck. You."

"Aw, come on, Cap. I just want a name. Tell you what; give me the name, and no one has to see the video."

"I said, *fuck you.*"

"Okay," Dora said. "But you know I can put this in front of just about every cop in the state. What will they think? What will your union—"

"Hagen. Jon Hagen. He's a lawyer. Works for the city."

"Thanks, Cap. And no, I'll keep my word. No one will see this. But I'll tell you what..." She bent down so her face was inches from his. "I'm going to make sure your corrupt ass will never wear the uniform again, startin' real soon."

• • •

C3 sat in his father's BMW outside the police station, lifting his mask and sipping from a coffee that he had brought from home, his eye caught by a poster for a designer vodka in the window of the liquor store across the street. He had never liked vodka. He had never much liked alcohol, but it would do in a pinch. He found that as long as he made his meetings, even if they were on video chat, alcohol held no attraction for him.

A reflected movement in the window caught his eye, and he turned to see his father emerging from the police station with Luis Martinez, both wearing N95 masks. As they got in the car, Luis was talking. He nodded to C3 and went on with what he was saying.

"I have no idea what happened to Franky. He was gone before the cops came. He doesn't tell me anything, and I don't want to know."

Charlie glanced at his son in the mirror then back at Luis as they pulled away from the station.

"Look, he was my tenant," Luis continued, "but it's not a legal two and, with Franky ... well, you don't want to bother him. He's crazy, but he pays his rent. I leave him alone. That was our deal."

Charlie's phone buzzed. "Just a second, Luis." He glanced at his phone, frowned, and then pressed it to his ear.

"Hello?" A pause. "What? When?" Another pause. "Well, where is he now? Is he conscious?" A pause. "No. He's with me ... On my way."

He caught his son's eye in the mirror. "Your grandfather's had a stroke. We're going to the hospital."

He looked at Luis. "Looks like you're along for the ride. Sorry."

"No worries, man," Luis said. "It's a big improvement from a jail cell."

• • •

Charlie Senior was in the ICU, where no visitors were allowed, due to Covid protocols.

C3 and Luis sat silently together in a corner of the waiting room, which was otherwise deserted. Every other chair had been turned backward to enforce the social distancing that was still required by state law.

A nurse had stepped into the waiting room and was talking to Charlie Jr. near the door. When they finished, Charlie returned and remained standing.

"Not much information, other than that he was able to dial 9-1-1 himself, which is encouraging."

C3 searched his father's face. His grandfather had been a powerful influence on him when he had been a child, instilling confidence that he could do anything he set his mind to. That his grandfather was now incapacitated in a hospital bed was beyond his comprehension. He could see that his father was also struggling.

"Luis, if you've gotta be somewhere, I can call you an Uber. I'll take care of it."

"No, thank you, Mr. Bernelli. I'll wait with you guys."

"You sure?"

Luis nodded.

"Well then," Charlie said, "we wait … and maybe pray."

Chapter 30

"Where'd you find that?" Missy asked.

"Back of your coat closet," Dora answered. "I didn't know you liked puzzles. Oh, maybe I did ..." She had completed half the puzzle, which had been made from a photo of the Amazon rainforest. The puzzle was especially challenging because so much of it was green.

"I do like puzzles," Missy said. "In fact, I think I might have just solved one. Come here."

Dora came over to the table, on which was one of the bizarre postcards that made accusations against unnamed conspirators, though it was plain they were referring to Dora and Agatha Raines, among others.

Missy didn't answer, but she got up and went to a narrow table that was against the wall just inside the front door. She and Dora had left their shoes beneath the table, on which were stacks of mail, which Missy now sifted through.

"Aha!" She took two pieces of what looked like junk mail back to the table and lay them next to the postcard. "Okay, puzzle girl, what matches?"

Dora studied each item carefully. "Well, they're all on white paper." She looked at Missy, who was still waiting. "They're not all in color. They're different shapes and have different numbers of pages. I don't know ... they all contain the letter 'O'?"

Missy was triumphant. "They all have the same bulk mailing permit!"

"Just a sec. I'm getting a text." Dora looked at her phone then typed a few keys. "Bishop's stopping by to talk to me for a second. That okay?"

"Sure," Missy said.

Dora nodded toward the postcard on the table. "So, what's the big deal about a mailing permit? They all use the local post office?"

"Probably." Missy nodded. "But that's not it. These, which I got last week and the week before, are obviously from the city, right?"

"Right."

"And this."

"We don't know who it's from."

"Oh, but we do." Missy pointed to the small square containing the bulk permit number. "Same permit number. All from the city."

The doorbell rang.

Missy went to answer it, peering first through the peephole. She opened the door as far as the chain lock allowed.

"I think that's for me," Dora said, getting up and going to the door.

"If he has a mask, you can let him in," Missy said.

"Maybe I'd better wait out here," Bishop said.

"Right. I'll get a mask and come out," Dora said.

Dora stepped outside, leaving the door open a few inches. A chilly drizzle had begun. "What's up?"

"I've put some things together and wanted to discuss them in person."

"Okay."

"You and Agatha are both being targeted by PR attacks in the newspapers and by mail, designed to distract and cover up corruption and criminal activity involving Julienne Inc., and numerous public servants."

Dora slowly nodded. "We were just talking about the postcards. Missy figured out that they're using the city's bulk mailing permit."

"Makes sense," Bishop said. "Speaking of Julienne, the supposed witness to the vandalism reported at Julienne was an employee there."

"Do you think that person was pressured?"

Bishop shrugged. "The more I learn about this town, the more possible connections I see. Agatha Raines is known for being a bit of a gadfly, someone the powers that be around here aren't too fond of."

"Because she tells the truth, things they don't want to acknowledge. Bet what happened to her is meant to distract from the pollution they dump in the channel."

Bishop nodded. "Possibly. Agatha has come up with evidence that, though circumstantial, ties chemicals at the Clean Acres site to Julienne. As to your case, the neighbors who say they heard you and Officer Hart fighting shouldn't be a problem. I suspect that, under questioning, they won't be quite so sure of what they heard. It's the witnesses who say they saw you in the car that ran her down that concern me."

Dora held up her hand. A tall, thin young woman was walking a beagle past the house. Dora waved. "Hi, Clara. Hi, Rocky."

Clara paused, waved, saw that Dora was with someone, and then continued on her way.

Dora turned back to Bishop. "Witnesses? There's more than one?"

"Yes. And they've both correctly identified the make and model of your car, and one wrote down the license plate. It's yours."

"They're ... they're lying! I wasn't there. I was home!"

"I have no doubt of that. I'm going to look into just who these witnesses are and what their motives might be. If there is anything you can do to prove you were home, the details of a TV show at the time, anything, please let me know."

Dora's cell phone rang. She looked at the number and frowned.

"Hey. What's up? We working tomorrow?"

It was Mo. He sounded frantic. "Dora. No—I mean, yes, we're working. Listen, I need to tell you something. I'm the one who made those calls."

Dora squinted and shook her head. "What calls? You okay, Mo?"

"To Franny Hart. To you. I have information about what happened"— he dropped his voice to a whisper—"to Anne Volkov. But I don't want to discuss it on the phone. I have other information, too, about Julienne, but I need to show it to you. Can you meet me at their front gate?"

"Of Julienne? When?"

"Fifteen minutes."

She glanced at Bishop. "Okay. Sure."

"There are people watching me. And trust me; there are people watching you."

"People ... won't they see us?"

"Won't matter. I'll have a key, and they won't have any way to get inside."

"How did—"

But Mo was gone, and Dora never had the chance to ask him how he came to have a key to the front gate of Julienne Inc.

• • •

The hospital lobby was nearly empty at midnight. The few people waiting there were grouped in small enclaves, well away from one another. All wore masks.

"What will you do for work?" Charlie Jr. asked Christine. He was sitting next to C3, who was dozing. Next to him, Luis was reading something on his phone.

"Oh, I'll find work," Christine said. "I'm on good terms with lots of businesses in the city. I'm sure someone can use an office manager, especially one with inside knowledge of City Hall."

"But you didn't leave on good terms."

"No, I didn't," Christine agreed. "In fact, I'd like to head over there and give the powers that be a piece of my mind. I was put in a terrible position on a regular basis. If they hadn't let me go, I would have quit." Her face was flushed. She was as angry as Charlie had ever seen her, which turned him on.

He pressed back into the chair to distract himself.

"It's bad enough that this city is run like a ... like a—"

"Like a mob family?" Charlie offered.

"Exactly! Like a mob family. They put a lot of pressure on me every day."

At that moment, Charlie realized that he loved her. He had been enjoying their time together since his return to Beach City, and the current incarnation of Charlie Bernelli saw exactly who he wanted to build a life with, sitting right there in front of him, spouting angrily and accurately about how badly her job had treated her.

"You know what?" she asked.

"Hmm ...?" He awoke from his reverie, realizing she was expecting an answer.

"I'm going down there tomorrow, find this Jon Hagen big shot who nobody knows, and give him a piece of my mind!"

"You should always, always speak your mind. Speak your truth." He held up a finger. "Just be careful."

"Why? I'm already fired."

"They're a pretty revenge-minded bunch, from everything I've seen."

She sat back, her lips pressed together. "We'll see about that."

After a moment, she turned to Charlie, keeping her voice low. "You know, no one told anyone anything in that place, except whatever the official line was—the mayor's line. And, quite frankly, he's a phony. He comes off as this cheerful, benevolent force, but it's an act. He had a way of figuring out what people really wanted, or their vulnerabilities, or what would make them look bad, and using it against them. I'm seeing it now. How come I didn't see it before?"

"Maybe," Charlie said, "because you didn't have all the information. Or maybe he's that good at it."

"Charlie, you have no idea! I went out with people from different departments now and then, and after a few drinks, they'd tell me things. Not a lot, but enough to know we were all getting different stories."

"Damn," Luis said.

C3 opened one eye. "Good thing you're out of there."

"And you think it comes from this lawyer?"

She nodded. "Hagen, yeah. Not from him, but through him. There was always a threat that if you didn't do something—"

"You would lose your job?" Charlie Jr. asked.

"Worse! No, if you didn't do what you were told, you'd be personally humiliated in a group meeting that supposedly had some purpose or other but was really called for just that reason. Worse than losing your job. They wanted to keep you around to humiliate and manipulate. And now that we do things on video chat, the meetings are all taped and could be leaked onto social media. They could be made public."

Charlie took her hand and leaned against her. Christine lay her head against his shoulder.

"Mr. Bernelli?" A nurse had stepped into the room and was waiting just inside in the doorway.

Charlie went to her. The nurse spoke quietly for a moment then left. Charlie returned to Christine and C3.

"He's resting. They won't know how much damage the stroke did until they do some more tests, but his vitals are pretty good."

C3 had opened his eyes and was smiling with relief.

"Thank God," Luis said.

They all stood up and began walking toward the exit.

Charlie turned to Christine. "Was the person doing the shaming always the mayor?"

She shook her head. "It was sometimes the mayor, but rarely. More often, it was a department head who, if he or she didn't do a good enough, or bad enough, job, would be next on the chopping block. And above them was the lawyer, Jon Hagen. I'm telling you, I'm going down there."

"But if Hagen is the mayor's errand boy ..."

They began walking again. Once they were outside, Christine looked around then continued.

"Hagen's a lawyer, but really, he's a fixer, and not in a good way. See, sometimes it goes beyond shaming."

"What do you mean, *beyond shaming*?" Charlie asked.

"First of all, nothing—absolutely nothing—happens at City Hall without the mayor's blessing. That nice guy shit is an act. He's basically a mafia boss whose mob is the whole of Beach City government. You know, now that I think of it, this whole thing—all of it, has gotta come from him. I cannot imagine Hagen and the city directors manufacturing a system of lies and revenge, and maybe murder, without the mayor's approval, if not his instigation."

Luis had been listening. "Know who also works for the mayor ... as in, directly? My former tenant—Cranky Franky Patella. Unofficially. I don't know exactly what he did, but everyone—and I mean *everyone*—stayed out of his way."

• • •

Dora was a block from Julienne when her cell phone rang. She saw the caller's name and picked it up. "Missy."

"Listen, I found something in an old newspaper archive." She sounded breathless, excited. "And I'll bet it's exactly what Franny found. In fact, I'm sure of it."

"Okay. What is it?"

"I'll get to it. Let me tell it. It's something that wasn't in the main *Chronicle* article about Anne Volkov's death, but it *was* in the original police blotter, where no one was likely to notice it, including whomever at City Hall was supposed to cancel this particular bit of information."

"Well? What was it? What did Franny find?"

"It's about the original police response to Anne Volkov's death. The officer who handled the call was Sergeant Mark Morganstern."

"Sergeant, as in *Mayor* Mark?

"Yep. The same. Dora, this should be enough to at least get Bishop focused on the mayor. Forget what you're doing and come on back."

But Dora was no longer listening. She thought she understood the truth behind decades of city-led vendettas and was beginning to see when it had all started. Her questions were: how and why? How did Anne Volkov really die? What role did the mayor play as the responding police officer? And what did Mo have to do with any of this? The young man had some explaining to do. She looked forward to hearing what he had to say for himself.

She parked a block away from the Julienne grounds. She walked and listened—she wasn't sure for what, but her senses were tuned in to her surroundings. Any sound of her footfalls on the gravel was swallowed by that of the waves gently lapping at the docks at the other side of the lot.

As she expected, she found the gate unlocked. It opened silently then clanged shut behind her.

She hadn't thought much about what Mo had said or what he might want to show her. She had some ideas but cleared her mind so she would be able to focus on the moment and better understand the big picture.

She went around the side of the main building, which held conference rooms and offices, to the rear parking lot, and walked lightly, on the balls of her feet, just outside the steel railing that served as a stop for parked cars. The tall, ground-floor windows on the smooth stone building were dark. She passed an outdoor dining area then walked through the boatyard, to the bulkheads, where she stopped and listened.

"Oh, here she is!" a voice called.

"Well, hello, Franky." She looked around for a second person. "Where's Mo? I'm here because he called."

The lanky young man with the floppy bangs and fake grin stepped into the light. He held a stick-shaped implement in one hand. Like Dora, he walked on the balls of his feet. She could see he was an athlete, his messy appearance probably belying some degree of skill.

"Mo wanted to be here, but was … detained."

While alarms were going off in her thinking brain, her lizard brain was delighted.

"And I know your MMA background," Franky said. "I've been keeping tabs on you. Very impressive."

"Keeping tabs? On me? How sweet."

"But here's the thing about MMA ... Have you fought against weapons? Have you fought in the street? Have you fought ... men?"

She didn't answer but retraced her steps back toward the outdoor dining area. He followed, staying close to the center of the parking lot, parallel to her, maintaining the distance between them.

"A weapon? Really? You're a coward, Franky."

He ignored her. "I know the weakness of MMA." He didn't wait for an answer. "Rules." He pulled out the baton and, in the same motion, leaped forward, as a fencer would, covering nearly ten feet of ground, all of the distance between them. Then, he whipped the baton across Dora's face, leaving a raised red welt above her eye. The welt began to bleed, and the blood ran into her eye.

My God, he's fast, she thought as she moved beyond some large, stone planters and into the dining area, where she could maneuver between and around the furniture.

"I'm going to whip you like a little girl, like your daddy should have."

"What do you know about my daddy, asshole?"

"And I'm going to do it slowly. So slowly. And then, when you are beaten, when you're whupped and crawling, I'm going to cut you even more slowly." He turned the baton in the light, and Dora saw the long, narrow blade opposite the whip end.

Dora pressed a finger to the cut and wiped away some of the blood. "I don't think so."

"And what do you think you can do about it? You and your MMA?"

"MMA? Yes, I'm involved in that sport. But you're right; it's a sport. With rules. Which can be a hindrance. I'll give you that." She lifted a chair by its back, holding it between them, like a lion tamer. "Frank—"

"Franky. My name is Franky."

"Here's your problem, Frank."

"It's—"

"You just don't scare me. Really! Not even a little. You're a little boy with his toy. I mean, do I look at all frightened? But you're right about rules. I don't like MMA rules any more than you do, *Frank*. Did you know I was thrown out of an MMA organization for ignoring the rules? For breaking them on purpose?" She closed the distance fast and jabbed the chair at Franky's face, then instantly at his knees, cutting his legs out from under him.

Franky slid backward to avoid the chair and fell forward, grabbing for a chair leg. Dora retracted the chair then shoved it forward again, catching and slicing the bridge of his nose.

Franky spun, with one hand on the ground, and flipped the baton in his hand, catching Dora with its blade and slicing a long furrow from her right arm to her thigh. He laughed, pulled the blade back, then hard toward her midsection, but his thrust was low, and his blade sliced her calf muscle.

Dora grunted from the pain then laughed.

Franky watched her, his eyes wide. "Something funny?" he demanded.

"You! You misjudged me. You thought I fight MMA and stick to their rules." She shook her head. "But you were wrong, *Frank*." She still had a hold of the chair, and now she stepped forward, raised the chair straight up, and brought it down, legs first.

Instead of stepping back, Franky flailed at the chair, but his baton was thin and no match for the chair's thick, oak legs. Dora was pretty sure she had broken his collarbone.

As he tried to roll away, she timed her strike just right, bringing the chair down on his abdomen and forcing the air from his lungs in a long moan. Then she raised the chair high above her head and slammed it down on his groin, using so much of her considerable weight that she was driven up into the air.

Franky screamed then whimpered.

"Can't do that in MMA. Against the rules," she explained, as though this had just occurred to her.

She left him on the ground and began walking toward the door. A faint sound made her stop. It was the click of a safety being flicked off.

Dora turned then ran right at him in a zigzag pattern, each step more of a leap, until she leaped on top of him, like a big cat on its prey.

"I'll kill you. I'll—"

Franky's scream was cut off. His trigger finger no longer worked, because much of it was gone.

Dora had bitten down on it with her front teeth. Then, with a second bite, she had pulled his finger farther into her mouth, where her molars could grind, and then she bit again.

She spit the tip of his finger into his face. "Not today, *Frank*, not today."

Chapter 31

"You really *are* crazy."

Dora opened her eyes to find Charlie Bernelli and Missy sitting across the hospital room, wearing masks, with more than six feet between them.

"What time is it?" she asked. "What day is it?"

"Ten forty-five a.m.," Missy said. "Monday?"

Dora nodded.

"Your name got us in here," Charlie marveled. "Technically, no visitors under Covid protocols, but you, girl, are a celebrity! Even so, they don't want us staying long."

"All I remember is that sick bastard having a knife, and I got cut." She looked down at herself for the first time and saw the bandages, which were soaked with dried blood.

Charlie saw her stunned expression. "You should see the other guy," he said.

Missy took an iPad out of her bag. "Gotta show you something." She held it up. On it was *The Beach City Chronicle*'s news app, whose headline read:

News Conference, 11 a.m. Today!
Local Murder Case and Corruption To Be Addressed
By City.
Breaking News!

"Wow," Dora breathed. "That's in like—"

"Twelve minutes," Charlie said. "Mind if I pull it up, and we watch together?"

Dora shook her head. "So, Patella is—"

"Probably in surgery," Charlie continued.

"How'd I get here?" Dora looked around, her eyes landing on Missy.

"You said you were meeting Mo at Julienne, and with what I found out, I just knew that wouldn't be a good thing. So, I went looking for you. Found you just as you were wandering out the front gate, dizzy from blood loss. Brought you here."

Dora reached for Missy and squeezed her arm. Then she pulled Missy to her and kissed her on the mouth, a long, tender kiss. "Mmm ..." Dora said. "Now that's what I'm talking about."

Missy blushed and looked down at her hands.

Dora looked suddenly embarrassed. "Sorry."

Charlie cleared his throat. He had set the iPad on Dora's movable table and turned up the sound. On the screen, Tom Volkov could be seen sitting behind a news desk. Next to him was Mo Levinson, who had a gash of dried blood that ran across most of his forehead and a left eye that was black and swollen shut. Both their names were on a graphic below the video:

Tom Volkov, Chronicle *Editor, and Mo Levinson, Beach City Sanitation Engineer*

Dora shook her head. "Sanitation engineer," she muttered, shaking her head. "Stupid."

From the tablet came Tom's voice. *"Thank you for meeting with me, Mo, and for agreeing to do this broadcast."*

Mo nodded.

"Why don't you tell us what you came here to say, Mo?"

Chapter 32

The young man took a deep breath. "Well, nineteen years ago, I was friendly with your daughter, Anne. She had been involved with someone who became a city employee—"

"And who is now in the hospital and under arrest," Tom interrupted.

"Yes. Frank Patella. At first, the three of us were friends—really good friends. Then, when Anne and I were … involved, Franky was jealous. He wanted nothing to do with us. He really liked Anne, and I think he kind of lost it when he saw we were together. Anyway, it happened on a Saturday evening in the spring—April, I think—we were at my parents' house, as I remember it."

"Go on."

"Well, this part's embarrassing."

"It's okay, Mo. It's been a long time, and Anne's not around to be embarrassed anymore."

"Well, we were involved—"

"Sexually."

"Um, yes. She had been involved with Frank, who had just started working for the city. But she was scared of him. Frank never really accepted that she was with me. He — well, I don't want to get too into what he thought. I'm here to tell my own story. Anyway, that's right. We got a little carried away, and she fell and hit her head." His eyes welled with tears. "I swear, Mr. Volkov, it was an accident. We were … we were in love, and we wanted to be with each other."

"I don't doubt that. No one doubts that. But please, continue. What happened then?"

"Well, she hit her head. I didn't realize how hard. I didn't realize she'd passed. I just knew she was hurt and was unconscious." His voice broke, and he covered his face with his hands.

"So, what did you do?"

Mo wiped his eyes and swallowed.

"Did you call the police?"

"I didn't have to."

"You didn't have to? And why was that?"

Mo went silent for a moment. "My father came home just afterward."

Tom nodded slowly. He already knew. "Tell us about your father, Mo."

He took a deep breath. "My father is the mayor of Beach City. My real name — my original name, I should say — was Maurice Morganstern."

"Why did you change it?"

"My father wanted me to change it. He said it was to protect me."

"Your father, Sergeant Mark Morganstern, of the Beach City Police Force, who is now our mayor, came home and found you, his son, with my daughter—" His voice broke, and he paused. Then he regained his composure and continued, "With my daughter, who had passed. Was she … already gone at that point?"

"Yes. Yes, sir."

"Should we believe you? There has been so much dishonesty surrounding this situation … from myself, as well. How are we to know—"

"I'll take a lie detector test. My father checked her pulse and … and there was none."

"I see." Tom looked at Mo, deciding what to say next. "What happened then?"

"My father … my father handled the situation."

Tom frowned. "He handled the situation? What does that mean?"

Mo continued, "He handled the police report, dealt with the medical examiner and the press, and he contacted Anne's family—you and Mrs. Volkov."

"Okay."

For everyone watching, now the camera zoomed in on Tom Volkov's face, excluding Mo from the picture.

"The rest of the story," Tom said, "is really my story—mine and Mayor Morganstern's."

He took a deep breath. "I have to thank my wife, Irene—my Rene—for convincing me to come clean about my part in a situation that has snowballed and hurt so many people. You see, Officer Morganstern, now Mayor Mark, I believe was, at that moment, more father than police officer, and I can hardly blame him for that."

Tom continued, "You see, what happened was, Mark convinced me to keep quiet about Mo's part in what happened to Annie. At first, he asked me to wait just a few hours, which seemed reasonable. Then he said a few days, which also seemed a reasonable request at the time. Annie was already gone, and Rene and I were so devastated; what did it matter? And, truth be told, I barely paid attention to anything except making funeral arrangements and seeing to Irene, who was even more devastated than I was. She became ill and never really recovered. I lost my daughter *and* my wife.

"Up to this point," Tom continued, "I think we were all okay, but something happened to Mark." He sighed. "You see, what I did was participate in a coverup. Even if I didn't think it would hurt anyone, it was wrong. I don't blame Mo. I realize that he and my daughter had a relationship and were expressing love for one another, and she got hurt. While I didn't like it, I accepted that as what happened. But Officer Morganstern wanted to do more than protect his son. He was ambitious. He wanted to be mayor. On the face of it, there's nothing wrong with that. I'm sure that, on some level, he wanted to help Beach City.

"Mark always seemed, to me, to be a very good man. A civic-minded man. But he also wanted to help himself. At first, it wasn't very much. He wanted positive press during his election campaign, and when I explained that I had to report the facts of what happened to Anne, and nothing more, he put pressure on me. He said I had already participated in a coverup of the facts surrounding my daughter's death. He accused me of instigating the coverup, which was just not true. He said I had not met my legal obligations around Anne's death, and he promised to let the whole city know that."

Tom blinked into the camera. "I was stunned. I told Mark that I couldn't skew stories. I had to tell the truth. So, Mark set about showing me why I had to veer from the truth. He put together a version of a police report, alleging that I had knowingly falsified information about Anne's death, and he said it would ruin not only my career, but my reputation in Beach City. But if I did as he asked, he would not file the report."

Tom shook his head. "Now, I wish I would have told him to go ahead and let the chips fall where they may."

He looked down, gathering himself, then stared into the camera. "You see, from there, it got worse. Mark ran for mayor, with my help, and won.

And he began asking for more press coverage and wanted more control over that coverage. Now he had not only my original coverup of Anne's death and Mo's involvement; he had each of the ensuing stories I published that were less than true. Each time he came to me, he had more evidence of my own wrongdoing. The pressure on me to continue to lie and to support our new mayor, no matter the circumstances, was snowballing. I knew, of course, that he was lying, too, but he had documents that he generated to support him, and I was pretty sure he would be able to get police and legal support. I was also pretty sure he would be believed, not me. He's a smart man and was good at this. Soon, others were drawn in. Names everyone in town knows.

"I might get in trouble for naming names, but I'm through with the secrets and lies, and I've spoken with RJ Bishop, my own attorney, who understands the risk I'm taking. My hope is that we can cleanse our city of this ugly corruption."

Chapter 33

Dora looked at Charlie and Missy. "Whoa."

Missy shook her hand.

"So, Mayor Mark buried Mo's part in this?" Dora asked.

"And his own part," Missy said.

Charlie nodded towards the iPad and gave a low whistle. "Unbelievable."

Dora and Missy exchanged a glance.

"So, it's been the mayor all along," Dora said.

Missy nodded. "So it seems. Of course, we're just hearing Tom's side. I haven't heard anything about the mayor being arrested, so he might have a thing or two to say."

Tom Volkov went on, grabbing their attention.

"Captain Cobb, with the Beach City Police Department; Jeremy Anderson, the former council person; and some of the people at Julienne Inc. were also involved. Apparently, there is some truth to the accusations that Julienne illegally dumped chemicals into our waters. I will leave any further comment to Beach City Police Chief Terry Stalwell. I suspect that Cobb, Anderson, and the directors at Julienne were being blackmailed by the mayor and his lawyer, who were clever and unrelenting in finding leverage to force people to do their bidding. The mayor's lawyer is Jonathan Hagen, whose name might not be widely known but who was a prime mover in the mayor's plans."

"Man, oh man," Charlie said.

"What then occurred was a system of racketeering, a reign of lies, corruption, and retribution that's lasted decades. Anyone who opposed the mayor, anyone who spoke out publicly against city policies, was targeted, often by having permits or licenses denied or revoked, by having their city taxes examined and penalized, by having services cut off, and with summonses. The mayor essentially became a mob boss. That might sound a little crazy because it is crazy, but it's true. And the worst of it is that one of Beach City's finest, Lieutenant Francesca Hart, a model police officer, was targeted and killed."

"Oh, Franny," Dora whispered, her eyes brimming with tears. Missy squeezed her hand.

Chapter 34

Back in the studio, Tom blinked back his own tears. "I deeply regret that I was party to such corruption and violence. My hope is that my testimony will help to set the city right and will help to bring the perpetrators of these crimes to justice. My hope is that others will follow my lead and speak up. If not, so be it. I am here to speak up, despite it being too late for Lieutenant Hart. Maybe others can be saved and protected.

"One individual, a city employee, who was a direct perpetrator of violence and intimidation, and who was, I believe, directly responsible for Lieutenant Hart's death—a Beach City hit man in a real sense—has been hospitalized and, while in the hospital, arrested.

"The evidence police have in their possession includes recordings of the perpetrators' planning sessions. Recordings that I took it upon myself to make. I believe that evidence will show that Lieutenant Hart had discovered Mayor Mark's original coverup and some of the racketeering that has been official policy since that time. As a result, she was targeted and killed. Several other Beach City citizens attempting to learn more about the city corruption were also targeted, albeit unsuccessfully."

The camera pulled back so that both Tom and Mo were again both visible.

"I believe that the person at the root of all this meant well, at least at first," Tom said. "He was my friend. We had planned to lift this community out of the racial tensions and high school riots we had here in the sixties, while steering clear of the corruption that tends to take over city governments. I'd be the journalist, and he'd be the law, but a more compassionate law. We had planned on cooperating, being honest. We had planned on serving the public."

"He was a good father," Mo said, "who wanted to protect his son. But it got out of control, took on a life of its own."

Tom nodded. "But I believe that, when Anne died and he found out how she died, that you were there, fear took over and grew. Fear of his only son paying a price, then fear of the consequences of protecting his son. And you're right; eventually, it snowballed and took on a life of its own."

"Please believe," Mo said with tears in his eyes, "I loved Annie."

"I do believe you, or I believe you thought you loved her. I'm not sure teenagers truly understand the depth of real love."

He looked into the camera. "I want to apologize to Beach City for my part in this mess. I know I betrayed your trust, and I deeply regret the part I played. I hope that you, our citizens, can forgive me."

Mo looked grim. "I feel the same." He looked into the camera. "I'm so sorry."

He then turned to Tom. "And I'm sorry, Tom"—he looked into the camera again—"and Mrs. Volkov, for my part in covering up what happened to Anne."

As Tom reached to his right and patted Mo's shoulder, the broadcast ended.

• • •

"Poor Annie Volkov," Charlie said.

Missy was looking at Dora. "Volkov helped set you up, as did Mo."

Dora didn't answer. She was still staring at the iPad, though the broadcast had ended. Finally, she looked at Missy, taking her hand. "Maybe it's time to let all this go. It's over, right? Let Chief Stalwell handle it, let the law take its course, and let the rest go. Anyway, I'm sure I'll have my own legal troubles, given what I did to Frank Patella."

Missy squeezed her hand. "How would anyone know? I found you there, and I'm not telling anyone. And if you think Patella wants anyone to know—"

Dora smiled. "He's no better than George Cobb."

"George Cobb?"

"Never mind."

Missy looked at her phone. "Here's a tweet from the city. '*Mayor Mark Morganstern will hold a press conference this afternoon at four thirty to refute* The Chronicle's *ridiculous charges.*'"

EPILOGUE

At four thirty-three, Mayor Mark Morganstern was about to begin his press conference on the Beach City official website and Facebook page. *The Beach City Chronicle* was live streaming the feed from the city on its home page. The mayor sat at his polished wood desk with the American and city flags on either side of him. Eschewing his usual sweats, he wore a white shirt and a red, white, and blue tie. His smile was confident ... and empty.

"Earlier today," he began, "*The Chronicle* broadcast a combination interview, accusation, and confession. I understand Tom Volkov's grief, even now, after decades have past, and I understand and forgive my son, Maurice—Mo—for being a part of what was a tragic accident. I take full responsibility for keeping the complete details of that accident out of the police report and news coverage and for protecting my son by changing his name. I was also protecting Anne and her family from what I believed would be the public's damaging rush to judgment. I've always been a good father to Mo and friend to the Volkov family." The mayor's expression changed from benevolent magnanimity to a chilly, grim focus.

"I will not, however, allow my name, my career, and my family's name to be a part of the spurious and specious accusations of *The Chronicle*'s broadcast. While I did keep my son's name out of the original police report and news coverage, that came from a place of love—the love of a father for his son. Yes, Mo was there when Anne died, but he was a bystander to an accident. He did not, in my view, commit a crime, and I utterly reject the notion that any of my or my administration's actions from that day forward were anything but the honest work of government. I will not let my work on behalf of Beach City, and my family's name, be fodder for anyone else's political gain. Whether one agrees with my and my administration's policies and decisions, they were all arrived at and carried out honestly by myself, your humble public servant." His expression changed again, to one of simple humility.

"You lie!" a shrill voice cried.

Startled, the mayor looked to his left, his eyes wide, his mouth opened, but no sound came out.

"There was no accident. It was murder! And you've been lying and screwing the public ever since!"

The camera pulled back and revealed Irene Volkov, pointing a handgun at the mayor, with a surprisingly steady hand.

Finally, the mayor found his voice. "Irene! No, I only did what was right. I protected my family and yours!"

"You're a corrupt piece of garbage, and you've been cheating and lying to the public ever since your boy killed my Annie. Admit it! For once in your miserable life, stop lying! Tell the truth!"

A pounding and muffled voices could be heard off camera.

"Irene … Irene, put down the gun. I'm telling the truth. I never meant to hurt anyone, only to save my boy. It was too late for Annie, but my boy —"

"You've held everyone's feet to the fire starting that day, starting with my Tommy. You told him he'd been part of a coverup, and you forced him to do your dirty work. Then you forced the directors at City Hall, and they forced everyone else who worked there! Admit it, Mr. Mayor!"

The mayor looked around frantically. "Irene," he begged, "let me get you a doctor." He picked up the phone, looking into the camera. "Tom, if you're watching this … please, Tom, come and get your wife. She's barricaded the doors. She's not well. She needs help! If any doctors are watching, please, come to City Hall. They'll let you in. John, please, send up any doctors who respond."

"Enough," Irene cried, advancing on the mayor.

The gun went off, and the mayor lurched backward against the back of his seat, a hole blossoming on his forehead, surprise on his face, followed by the light in his eyes dimming and going out.

Two police officers rushed into view. One took the gun from Irene and handcuffed her, while the other rushed to the mayor's side and cradled his head, as the screen went blank.

• • •

Rudy's, now open thanks to RJ Bishop, was closed for that evening, and tables had been set up with place settings six feet from one another.

Clear plastic partitions separated the tables. A mixed greens salad had been followed by a choice of prime rib, rigatoni a la vodka, or salmon, with sides of potatoes, baked beans, and broccoli. It was the best he could do, given the ongoing pandemic restrictions.

Rudy's was as quiet as it had ever been, given that the place was as full as was allowed under the current Covid-19 guidelines. Everyone was too busy, for the moment, to talk, except in murmured whispers.

Rudy sat next to his wife. He surveyed the room then dialed his cell phone. After that, he donned a mask and walked to the back of the room. He had a glass of bourbon in one hand, and a fork in the other. He took a swallow of bourbon then tapped the side of the glass with the fork.

The whispers and sounds of people eating subsided.

"I want to thank everyone for coming," Rudy said. "But, more than my thanks, I know someone who wants to thank you all even more than I do. I'd like to introduce our special guest this evening, Chief Terry Stalwell." He nodded toward the opposite end of the room.

The front door opened, and the chief entered, wearing a tailored charcoal grey suit and a broad smile.

"My friends," the chief said, when the applause subsided, "I cannot tell you how grateful I am, and the city is, to you all. On behalf of our citizens, on behalf of what will soon be a new, incoming Beach City administration, and on behalf of the Beach City Police Department, I am humbled and honored to say a heartfelt thank you." He began to applaud slowly and with force.

Agatha Raines rose and began to applaud with him, followed by Charlie Bernelli, C3, Christine, and then everyone else. The chief nodded to each of those attending and extended his applause in their direction.

When the applause died down, he continued, "I am here tonight to express gratitude, but also to bring you all up to date, and to answer any questions I can about this strange, tragic set of circumstances that you have all helped our city to overcome.

"So, here is what I know. My dear Agatha, Charlie Bernelli; your son, C3, as we know him; Christine, Luis, Michele, Missy, and Dora … I want to especially single out Miss Deborah 'Dora' Ellison, for bravery far beyond what any citizen would be expected to display."

Dora smiled and nodded. She had just that day stopped taking painkillers for her wounds.

"When you are fully healed, the department would be honored to consider you for the position of Beach City Police recruit. But that is a discussion for another time."

The chief continued, "First of all, we have quite a bit more information about both the inner and, until now, secret workings of City Hall. We have had a number of sources come forward. One, an employee at Cobb's Diner, was privy to many of the conversations that were behind the mayor's and Cobb's agendas."

"Will there be arrests?" Missy asked.

"Good question," the chief said. "The short answer is yes. RJ Bishop is working to determine who will be charged with what crimes. I believe that several of the departmental directors will be charged with racketeering, accepting, and offering bribes."

"What about influence peddling?" Christine asked.

Stalwell pressed his lips together. "That's where it gets complicated. For several years now, influence peddling—that is buying influence with campaign contributions—has been legal."

"What about the death of Anne Volkov?" Dora asked.

Someone's cell phone rang.

Agatha stood up. "Sorry. Gotta take this." She hurried from the room, Rudy following her with his eyes.

Stalwell went on. "The mayor, when he was a police officer, did file a false report, and in due time I suspect he would have had to answer for that. There's no statute of limitations where murder — or manslaughter, which I suspect is more likely in this case, is concerned. Mo will have to answer for his part in this tragic situation which, I'm afraid, remains a criminal case."

"So, who will be the new mayor?" Charlie asked as Agatha returned.

Rudy looked at her, but she avoided his eyes.

"Well," the chief said, "from what I gather, the council will be meeting tomorrow evening to address that very question." He looked at Agatha.

"That's right," she said. "The charter was amended several years ago at the mayor's request, to make the lead attorney serving the city our temporary mayor until an election could be arranged."

"Jonathan Hagen?" Missy began.

"Jonathan Hagen resigned his position effective last night," the chief explained, "very likely to distance himself from these events and to avoid prosecution."

"Devious," Christine stated.

"No doubt," the chief agreed. "Also of interest, in the year prior to Anne Volkov's death, Sergeant Morganstern was brought up on charges of unnecessary brutality several times. He was able to bury that information."

"As he buried the truth about Anne's death and his own involvement," Agatha added.

"I have something of interest," Missy said.

"Go ahead," the chief encouraged.

"I FOIA'd the most recent permitting and environmental impact studies for Julienne. There don't appear to be any studies at all, which is impossible. They make plastic molds. They work with resins and all sorts of petroleum-related products, the disposal of which is closely regulated."

"So, no permits were issued?" the chief asked, frowning.

"Oh, permits were issued, but the studies underlying them. Well, they don't seem to exist."

"How can that be?" the chief asked.

"It can be, if the person signing off allows it to be."

"And that would be—"

"The Building Department supervisor, name of Clyde Franklin."

The chief nodded slowly. "I see. Well, thank you for calling this to my attention. I will relay what you've said to Bishop. You would be available to meet with him, if he so desires?"

"Absolutely," Missy said.

"Mm …" The chief took a sheet of paper from his pocket and looked at it. "Jeremy Anderson's company, Anderson Consulting, has long handled the marketing for Julienne Inc."

"We know," Dora said.

"What you may not know is that Anderson is also one of Julienne's owners."

"We know that, too," Missy volunteered. "Actually, I've already discussed that with Bishop, along with the fact that Julienne was one of Jeremy Anderson's major campaign donors."

The chief laughed. "Well, we're all on the same page. Thank you."

• • •

Agatha hung up the phone and came back into the bedroom to find Rudy sitting up in bed, the covers pulled up over his legs the way he liked them, and Folami, their ancient Labrador, resting his head on Rudy's leg. On the TV was a Yankees game.

"Who is calling you at this time of night?" Rudy wanted to know. "And why do you need to speak to him or her—I hope it's a her—in the other room?"

She lay down on the bed and turned toward her husband, with Folami between them. The dog lifted a paw and placed it gently on Agatha's thigh.

"No, it was a man."

"A man," Rudy repeated.

Agatha nodded, her expression grave, but then she laughed. "I can't do this. Yes, it was a man. It was Reverend Bailey, getting back to me."

"About?"

She took a deep breath then let it out slowly, centering herself. "I've been talking to him about ... our situation."

He took her hand. "That's good. Talking about this thing is good. Talking about pain is good."

Agatha's eyes welled. "I know. Anyway, just yesterday, he called and told me about a young woman in our church ..." Her eyes overflowed, and her voice broke. "A woman—"

"Shh, shh ..." He pulled her head to his chest.

Agatha pulled away and looked at him. She spoke quickly, determined to get the words out before emotion got the better of her. "Reverend Bailey knows a young woman who just had a baby that she cannot keep. He was wondering if we—"

242

She sobbed, unable to continue.

Rudy sat up and took her face between his hands. "Agatha ... Agatha, listen to me. Hear me. Yes. Tell him, yes."

• • •

Charlie had decided not to drink. The fact that his father was an alcoholic, who had just suffered a stroke, and his son had recently been living in a halfway house, had nothing to do with it. Well, maybe a little to do with it.

The real reason, or at least the reason he had told himself that he had decided not to drink, was that he would be spending the evening with Christine, who had repeatedly turned him down these last months. He saw this evening as perhaps his last chance to keep her in his life.

So, staying on his toes was a must.

His doorbell rang. He opened the door and there she was.

Why was his heart in his mouth, tying up his tongue? Why did he feel as though he needed to untuck his shirt so that it hung over the front of his pants whenever he saw her? Where was his cleverness, his sense of humor? Where were his words?

"Come in," he managed to say.

"I thought you'd never ask." She stepped inside, held out a suspiciously tall package, which he took from her and set on a counter, and began unbuttoning her coat.

"I, uh ... decided not to drink this evening, but that's got nothing to do with you," he said.

Christine's eyes twinkled. "Oh, we're not drinking? This is just a little Chateau Corton Grancey I picked up. Just wine."

"Ah," he said, removing the bottle from the bag. "Well, maybe just one."

He had put out some crackers, cheese, and dip, and for the next hour, they sipped, ate, and chatted, mostly about the changes at Beach City Hall, where the council would soon be installing a mayor, and about the city departments, most of which would need new directors. Christine knew them all, of course, and had plenty to say about the way they ran their departments and the fact that they had all been afraid of her. With each glass, she talked more, which Charlie found surprising. He thought of Christine as quiet, reserved, refined.

"Do you know why they were all terrified of me?" she asked. She had started slurring her words, and Charlie was relieved she was nearly done with the last glass of the bottle, whereas he was still nursing his first.

"Well, I didn't know they truly were."

"Mmm … well, they were. Mmhmm … They assumed I'd had an affair with the mayor; that's why!" She closed her eyes and sat back then opened them with a startled, slightly nauseous expression. "Oh, that wasn't good." Then she turned to Charlie. "They were right!" She barked a laugh, slapping Charlie's thigh.

He watched her, trying to understand.

"Don't worry. No, don't you worry. He wasn't anything to worry about." She leaned close. "Small hands. Ha!"

"Christine—"

"Wait, wait, wait. Before you say anything. I know, I know, I know. Why, why, why am I drinking so much. Well, there's a reason." She looked around then whispered, "Got any whiskey? No? Brandy? Good thing I had one … or three before coming over, right? Ha!"

"Christine—"

"Charles." She was suddenly serious and at least attempting to look dignified. "I'll have you know that the reason I'm drinking is that I decided to go to bed with you. And, because I am seriously limited in that area of experience, I thought it wise to have a little something first to … to … to summon up my courage."

He took her into his arms, swerving away when she made a lunging attempt at kissing him. "Christine, I'm going to put you to bed. Come on."

"Oooh … the plan worked! Where are we going?"

He had helped her up and was now guiding her by the shoulders. "To the guest room."

"Guest room? Or did you say guess room? Or maybe guess whom? Or is it who? My answer is: the bedroom! Ha!"

"The *guest* room. You need to get some sleep. We can talk about this tomorrow."

As he put her to bed, fully dressed, and covered her with a blanket, he kissed her gently on the cheek.

"Mmm …" she said.

He stood up, smiling down at her, then shook his head. "The mayor? Oh, Chris."

As he closed the door behind him, he heard her murmur, "No worries there, darling."

• • •

The next morning, when he woke up, Christine was already in the bathroom. He opened his eyes and, a moment later, she peeked her head into the room, while brushing her teeth.

"I used an unopened toothbrush."

"Ah," he said, a bit relieved.

When she finished, she came back into his room, wearing nothing but a smile.

And Charlie had one of the best days of his life. It was, in an absolutely true sense, the first day of the rest of his life.

• • •

The puzzle they were working on was of the Great Lakes: challenging because so much of it was blue.

"I wanted to apologize."

Missy looked at Dora, who was seated on the couch next to her, one leg folded beneath her, the other swinging inches from the floor. Comfort's head was in Dora's lap. She stroked the top of his head, and Comfort pressed his head back, reveling in her touch.

Missy looked surprised. "Whatever for?"

"For kissing you … again."

Missy smiled, and Dora loved that hers was a smile that hid no agendas or secrets.

"You don't owe me an apology. Kisses are nice."

"I didn't want to lead you on."

"Don't worry; you didn't."

"And ... I didn't want to disrespect ... Franny."

Missy nodded. "For what it's worth, I don't think you did. You expressed your feelings in that moment, and I thought—and still think—it's nice that you did."

Dora smiled. She was well on her way to healing—both the scars that showed, and those that didn't. "Well, I'm glad for the part you played in putting away the guy who—"

"The part *we* played," Missy correct. She added two pieces she had been looking at to one side of the puzzle.

"Yeah," Dora agreed.

"I like puzzles." Missy looked at Dora.

"Mmhmm ..." Dora agreed.

"So, I have a question. Sounded to me like the chief was offering you a job."

Dora didn't answer right away. She found and added a puzzle piece. "I don't know. That might have been kind of a show of gratitude."

"Justified."

"Maybe ... with your help. And others'."

"Do you have any interest?" Missy began.

Dora looked at her. "In being a cop? I don't know. Maybe. I sure like the idea of helping put people away who need to be put away. But don't you need to pass psych exams or something?"

Missy scanned the puzzle. She found a few puzzle pieces from the states of Michigan and Wisconsin. "Trauma from a violent childhood isn't wrong. You might have to learn a bit of restraint, is all."

Dora looked up quickly.

Missy held up a hand. "It's not always necessary to go from zero to a hundred the first second."

Dora broken out in a grin. "Really?"

Missy leaned toward her, and Dora could see that she was meaning to kiss her. She offered Missy her cheek, but Missy took Dora's chin firmly between in her hand and kissed Dora on the mouth.

"I think you'd be an outstanding member of the force."

THE END

Dear Reader: Thanks so much for reading NOT TODAY!

I hope you enjoyed it and my new heroine, Dora Ellison.

If you did, I would be grateful if you would
post a review online and join my newsletter at:
https://www.davidefeldman.com/books.shtml
See you again soon!

-DF

Acknowledgements

Thank you to my wife, Ellen, who is forever supportive, and to my sons, Michael and Daniel.

Thanks to my parents, who were supportive of my love of writing from the beginning.

Thanks to my brother, Matt and sister, Cindy. I love you both.

Thanks, as always, to my late, great Grandma Nettie.